Ralph Compton
The Guns of Wrath

A RALPH COMPTON WESTERN

RALPH COMPTON
THE GUNS OF WRATH

TONY HEALEY

THORNDIKE PRESS
A part of Gale, a Cengage Company

GALE
A Cengage Company

Copyright © 2022 by The Estate of Ralph Compton.
The Gunfighter Series.
Thorndike Press, a part of Gale, a Cengage Company.

Thorndike Press® Large Print Hardcover Western.
The text of this Large Print edition is unabridged.
Other aspects of the book may vary from the original edition.
Set in 16 pt. Plantin.

LIBRARY OF CONGRESS CIP DATA ON FILE.
CATALOGUING IN PUBLICATION FOR THIS BOOK
IS AVAILABLE FROM THE LIBRARY OF CONGRESS.

ISBN-13: 979-8-8857-8479-5 (hardcover alk. paper)

Published in 2022 by arrangement with Berkley, an imprint of Penguin Publishing Group, a division of Penguin Random House, LLC.

Printed in Mexico
Print Number: 1   Print Year: 2023

THE IMMORTAL COWBOY

This is respectfully dedicated to the "American Cowboy." His was the saga sparked by the turmoil that followed the Civil War, and the passing of more than a century has by no means diminished the flame.

True, the old days and the old ways are but treasured memories, and the old trails have grown dim with the ravages of time, but the spirit of the cowboy lives on.

In my travels — to Texas, Oklahoma, Kansas, Nebraska, Colorado, Wyoming, New Mexico, and Arizona — I always find something that reminds me of the Old West. While I am walking these plains and mountains for the first time, there is this feeling that a part of me is eternal, that I have known these old trails before. I believe it is the undying spirit of the frontier calling me, through the mind's eye, to step back into time. What is the appeal of the Old West of the American frontier?

It has been epitomized by some as the dark and bloody period in American history. Its heroes — Crockett, Bowie, Hickok, Earp — have been reviled and criticized. Yet the Old West lives on, larger than life.

It has become a symbol of freedom, when there was always another mountain to climb and another river to cross; when a dispute between two men was settled not with expensive lawyers, but with fists, knives, or guns. Barbaric? Maybe. But some things never change. When the cowboy rode into the pages of American history, he left behind a legacy that lives within the hearts of us all.

— *Ralph Compton*

PROLOGUE

Eden's Ridge

"You're shaking," Tobias said.

Hope used her other hand to steady the gun, hold it true. She straightened her aim. "Better?"

"Much," Tobias said. "Don't forget your breathing. You are immovable."

"I am immovable," Hope repeated in between inhaling and exhaling slowly as he'd taught her.

"Remember, there's a slight crosswind, so —"

Hope pulled the trigger. The gun shuddered in her grip. The bullet hit the tin can dead center, sending it flying up into the air. The metal caught the light, flashing like polished chrome as it fell, turning over and over to land in the brush a second later. The sound of the gunshot echoed like a thundercrack in the open space, repeating itself over and over. She shot the other two cans in rapid succession, clearing the top of the fence posts of their targets.

Her father whooped. "Thatta girl! Damned if you ain't a daughter of mine!"

"I take it you approve," Hope said coolly, holstering her pistol.

"Damn right I do! Now how's about you show me what you can do with that cat-o'-nine-tails you favor."

Hope rolled her eyes. "It's not a cat-o'-nine-tails, Pop. It wasn't funny the first time you said it, and it's not funny now."

Tobias set three more tin cans on the fence. "Well, it's funny to me." He stepped back, far enough away that she would not catch him with the whip. "Go on, then. Show me what you've got. Let's see if that fool uncle of yours has taught you anything."

"Gladly," Hope said, freeing the bullwhip from her belt.

With a quick flourish of her left wrist, she brought the tongue of the whip to bear on the first can. The braided leather made a sharp snapping sound as she repeated the move, knocking the other two cans clean off the top of the fence. She slowly coiled the whip back up in her hands.

"As you can see, I've been practicing."

Tobias Cassidy shook his head in stunned

disbelief. "Well, I'll be . . ." He reached inside his jacket and retrieved his hip flask. "I reckon this calls for a toast."

Her father unscrewed the cap, took a hearty swig, then handed the hip flask to her. Hope lifted it to her lips and gulped the whiskey down, the fire in her throat catching her breath. She coughed and spluttered as she passed the flask back to him.

"Good for you, eh?" he hollered, patting her on the back.

"I don't know how you drink that all the time," Hope said, wiping her mouth on the back of her hand.

Tobias shrugged, took another drink from the flask, then screwed the cap back into place. "Let me tell you something. There's been times the only thing keeping me going is a toot from that flask. Especially when I'm tracking some murderer down or chasing the tail of a bandit. The ride gets lonely. It can eat at you sometimes, get right under your skin. A man's gotta have his vices."

"I guess you would know all about that."

Tobias cocked an eyebrow. "Know about what? Chasing criminals or chasing vices?"

"Both."

Her father's mouth curled up into a wicked smile. "You're cut from the same cloth all right."

11

They walked back to their horses, hitched securely to the posts at the back of the field.

"When do you ride out again?" Hope asked.

"Not for a few days at least."

"It'll be good to have you home. I think Father Flanagan wants to see you."

"He does? Well, if he thinks I'm about to enter the confessional, he's got another thing coming." Tobias stopped walking. He laid a hand on his daughter's shoulder. "I know it gets lonely, you know, at the house. Especially with your mother gone. I'm sorry I have to do what I do . . . that it takes me away."

"Don't apologize," Hope said. "You know we always understood what you do."

"I know, I know. I just . . ." Tobias frowned, searching for the right words to use. "I worry about you. I guess that's what I'm trying to say here. I don't like leaving you. I know it's been hard since your mother passed, and I haven't exactly been around to help you through it. It ain't been easy. I know that. Believe me, that reality ain't ever far from my thoughts."

Hope patted his hand. "Like I said, there's nothing can be done about it. You have to do what you do. And I've got to get used to life without her, Pop. It's nobody's fault she's gone. Certainly wasn't hers. It just worked out that way."

His face softened. "You mean that?"

"I miss her all the time. The house is empty without her. *I'm* empty without her. But we have to keep going."

He regarded her a moment. "How did you get to be so damn wise, Hope? You certainly didn't get it from me!"

They continued on to their horses. "I guess I'm plenty like Mom, too."

Tobias threw his arm around her shoulders as they walked together. The sun was a ball of red flame on the horizon, casting long blue shadows as it sank beneath the lip of the world. "You are indeed," Tobias told her. "You're the best of us both."

Maria Cassidy passed in June.

Hope sent word to her father but he didn't receive it for two weeks. By the time he read the telegram and rode back to Eden's Ridge, the funeral had been held and Maria buried in the town's cemetery. After all, the dead do not keep.

Tobias reached the house late one evening, his horse covered in foam and breathing so hard from exertion, it sounded as if it were at the brink of collapse. Hope opened the door and her father wrapped his arms

13

around her, holding her close to his breast.

"I tried to make it back in time," he said.

"I know," Hope said.

Together they rode up to the cemetery and Hope looked on as Tobias fell to his knees by Maria's graveside, weeping like a child. She had never seen him cry, and it was hard to witness such a big, burly man so diminished by grief. He had always been a transient presence in her life, coming and going between assignments, riding out into the wilderness to chase the bad men, the specters of the night, a hero fighting evil. But when he was home, Tobias was a wonderful father. He took her fishing, taught her how to hunt, to handle a firearm. He imbued in her his knowledge, his wisdom, and he was always available with answers to whatever she asked of him. The only thing was, he never spoke of the past, never told her stories from his youth. She had no idea where he came from or what he had been before becoming a US marshal. Hope's mother warned her never to ask. She said, "For your father, the past is painful to recount. Best to leave it where it belongs. Focus on the here and now, Hope. Do not make him dredge up what was. He's a better man for it."

She wasn't the traditional daughter of a

traditional father — she was more like his understudy — but it worked in its own way and neither Hope nor Maria resented him for his absences. They understood that his was a life of service, however much they might have wished it to be otherwise.

Tobias had been called away while Maria was sick. At the end, it was just Hope and her mother facing the inevitable alone. At times it was like staring into an abyss, into an all-consuming darkness from which there was no turning back. Still she did not resent her father for not being there. He had his service and she had hers. And when her mother had gone, Hope wondered what would be next for her. She would have to forge her own path in life; she just didn't know what that would turn out to be.

As they rode for home with the light dying around them, Hope's thoughts once more turned to her future. It was November. The days were getting shorter, the nights longer. The wind had a decidedly frosty edge to it that had not been there before. The last foliage from the trees had settled on the ground, the bare trunks and branches like skeletal imitators of what they had once been. Her father would soon be off again, she knew. There'd be a bank robbery somewhere, or a murder, and he would be called away to wield the might of the law against the perpetrator. She looked at him smoking a cigar as they rode casually across the fields and met the road.

"Tell me about your last job," Hope said.

"I'm sure you don't want to hear about all that."

"If I didn't, I wouldn't have asked."

He smiled. "Well, for a start, you know perfectly well they're not *jobs,* Hope. They're assignments. Cases. I'm not a bounty hunter or a gun for hire. I'm a lawman."

"Sorry. Tell me about your last *assignment.*"

Tobias drew on the cigar, exhaling slowly from his nostrils. "I was out at this place. Little town called Delphine. Way out in the sticks."

"What happened?" Hope asked.

He drew one last time on the cigar, extinguished it by pinching the end of the stub between the forefinger and thumb of his left hand, then pitched it away. He held the horn of his saddle as the horse moved beneath him. "Two bandits. Turned over a farmhouse, took everything they had, then burned the place to the ground."

"Really?" Hope gasped. "What about the

16

family?"

Tobias shook his head slowly, heavily. "Gone. They killed them all. The father, the mother . . . the children, too. Left 'em where they fell, outside, like culled cattle, for all the world to see."

"Why?"

"There's evil everywhere," Tobias said. "Men that'll do whatever they please, no matter who they hurt, no matter the consequences. I tried to find 'em, but they were long gone. I searched for days. They were headed in this direction, but I lost their trail. Sometimes that happens."

"What will you do when you catch up with them?"

"*If,*" Tobias corrected her.

"Okay, *if* you catch up with them."

"I doubt I will." Her father's face hardened. "But let me assure you, they ain't gonna make it to no court. That's for sure."

Hope looked ahead.

"You know, you should ride out with me one time," Tobias said.

"Really?"

"Why not? You just proved to me you can shoot the whiskers off a mountain lion. And if your gun slips out of your hand, I'm confident you could learn that mountain lion some manners with a few licks of that whip you've taken to. You been ridin' since you were a kid. I think you can handle what's out there. Maybe I'll teach you my line of work, not that you don't know a lot of it already. But there's some things you have to pick up as you go along. You know, as you live 'em, so to speak. Think of it as being like boots."

"Like boots?"

"Yeah, the way you have to wear 'em in. It's no good just puttin' 'em on. You gotta cut your feet to ribbons first. Understand?"

"Yes."

"So come with. I'll teach you what I know. If you're lookin' to get in my line of work, that is."

Hope laughed dismissively. "I don't think they're about to appoint lady marshals to the service, Pop."

"I've heard tell of several women who've been made deputy marshals, matter of fact. It's not beyond the realm of possibility."

"Really?"

"Damn straight," her father said, peering at the horizon. "The world moves on. That's what I've come to understand about life. The world moves on, and we all have to move with it, or get stuck in the past. Some folk are happy doing that. Sticking with what's comfortable. That ain't never sat right with me."

"Perhaps you're right, Pop."

"Do you know how many lady bounty hunters and gunslingers I've come across over the years?"

She shook her head.

"I've lost count. The world ain't like Eden's Ridge, where there's hard-and-fast rules. Everything in this town operates a certain way, and it works because there's law and order, very little unrest or criminality. That's why when it came to settin' down roots, your mother and I chose Eden's Ridge. It felt like a good place, and it is. We weren't proved wrong on that score. But when you're out there, you soon realize the world don't necessarily work the same as it does back home."

"What d'you mean?"

"Anything goes. I can't begin to tell you the strange stuff I've seen over the years. If it's possible that a thing can be, you can guarantee that it *is* somewhere."

Hope wondered if it might open her mind to what she could do with her life. Perhaps riding out with her father would help her decide what to do with herself. It would at least allow her to see a little more of the world. When her father described that world as always moving, she pictured one of those globes important men kept in their offices, and herself as an ant running on its surface, struggling to keep pace.

"I guess I could ride out with you when you leave," Hope said.

"You'll see things that might disagree with you or upset you in some way, but I know you're not naive," Tobias said. "You've listened to enough of my stories to have a notion of what the criminal world is like. But it'd feel good having you with me, rather than leaving you here all by yourself. You're seventeen. Home ain't gonna be your anchor forever. Might've been different if your ma were still alive. But she ain't, and we both gotta adapt to a new way of living."

Hope felt a lump rise in her throat. "I wonder if she'd approve."

"Probably not," Tobias said with a chuckle.

They crested a rise. A column of black smoke rose up into the slate gray sky.

Hope frowned. "Oh, no, where's that coming from?"

"Come on!" Tobias said, jamming his heels into the sides of his horse.

The beast neighed, bucked a little, then surged forward at a gallop. Hope followed suit, quickly catching up with her father.

"Pop, what is it?" she called.

"It's coming from home."

"Are you sure?"

He drew his pistol. Held it at the ready. "I'm sure."

"What do we do?"

"You got anything left in that shooter of yours?"

Hope held the reins tight as she followed him off the road and across a meadow. The sun was now bloodred, spilling its deep crimson light over everything.

"I got three chambered. Didn't bring no spares."

"It'll have to do."

"You expectin' trouble?"

He didn't answer.

Hope drew her pistol and followed him across the meadow, downhill at speed, both of them reaching the bottom in a thudding cacophony of hooves and jostling gear. Their home stood before them, flames licking the air from the windows on one side and peeking from within the structure of the roof itself. The smoke rose thick and fast, giving the air a cloying, oily quality.

Tobias pulled up, swung his leg over the saddle and hopped down. Not for the first time, Hope marveled at the unexpected agility of the man. He moved with an ease that belied his size, his heft. Hope got down from her horse, adjusting the gun in her hand. She made to run toward the furnace that had been their house, but Tobias stopped her.

"You can't!"

"But the house . . ."

"It's gone. It's gone, Hope."

She shook her head, refusing to accept it. "No. No, it can't be."

A memory rose, vivid and sure to her in that moment, of her mother drawing her last breath in the bedroom. If the world was always in motion, as her father claimed, then for sure it had come to a stop that day. Everything had.

Tobias held her by the shoulders and looked her square in the eye. "Listen to me. It's gone. Clear your head. You got to *own* the fear, not have it be the other way around."

Sucking in a deep breath, Hope stopped trying to move and focused instead on letting the panic dissipate.

Tobias let go of her. "Hang back," he ordered.

His voice had changed. His entire demeanor. It was no longer her father speaking to her — it was US Marshal Tobias Cassidy, and she was his protégé.

Hope did as he told her.

Two black horses stood to one side of the house, far enough away from the fire raging inside not to feel threatened. They were rides she did not recognize.

"Take cover," Tobias barked.

An old trailer they hadn't used in an age was parked on the grass. It sat at an angle, its front end up, both arms jutting into the air. Hope scooted in behind the trailer, expecting her father to follow suit. But he continued walking cautiously toward the house, eyes flicking here and there, watching for any sign of movement.

"Pop?"

He shushed her. "Stay low."

"Pop . . ."

Two men stepped out from behind the house, their faces blackened by proximity to the smoke pouring from inside. They made themselves apparent, one either side, as if they'd been waiting for Tobias to ride up.

They had their weapons drawn.

Tobias stopped moving.

The man on the left grinned, showing several gold teeth, while the man on the right showed no emotion at all. He had a deep, angry, jagged scar running down one side of his forehead, as if he'd cracked his skull open at one time.

Goldie pointed at Tobias. "There he is.

Like seeing a ghost."

Tobias stared at them in disbelief. "What in the hell . . ."

"*Hell* would be right," Goldie said. "You're good, Cassidy, but we still managed to give you the slip and circle back on you."

Scar leered at him. "Damn straight we did. 'Member me? Puck Cosby, and this here is Lance Knox."

"You don't have to introduce yourselves. Not to me."

"We thought you might've forgotten, is all," Knox said, raising his arm to reveal a black tattoo of a scorpion on his wrist.

"There ain't no forgetting." Tobias breathed steadily, calmly. "You two did this? You set fire to my house?"

"Sure did," Lance said.

"Who's the pretty little thing hiding behind that old cart?" Puck squawked.

Tobias turned his head. "You stay where you are. D'you hear me?"

Hope nodded.

"Aww, she's all scared," Puck said. He cocked the hammer back on his pistol. "Don't worry. We ain't gonna hurt her bad. Not all at once anyway. Not straightaway."

"You're not touching a hair on her head," Tobias growled. He looked from Puck to Lance.

24

Lance's golden smile vanished. "Enough. We came here to see this done." He raised his pistol.

Tobias moved, taking aim as he cut to the right.

Lance fired.

The shot whirred past the marshal's head, catching the top of his ear. Grimacing, Tobias fired back. The shot swung wide of the mark but caught Lance in the left arm, sending him spinning about from the force of the bullet tearing through his flesh.

Puck fired once, twice.

Tobias turned to face him down.

Both of Puck's shots were on the money, plunging into the marshal's rib cage at an angle. They tore through his lung on his right side and exploded out his back. Tobias landed on his side on the cool grass, gun falling from his hand.

Puck helped Lance to his feet.

"You all right?"

"Winged me, is all," Lance said, clutching his arm.

Puck looked at the cart. Hope remained hidden behind it, following her father's order despite her desperate desire to avenge him. She bit her knuckles to stop herself from screaming. She could open fire, but she had only three shots. She could run for

25

her horse, but they'd shoot her in the back before she got there.

Her father groaned as he pushed himself up to his knees, somehow still alive.

But before he could aim his gun, Puck ran over, kicked him in the stomach, sent him rolling onto his back.

Hope couldn't remain hidden. She sprang up, gun in hand, and cried out in fury as she leveled her pistol at Puck. Lance stepped into her field of vision from the left, and before she could let off a single shot, or do anything to defend herself, he kicked the gun out of her hand with his boot. She cried out in pain, clutching her hand. Lance pounced on her, pinning her arms behind her back and applying enough pressure to prevent her from wriggling free.

Puck dug the heel of his boot into Tobias's chest as the marshal spewed blood from his mouth, struggling to breathe.

"You had us right, Cassidy. We take. We kill. We burn," Puck said. He aimed his gun at Tobias's face.

Her father did not beg for his life. Did not try to stop what was coming. He lay on the ground and stared into the dark chasm of the gun. Then he turned his head and looked at Hope, eyes focusing on her. He did not have to tell her that he loved her.

He did not have time to say goodbye or offer any last wisdom.

There was just one look.

One last connection between them.

Puck pulled the trigger. The gun erupted in his hand. Hope flinched from the sound, squeezing her eyes shut. When she opened them again, her father was unrecognizable.

She screamed. Mouth wide open, straining against the hands holding her in place, against the horror before her. The air was thick with smoke and heat. Filled with the sound of every last thing they had succumbing to the fire eating through the house.

Lance struggled to hold her still. He forced Hope's head sideways so that she had to look at the ruin of Tobias's head. Then he bent toward her ear and whispered, "Killed him like a dog. Because that's what he was, a good-for-nothin' dog. When a dog got no use, you put it down. Just like we did your pop. We put him down good."

"I'll kill you both!" Hope snarled wildly.

"Don't play with her, Lance. There'll be time for that later," Puck said.

He stepped over Tobias's body and flipped his gun around. Holding it by the barrel, he brought the butt of the gun down in one sharp motion against her head. Hope went limp in her captor's arms, the fight draining from her in an instant. Consciousness ebbed and flowed.

She heard Puck ask if she was dead.

"No, just out," Lance told him.

"Near cracked her damn skull," Puck said, followed by a cruel guffaw.

"Yeah. Almost," Lance said, stroking her head. "When she comes around, we're gonna have some fun with this pretty little thing."

Puck laughed some more. "She gonna wish she was dead. Oh, boy, she gonna wish she was dead ten times over!"

Both men laughed cruelly together.

Hope listened as their voices faded, eventually hearing nothing at all. . . .

When she opened her eyes, there was no more fire.

It was still dark, and it took a moment for her vision to adjust — to realize she was riding horseback in the dead of night, wrists bound, facing the back of the rider. She squeezed her eyes shut again, head throbbing painfully from the hit that had been administered. She saw her father on the ground looking at her seconds before he was shot dead. She saw his eyes, and all that was unsaid resting in his sad dark pupils. Hope recalled the gunshot, loud as thunder, knowing the memory of that sound would ricochet inside her skull for the rest of her life. As would the despicable laughter of the men who'd committed the crime.

She gonna wish she was dead.

Hope's eyes snapped open again, clarity descending upon her like a cooling mist. She looked to the left. A field with trees at the far end and more rolling hills behind. The mountains in the distance. To the right the ground seemed to stop dead less than fifty feet away. She heard running water. Not the trickle of a stream winding its way downhill, but a surging river. She tried to think where they might be. There were several rivers of various sizes near Eden's Ridge. The river she heard down there could have been any one of them . . . not that it mattered. Whichever it turned out to be, Hope knew the river was her only chance. When Lance and Puck found somewhere secluded to stop for the night, it was obvious what would happen to her. What they had in mind for her would be drawn out, painful, torturous, and she would be dead by the end of it. Hope was not so innocent to the ways of the world to know she'd not make sunrise.

She gonna wish she was dead ten times over!

29

Her wrists were bound before her, and there was a gag across her mouth, but her legs were free to swing either side of the saddle. That meant she could run.

"You awake back there?" Lance asked.

Hope froze.

"I feel you wriggling about. You gotta be awake. Best be ready for what's coming. Me and Puck sure are looking forward to gettin' acquainted with you, sweet thang."

She must not cry, scream, let herself give in to the hysterics threatening to burst free from her core. She raised her bound hands to her mouth and bit into the rope pinching her skin. To her surprise, when she gnawed at it with her top teeth, the rope did loosen ever so slightly. They'd bound her tight, but not tight enough.

Lance continued: "It's been so long since we had ourselves some company."

The panic fell away, and once again Hope felt calm. Every instinct in her body burned to lose control, but she could hear her father telling her to keep her head clear. The voice of Tobias Cassidy, US marshal, resonating through her.

You got to own *the fear, not have it be the other way around.*

"Yeah, we gonna hurt you bad, angel . . ." Lance told her.

Hope worked at the ropes around her wrists. She thought her front teeth might snap before she ever got them loose enough, but to her surprise, they worked themselves apart. She moved her wrists this way and that, pulling them away from each other, and the ropes slid free. She had her hands back.

"And when we kill you, it ain't gonna be too bad for you. Not too bad at all. Know why? 'Cause you'll be beggin' for death anyway. So it ain't gonna much matter."

Hope leapt from the saddle. She hit the ground awkwardly, rolling to break the momentum of her fall, just as she'd been taught. But she still hit the ground too hard and felt something in her give way from the impact. She cried out in agony but forced herself to get up, to move.

It isn't broken, she told herself.

Lance stopped his horse, pulling hard on the reins. "Whoa!" he said. "Whoa! Hey, Puck, we got a runner!"

Hope hobbled away, her ankle singing from the pain. She focused on the sound of the water churning below. The moon was big and white ahead of her, beckoning her to follow it to freedom. She did not need any convincing. If she stayed, she died. If she took her chances with the river, she might still die, but she might *live,* and that chance of life was better than nothing. It was a shot and she had to take it.

Hope reached the edge and looked down. It was more of a drop than she'd realized. There was a hundred feet of empty air between where she stood and the water. The moonlight shimmered on the river's roiling surface, making the fast-moving water look like molten silver. She wondered how deep it was; if there were obstructions beneath the surface; how strong the current would be; and how well her ankle would hold up. All of these concerns flashed through her mind in the time it took to look over her shoulder and see Lance and Puck race toward her, looking meaner than hell.

Hope had seconds to decide. Seconds before they got to her and prevented her from ever escaping again. Seconds to decide in whose hands she placed her life — the hands of her father's killers, or the hands of fate.

She chose fate.

Hope stepped off the edge. Fell through the air, remembering to hug herself and keep her legs straight so that she plunged *into* the water rather than smack against the surface. She held her breath and waited to find out which it would be. If she hit the water, the force would wind her and she would drown. The fall seemed to last an age, as if she were floating in a void of night with no sky, no ground, just endless black, and the air rushing in her ears.

But then she slid into the water at an angle. She remained beneath the surface for a moment, the strength of the current thrusting her forward. Hope used her arms to push herself to the surface, her head breaking free. She gulped at the air, thankful to be alive. As the water spun her around and around, she got a glimpse of Lance and Puck leaning over the edge, shouting to each other and pointing. By the time she'd done another full pivot, Puck had his gun aimed at her. The gunshots sounded distant, but she felt them zip into the water around her and flinched. There wasn't anywhere she could go, no way of taking cover. Up on the ridge she spotted Lance taking aim.

She was completely exposed. Hope drew a breath and dipped beneath the surface, believing it would protect her. But she did not know how long she could keep herself submerged before she could no longer hold her breath. Before she had to give up.

Shooting at a moving target had never been Puck's strength, plus they had to keep pace with the furious surge of the river. It was like trying to hit a target nailed to the side of a wagon.

"Damnation! Keep missin'!"

"Allow me," Lance said.

He ran along the edge of the drop ahead of Puck, paused, leveled his pistol at her with both hands and fired.

Cassidy's girl slipped beneath the water.

"Did you get her?" Puck asked.

Lance stared hard at the water. He was certain he'd gotten her. There was no sign of her breaching the surface that he could see.

"Well?" Puck demanded impatiently.

"Don't see her. Unless your eyes tell different."

"No."

"Punched her full o' holes, for sure." Lance drew a more relaxed stance. The river below sounded like rolling thunder. "Think she's gone."

Puck stood next to him. "Aw, hell. Too bad. I was lookin' forward to havin' some fun."

"Me, too. But there'll be more."

"True enough."

Lance was disappointed, too. More than he'd ever let on to Puck Cosby. "Come on.

34

Let's get back to the horses before we lose 'em."

Puck spat over the side of the ridge. "If they ain't scarpered already, what with all the shootin'. They can get awful flighty."

"That they can," Lance said.

The bullets punched through the water and a burning sensation lit up her insides. The pain didn't make sense to her at first. Then the same hot, focused agony blossomed in her right shoulder, rendering her arm useless to her. She cried out, expending what was in her lungs, forcing her to push herself to the surface once more.

Hope burst through, coughed up water, spat it free. She could no longer see either of her captors. The current continued to shove her along and it took all her strength just to stay afloat. She sank back underneath, got spun about, but somehow managed to get her head back above water.

Something long and gnarly bobbed up and down ahead of her. Hope knew from its thickness that it had to be a log or tree trunk. It was covered in the sharp remnants of lesser branches. They cut her left arm and hand when she grabbed onto it, but still she held on, knowing it was her only chance of keeping afloat. The pain coursing through

35

her body told her: *I've been shot.* The pain was new to her, but she understood what it meant. One in the gut and one in her shoulder. Hope wondered how long before she bled out, how long before she passed out. She tried to think. There was no way she could swim for the shore, not with one arm. If the log hadn't been there, she'd most likely have drowned already. She had to keep hold of the log and wait for an opportunity to somehow get to land.

She didn't know how long she continued that way, hugging the log as it was jostled along on the back of the water, kicking with her legs to assist her own buoyancy. The river curved ahead of her, the current surging. The fury of the water increased to the point of being deafening. She tried to see what lay ahead, but her vision had gone bleary and it was too dark. A thick bank of clouds rolled in against the moon, blanketing its light and leaving the world suspended in deep shadow.

The water roared and boomed around her, building in intensity. At first it seemed as if the river came to an abrupt end before her. But she knew that didn't make sense. Rivers didn't just *end.* Which meant the water didn't stop; it *fell.*

Panic rose in her chest. Hope tried to kick

herself to shore, to steer the log away from the drop, but it was impossible. It was going to fall and she was going to fall with it, regardless of whatever she did to fight the inevitable.

In the seconds she had left to her, Hope made the decision to cling to the log. It was her best chance — her *only* chance — of making it at all. She couldn't fight the power of the water with just one arm. She had been shot. She was bleeding and felt steadily weaker with each passing second.

Her path was set and there wasn't anything she could do to change it. Hope saw the edge of the water. Saw it fall into the dark. With every ounce of strength left to her, Hope gripped hold of the log and braced herself for what was to come. And then the log was jostled off the edge of the waterfall. It dropped hard and fast through the darkness, and Hope fell with it, the night rushing past her ears.

■ ■ ■ ■

PART ONE:
IRONS IN THE FIRE

■ ■ ■ ■

CHAPTER ONE

Eight Years Later

Winter held the town of Fortune's Cross in its grip. Snow lined the main street and the roofs of the storefronts either side. Icicles hung from the gutters and the busted down-pipes. Some of the snow had melted to a muddy slush during the day and refrozen overnight to treacherous expanses of uneven brown ice. The smoke rising from the chimneys spoke of the nip in the air, and the warmth and comfort offered by the fires within.

Hope Cassidy took no heed of the stares she attracted from the locals as she rode into town and brought her horse to a stop in front of the local saloon. The sign out front read:

**FORTUNE'S CROSS
SALOON & INN
GOOD CLEAN ROOMS AVAILABLE**

SPITTING FROM WINDOWS
PROHIBITED
BATHHOUSE AND STABLES
AROUND BACK

Hope made a quick assessment of the place. She'd stayed in better — and she sure as hell had stayed in worse. She climbed down from the saddle and hitched her horse to one of the porch posts. She took a moment to run her hand across the creature's neck and feed him an apple.

"Once I get a room sorted, I'll see to your stable," Hope told him. "It's been a long journey and we could both do with —"

She heard a man's startled cry and turned to see a woman with a pistol in her hand the other side of the street. The woman booted a man with a short gray beard in the small of his back. He flew forward, fell face-first in the snow and slush. The woman followed up the first kick with another hard kick to the man's ribs. He whimpered like a beaten dog.

"Care to give me anymore trouble, Bandanna? Or have you learned your lesson."

He mumbled something into the snow.

The woman kicked him again, though not as hard as the previous times. "Say that again."

42

The man lifted his head. "No, ma'am."

"That's more like it," she said, stepping back, gun raised and at the ready. "Now get the hell up before I claim a bounty on a dead man. You're worth more to me if you're still breathing, but if your antics continue, I'm happy to take the lesser fee."

Hope walked up the steps of the porch and the woman peered across the street at her. Hope tipped the brim of her hat in greeting.

"Howdy."

The stranger nodded. "Howdy to you. Sorry you had to see this."

"Don't apologize," Hope said.

She walked into the saloon but not before she saw the woman drag the man up the street toward the sheriff's office.

"Help you, miss?" the bartender asked.

Hope approached the bar and stood with her hands braced against the top. A handful of old-timers played a quiet game of cards in the corner, nursing beers. A young boy was on his hands and knees scrubbing the floorboards with soap and water. He glanced up at the sound of her spurs as she strode past, but he did not attempt to make eye contact. He studiously went back to what he'd been doing. Other than that minor activity, the saloon was empty.

"I'll take a whiskey," Hope said.

The bartender nodded. "Whiskey it is."

"And a room, if you have one going."

"Sure do. Though they won't be free for long," the bartender said, setting a shot glass down in front of her.

Hope looked on as he proceeded to fill it with whiskey from an unlabeled bottle. "How so?"

"The contest. It starts in a few days. Things are gonna get real busy around here for the next week or so."

Hope sank her shot of whiskey and ordered another. "What contest is that?"

"You mean, you don't know?"

"I wouldn't ask if I did."

The bartender frowned at her. "I'm sorry. I just assumed you were here for the contest. What with your sidearm and all."

"I can't be the only woman around here with a gun."

"No, it's not just that. I suppose it's the way you carry yourself, too. Saw it the moment you stepped through those doors."

"And how would you say I carry myself?"

"Like you could shoot a gnat off the hind end of a stray dog."

Hope smiled. She fished out a coin and flipped it at him. "Tell you what. Get yourself a drink, too."

"Much obliged, miss."

"So, tell me about this contest," Hope said.

"There's six contestants. The sheriff is usually the master of ceremonies. He'll pull names out of a hat to determine who's fightin' who in what round. After the first day, when three have fallen, a coin toss decides the second day's rounds. Y'know, who's facing who. But ain't none of that matters because Cyrus Barbosa always wins."

"He's the reigning champion?"

"Sure is. The whole thing's his idea, after all."

"I'll bet it is," Hope said. "Now, about that room . . ."

The bartender poured himself a shot of whiskey from the same bottle. "Rooms are a dollar a night. But seein' as you're booking in now before the chaos begins, I can cut you a deal for staying the week."

"What's that look like?"

The bartender sipped from his shot glass. "Well, today is Wednesday. The contestants don't usually arrive until Friday. While the contest is in play, we usually charge two dollars a night."

"Two dollars?" Hope said in disbelief.

"They pay it, too."

45

"Fair enough. It is what it is."

"Tell you what. Since you got here early, how's about I keep the rate at a dollar a night?"

"Sounds more than fair."

"I can't have nobody hear of it, though. There'll be hell to pay. Possibly murder, too, if the players hear they're paying double what you are."

Hope figuratively crossed her heart. "I won't tell a soul. Promise."

"Good."

"How about the stables out back?"

"How's fifty cents a day sound?"

"Good to me. I can pay you a week up front. Just so we're square," Hope said, counting the money onto the counter.

The bartender swept it off into his hand and deposited it in the front pocket of his apron. "Much obliged," he said. He handed her a room key. "It'll be number five. End of the hall. Young Jasper there will see to your things."

"Appreciate it."

The bartender leaned on the bar and raised his voice. "Jasper! Go fetch the lady's belongings, will you?"

The boy stood up, brushed off his knees.

Hope walked over, pressed a few cents in the palm of his hand. "Mine's the horse out front. Take the saddle and bags up to room five, will you?"

Jasper nodded. "Yes, ma'am."

"Good boy."

Jasper went on his way. A second later, the saloon doors parted again to admit the woman from across the street. She eyed Hope and the bartender, then the old men in the corner. She joined Hope at the bar and ordered a whiskey, followed by a heavy sigh.

"Allow me," Hope said, sliding a coin across the bar top.

"Appreciate it," the woman said. She offered her hand. They both shook. "Katie Roper."

"Hope Cassidy."

"Your name rings a bell."

"So does yours," Hope said.

The bartender filled Katie's glass for her. She shrugged. "Small world, I guess," she said, lifting the glass. "Anyway. Cheers!"

Hope did the same. "Cheers."

They drank, both women bringing their glasses down at the same time.

"Looked like you had your hands full there," Hope said.

Katie Roper shrugged. "It is what it is. You in town for that damned contest?" she asked.

Hope shook her head. "You're the second person to ask that. No. I have other business here."

"You a bounty hunter, too?"

"Sometimes I am. When I have need to be. Not seen many other women in this line of work, though."

"We're a rare breed," Katie said.

Hope watched as Jasper hauled the saddle and saddlebags into the saloon and struggled to take them up the stairs. She went to help but the boy waved her off.

"No need, ma'am. I got this."

"Sure?"

"Yes, ma'am."

"Boy's stronger than he looks," the bartender said. "No surprise, given what he's been through."

"Does he live around here?"

"Yes, he lives here with me. I took him in about a year and a half ago."

"Not many would be so kind."

The man shrugged as he wiped at the bar with a wet rag. "Sometimes you just gotta help folk out, you know? It ain't glamorous work what I have him doing, but I give him a roof over his head, a hot meal in his belly, and he keeps whatever he makes. It's not a bad arrangement. Besides, I need the extra pair of hands. Couldn't run this place all by myself."

"If only everyone were so gracious," Katie said.

"I do what I can."

Hope watched Jasper haul her belongings across the top landing. "Where's his parents?"

"Dead."

She felt a lump in her throat. She knew all too well what it felt like to be alone in the world. "That's a shame," she said, and meant it.

Gunshots issued out in the street, causing Hope, Katie and the bartender to jump. Shots rang out again, this time louder than before. Katie was the first out the doors, pulling her pistol free from its holster as she stepped out onto the porch. Hope was close behind, taking in the scene as she stepped outside. The sheriff stood outside his office, blood running down one side of his face. One hand held a rag there to stem the flow, and with the other he attempted to draw a bead on Bandanna. But the sheriff's aim was marred by his head injury. He couldn't hit his target.

Bandanna, meanwhile, seemed to have acquired a pistol of his own since Katie Roper had left him in the hands of the law moments before. The bandit spotted both women on the porch and brought his gun to bear.

"Get down!" Katie urged.

They took cover as he opened fire. He was hell-bent on making his escape, and if it meant killing them in the process, he would do just that.

Katie popped back up to return fire, but she got the chance to let off only a single round before Bandanna sent two shots her way. They split the wood to the side of her, and she shrank down out of the way. Bandanna used Hope's horse for cover as Katie edged back out and tried to get a clean shot.

"Damn it, get the hell away from that horse so I can send you to your Maker!" she yelled.

"Not a chance!" Bandanna shouted back.

Hope ran to the end of the porch and swung herself over the rail, landing in the brown slush on the other side. She ventured out in time to see Bandanna attempting to free her horse from his post. She took her bullwhip in hand, circled around the back of him.

Bandanna heard her boots crunch on the snow and ice. He spun about, brought his gun up to shoot her, his teeth bared in anger. Hope snapped her bullwhip out like a dragon's tongue. It snapped around his wrist. With one hard pull, the pistol flew from his hand. She didn't see where it landed. Hope flicked the whip free, brought it back around and caught Bandanna by the throat with the end of the tail. His hands went there, trying to free himself.

Hope yanked him forward and brought her boot up under his chin. His jaws clattered together, eyes rolling up into the back of his head. He careened back, hit the ground with a decisive thud. Out for the count.

Katie ran down from the porch and unwound the end of the whip from Bandanna's throat.

She looked at Hope in disbelief. "Just when I thought I'd seen everything!"

"It's nothing," Hope said, coiling the whip back up and setting it back on her hip. She approached her horse and did her best to calm the beast by stroking his neck the way he liked.

Katie said, "Well, *you* say it's nothing. *I* say you're a dab hand with that there bullwhip. Best I've seen."

Hope smiled thinly. "I guess people are no different to cattle, are they?"

"I guess not," Katie Roper said, grinning.

The sheriff made his way over. Hope could now see that he'd been grazed above the eye. The blood made everything look a lot worse that it really was.

"Thank you, ladies. I tried to get him but I couldn't see straight."

"How did he get away?" Katie asked, her tone sharp edged. "It took minutes."

"Got the jump on me. He was quick. Smashed me in the head and made a run for it."

"Damn it," Katie said, irritably.

"Where's your deputy?" Hope asked.

The sheriff looked at her. "Quit last month. I haven't yet settled on a replacement. I got a few contenders . . . but none I'm particularly struck on, if you take my meaning."

"He take out your eye?" Katie asked the sheriff, frowning at the amount of blood that had coursed down the side of his face and begun to dry there like new skin.

"No," the sheriff said, lifting the rag. "Just had so much damned blood gettin' in my eye, I couldn't see a thing. Not to shoot anyway. I owe you both."

"We're just two law-abiding ladies doing what needed to be done," Katie told him. "Do you have a set of irons?"

The sheriff tossed her the handcuffs. "I'm in your debts anyway." He looked at Hope and offered his hand. "Sheriff Maxwell."

"Hope Cassidy," she said, shaking his hand.

Maxwell nodded in Katie Roper's direction. "Are you working with Miss Roper here?"

"No, no," Hope told him. "I have my own business in town."

"Ah," he said, looking her up and down. "Here for the contest, I take it."

"I'm afraid not."

Sheriff Maxwell looked from Katie to Hope. "If you're not collecting on this man's bounty, and you're not taking part in the contest . . . why are you here, Miss Cassidy?"

"It's a long story, Sheriff. How about we have somebody look at that head of yours, and I'll tell you."

"Sounds fair enough," Maxwell said, making his way into the saloon.

Katie lifted Bandanna's feet. "I'll get this sack of fodder stowed behind bars. Keys up on the peg, Sheriff?"

"Where they always are," Maxwell told her.

"Want some help?" Hope asked.

"No, I've done this before. You staying in town, then?"

"A few days. You?"

"A night or two. I'll be moving on before

53

that contest starts. That's for sure. I'd advise you to do the same."

"I'll take that under consideration."

"Tell you what. Let me buy you a drink later on before I go. You know, to say thanks."

Hope nodded. "Sure."

Katie dragged Bandanna's inert form across the main street toward the sheriff's office as Hope entered the saloon. She saw the sheriff had removed his hat and decided she'd better do the same. It was customary to remove your hat when entering a building, but she rarely did. It wasn't about standing out from a crowd. It was about making a statement. It was about defiance, in big and little ways. Because defiance meant freedom, and in a world of men, women could use all the little freedoms they got. Every victory was a victory nonetheless, regardless of size or importance.

The sheriff dabbed at his head with a wet cloth the bartender had provided him. He wiped away at the blood, revealing a small but not insignificant laceration above his eyebrow.

Jasper came down the stairs and the bartender waved him over. "Jasper, go fetch the doc, will you? Tell him the sheriff's got himself a nasty cut on the head. Gonna need some stitches for sure."

Jasper ran off to follow the bartender's instruction.

The sheriff groaned. "Not stitches . . . You know I ain't a fan of needles."

"Here, this ought to help," the bartender said, pouring the sheriff a measure of brandy. He set it down in front of him. "Y'know. For the nerves."

"Nerves?" Sheriff Maxwell said, eyeing the bartender in a way that was decidedly unfriendly.

"For the constitution, then."

The sheriff lifted the brandy to his lips. "Well, I never did refuse a drink when one was going."

"That's what I thought," the bartender said.

Hope stood at the bar. "I never caught your name," she said.

"Burt," the bartender told her. "Burt McCoy."

"This place has been a McCoy institution going back decades," Sheriff Maxwell said, draining the last of the brandy. "I reckon when they set down the first foundation of this here town, one of them folks doin' it was a McCoy."

"Well, the Maxwell name can't be far

behind, Travis," Burt said.

"True," the sheriff said. "We been here a long time."

Hope drew a breath. "And the contest? Has that been going on for as long?"

"No," Maxwell said bitterly. "I'd say the last ten years or so."

Burt nodded. "Sounds about right."

"Neither of you men sound like you approve of it," Hope ventured.

"If you were the law of the town, would you approve of a contest that results in blood spilled?"

"I reckon not."

"Right. But the town wills it. The council argue the contest brings much-needed revenue to the town's coffers. And who am I to argue? I'm just a man who went to war and came back to find there was a vacancy needed filling. So I stepped into this role. It was never my intent to be the regulator around these parts. I fell into the job, I suppose you could say. I can disagree with the contest all I like, but it ain't gonna stop until the council declares it don't want it here no more."

"And if that happened?"

Maxwell shrugged. "I do not know. I guess they'd hold it someplace else? I don't think I'd wanna be the one to tell folk it couldn't

56

take place here no more. Talk about putting yourself in the firing line."

"You sound like you don't have much say in it either way," Hope said.

"If I sound that way, it's probably because it's true," the sheriff said. He touched the wound on his head and winced. "Besides, I'm designated master of ceremonies. Bit hypocritical for me to be putting a stop to it when all these years I've been overseeing things."

"You said you're not here to participate in the contest," Burt said.

"That's right. I'm not."

Maxwell eyed her. "What're you here for, then, young lady? You sure have the look of a gunslinger to you. So it surprises me that you're not —"

"I'm here to observe."

"Oh? Just in town to watch, eh?"

Outside the winter winds picked up, whistling through the gaps in the windows. "I'm not here to cause trouble, Sheriff. Though trouble has a way of finding me."

Burt refilled the sheriff's glass. He lifted it, eyeballed the deep amber color of the liquid within.

"Just so long as you don't start something here, miss. There's gonna be enough blood-shed as it is. I don't want to add more."

The town's doctor arrived, carrying her bag of equipment. Hope got out of the way to let the woman work. But as Hope left the saloon to stand out on the porch, she heard the woman say, "Plying my patients with booze they shouldn't be drinking when they're injured, Burt?"

She didn't wait to hear the barman's stammered defense.

CHAPTER TWO

Despite the quality of her lodgings, it felt strange staying above the saloon and being the only paying customer to occupy a room. Hope saw that her horse was well cared for in the stable out back, then inquired about the baths. Burt sent Jasper up to knock for her when it was done, and the boy led her out to where the baths were kept.

"Hope it's hot enough for you, miss," Jasper said. She pressed a coin into his hand. Jasper tried to give it back, shaking his head. "No, no, you already tipped me once today."

"Well, I'm tipping you again."

"Much obliged," Jasper said, accepting the coin. "You're very generous."

Hope regarded him a moment. "If everyone in this life gave a bit here and there, folk would be able to get by. Do you agree?"

"I do."

Jasper made to leave, but Hope stopped

him. "I hope I'm not being forward, but . . . Mister McCoy told me how you came to be here. He told me about your parents. I'm very sorry."

"Thank you," Jasper said, looking away.

He was embarrassed, she realized. Ashamed, too, by the look of it. She recognized those emotions in him because she, too, had felt embarrassment and shame at the loss of first her mother, then her father, to forces outside of her control. When things don't make sense, people seek refuge in guilt. It never makes a whole lot of sense to those who haven't experienced it firsthand, but it made sense to Hope. And she knew, as certain as she knew the difference between night and day, that it made sense to Jasper, too.

"I lost my parents. Same as you."

Jasper looked up. "You did?"

"Yes," Hope said, nodding slowly. "My mother died of illness. I nursed her till the end."

"And your pop?"

A sour taste filled her mouth. Hope swallowed it down. "Murdered in front of me."

"That's awful," Jasper said. He looked at her curiously. "Miss . . . why are you telling me this?"

Hope rested a hand on the boy's shoulder.

"Because I want to let you know we have that in common and that you can speak with me, while I'm in town. Because it don't matter if it happened a year ago, or ten years ago, the hurt you feel every day is the same. It don't fade. It don't go nowhere. It just sits there, and there isn't anything you can do about it, except learn to live with it."

"Yes, miss," Jasper said quietly, and walked off.

Hope watched the boy go, then shut the door to the bath. The water was just hot enough, and had been scented with something sweet and unfamiliar, but not unpleasant. Hope stripped out of her clothes and slipped into the water, submerging herself up to her chin.

It was a rare treat, and she made the most of it, remaining in the tub until the water had turned too cold to stay any longer. So many times when she was out on the trail, making her way from one place to another, the only thing that got her through it was the thought of a long, hot bath. It cleansed the skin, soothed the muscles and generally made her feel more human than she had before.

Hope climbed out, towel-dried her hair and got dressed again. Her stomach gurgled and she realized that she hadn't eaten a

61

good meal for a day and a half. Chewing on jerky and candy didn't exactly count as a meal — much less a *good* one.

"Burt, do you serve meals and such here?"

The bartender was working at the bar top with a cloth and some wax, buffing it to a high shine. He shook his head with a grin. "Afraid not. I don't cook. If I did, I'm pretty sure you'd find the results inedible. If you're after getting some chow, the only place in town worth a spit is the café at the end of the street."

"The café. I didn't see it on my ride in."

"Oh, there's no sign or nothing. I guess they always figured they don't need one, on account of 'em being the only place in town to get something."

Hope worked her damp hair under her hat to keep herself from getting a chill. "Makes sense. They open now?"

"You bet. Right down the end of the street, like I said. Can't miss it."

Hope left the saloon and made her way up the street. There was a church at the far end, its tall white steeple overlooking everything. She could see a bell up in the very top of the steeple, waiting to be rung. The sun had sunk down behind it, its red glow casting the church's long, cool shadow up the length of the street. Hope smelled the café before she came to it. The hunger-inducing aromas of hot bacon fat, eggs every which way and fried bread were unmistakable — and the effect instantaneous. She was ravenous by the time she reached the door.

The windows were steamed up from the patrons inside. Every table was taken, bar one at the very back. Hope nodded in greeting to the husband and wife running the joint, and made her way to the empty table. She removed her hat, set it down at the end of the table and sat. Hope chose to face the door, to see every patron already inside the café, and monitor who came and who went.

An old habit of hers, and one that had kept her in good stead over the years.

The husband and wife were a portly pair. They were gray haired, the husband with a wiry beard that complemented the mop on top of his head. The wife had her own silver locks pulled back into a ponytail. She had a mole on one cheek the size and shape of a pumpkin seed. But it wasn't unsightly — it gave her character. She ambled over to take Hope's order.

"How're you doing?"

Hope smiled warmly. "Very well. I'm Hope Cassidy."

"I'm Ruth Rowntree and that miserable

63

son of a gun over there is my husband, Frank."

"Nice to meet you."

Ruth nodded. "Same."

"This is your café, I take it?"

"That's right. We've been here, oh, eighteen years now. Give or take a month either side," Ruth said, followed by lively laughter. "Now, what can I get you?"

"What do you have?"

"Everything we do is up on the board there," Ruth said, indicating a chalkboard behind the counter.

Hope made short work of assessing it. "I'll take the bacon, eggs, fried bread, an ear of corn and some biscuits. If you've got gravy going, I'll have that, too."

"Hungry, are we?"

"A bit."

"How do you take your eggs? We fry 'em or we scramble 'em."

"I guess I'll take them fried."

Ruth made a mental note of the order. "To drink?"

"Oh, hot coffee. And keep it coming."

"A woman after my own heart," Ruth said. She began walking away, then turned back. "By the way, just so you know, this table is usually reserved. When a table becomes free, or a spot opens up at the

64

counter, I'd move if I were you."

"How come?"

"There's a good reason this table wasn't taken when you walked in. The gentleman who sits here gets a little . . . territorial."

Hope smiled. "I'm sure he won't mind sharing."

"As you like, miss. It's all the same to me. Just wanted to drop it in your ear, is all. So as you're aware," Ruth said. "What you choose to do is entirely up to you."

"Thank you for letting me know," Hope said. "But I think I'll sit here all the same."

Ruth nodded. "I'll be back with the coffee."

While she waited, Hope made a point of scanning the faces of the locals crammed into the café. There weren't any who stood out, and she didn't notice anyone looking in her direction, apart from a man sat up on a stool at the counter. He nursed a cup of coffee, picking at the remains of a plate of what appeared to be chicken and some kind of mash. It didn't look to Hope that he had much of an appetite for it.

Perhaps he's in town for the contest, and the closer it gets to taking place, the more his nerves are getting the better of him, she wondered. *Or . . . he's just not hungry.*

He glanced over his shoulder at her once,

made eye contact, then returned to his coffee. He wasn't the biggest man in the room, but he was not small or weak, either. The way he sat, his posture, gave Hope the impression of a coiled spring. When he'd turned to look at her, she caught his profile — the edge of his nose, his thin lips and angular chin. She couldn't put a finger on the why of it, but she found the man attractive in a way she seldom did most men. He was only slightly older than her but completely bald. He wore good boots, high-quality clothes and heavy silver pistols hung either side of his gun belt.

Ruth returned with a mug of steaming-hot black coffee. "Your meal will be along shortly," she said pleasantly enough.

"Thank you."

The bell over the door to the café jingled. The chatter among the patrons died down, then stopped altogether as three men stepped into the warmth. Hope heard Ruth's voice catch in her throat as she greeted the eldest of the three men.

"Mister Barbosa, good evening."

Barbosa paused. Took out a pocket watch and flicked it open. "We're not quite there yet, Ruth, but I appreciate the greeting. How're you doing?"

"Very well, sir. And you?"

"Oh, you know," Barbosa said, smiling at the other patrons. "Tickety-boo."

He stood less than six feet and was as wide across the shoulders as he was across his considerable stomach. But everything about him seemed to be oversized. The size of his head, the thickness of his nose. As if he were a caricature of a man. He had a huge black handlebar mustache that dominated his face, and his graying hair was swept back and held in place with copious amounts of pomade. Hope could smell it from where she was sitting. It was stifling.

Barbosa stood with his thumbs tucked into his gun belt and Hope noted the size of the man's hands — they were like fat clubs.

"And how about you fine folks? Enjoying yourselves?"

A few murmured grunts of agreement.

Barbosa nodded. "Good to hear."

"Will it be your usual, Mister Barbosa?" Ruth asked.

"You know me too well. And the same for the boys."

The men either side of him were clearly there for protection. They were taller, if not broader, than their boss. There was no warmth in their eyes as they assessed each patron of the café in turn.

"I'll go get your order," Ruth said, moving away.

Barbosa looked directly at Hope. "There seems to be somebody occupying my table," he said, still smiling.

"I didn't realize it was anyone's in particular. It was free when I got here," Hope told him.

Barbosa's smile widened. "Was it? Well, it comes as no surprise. The people of this town know where I like to sit and when. They have the manners to keep that spot free for me, and I appreciate their courtesy."

"I see."

"But you are not from this town, are you?"

Hope lifted her coffee to her lips, blew across the surface and took a sip. "You have a keen eye. Mister Barbosa, was it?"

"Yes. Cyrus Barbosa. And I do not believe I caught your name, young lady."

"Hope."

His eyebrows rose. "Peculiar name. But a good one. Where would we be without hope, eh? How would we find the impetus to rise from bed each morning, face the challenges of this life, if it were not for hope?"

"A good question. I'll have to think it over," Hope said.

Barbosa's smile began to fade. "Are you here for the contest?"

68

"No. I have my own reasons for being in town."

"Well, I have business to discuss with my men here. And that is my table," Barbosa said.

It was Hope's turn to smile. "I'll let you know when I'm finished."

"You mean to say you aren't going to release that table?" Barbosa asked.

The café was so quiet, Hope could have heard a pin drop. "Correct."

Barbosa shook his head. "Unfortunate . . ." He did not have to look at his men to issue his orders. "Cotton. Ed. Show Miss Hope the advantages of giving up her table for us."

They advanced on her wordlessly.

The bald patron at the counter shoved himself back without warning, knocking the man to Barbosa's left off-balance as he collided with him. Then he stepped off the stool and swept the henchman's legs out from under him with one strong kick. Meanwhile, the man to Barbosa's right arrived at Hope's table in a single bound. Hope stood up from her chair. With one quick movement, she threw her cup of hot coffee in his face.

He shouted an oath and clutched at his

face, squeezing his eyes shut as he recoiled in pain.

Hope leapt out from behind the table and took aim at the man's jaw, landing a good hit that sent him stumbling to the floor. The bald man had Barbosa's other bodyguard pinned to the floor with his boot on his chest, and one of his silver pistols aimed at his head.

In the seconds the altercation had taken, Barbosa had not moved an inch. He'd calmly watched the scene unfold and looked at Cotton and Ed with a bemused expression. Both Hope and the bald man waited to hear what he would have to say.

"Well . . ." Barbosa ran a hand down his mustache. The silence stretched out. "This is interesting."

"What's *interesting* about it?" Hope demanded.

With the man she'd thrown coffee at out cold on the floor, she stood ready before Barbosa with her hand loose at her side, ideally placed to pull her sidearm free if she needed to.

Barbosa looked first at Hope, then at the bald stranger with the silver pistols who had intervened on her behalf. "You have come to my town, to the café that I frequent, sat at my table, and yet I am the one who is stood here at a disadvantage. Very interesting. This is not how I foresaw this playing out," Barbosa said, stepping over the man Hope had knocked out to stand directly in front of her, his belly protruding in front of him like a barrel. "Let it be known, were I not a player in the contest that will soon see the end of five other men and women, I would kill you where you stand."

"Is that meant to scare me, Mister Barbosa?"

He cocked an eyebrow. "No. It is meant to *educate* you. My word is unbreakable," he said, jabbing her square in the chest with one of his pudgy fingers. "I made a vow to confine bloodshed to the contest itself, but that vow does not hold beyond the borders of this town, and you cannot stay here forever. And where the offense is, let the great ax fall. That's all I'm saying, young lady. *Let it fall.*"

"Sounds poetic."

Barbosa grinned. His eyes searched her face. "I'll be seeing you. I'm sure of it."

The bald stranger released the henchman he'd pinned to the floor and allowed him to sit up. He stepped back, keeping the other man at gunpoint.

Barbosa helped the bodyguard to his feet. "Drag Cotton out of here. I'll meet you at the wagon."

"Yes, boss."

"Useless lumps," Barbosa muttered under his breath. He jabbed a finger in the air at Hope and then at the bald stranger who'd helped her. "I'll be seeing you both. Count on that."

He swept out of the café, followed close behind by Ed scooting backward, dragging the unconscious form of Cotton under the armpits.

The bald man remained fixed to the spot a moment, watching Barbosa and his men leave, then crossed the café to close the door after them.

Ruth hurried out from behind the counter and began mopping up the spilled coffee. "Heavens to Betsy, look at this mess."

"I'm sorry."

Ruth tutted. "You don't know what you started. I tried to warn you. But you haven't listened one jot to a word I've said."

"I'm not being ousted from a seat anybody has a right to. Surely you must see that."

Ruth shook her head as she cleaned. "You don't have no understandin' of the way things work around here. No understandin' at all."

"Maybe I don't. But I know the way the world works, and it ain't right to let a bully push folk around," Hope told her. "I've never backed down from a man like that, and I'm not starting now."

"This won't be the end of it," Ruth said, getting up off the floor. "He'll make sure of it."

"Don't you worry about me," Hope said. "I can look after myself."

The hum of conversation slowly returned and Hope resumed her seat. Frank brought over a plate piled high with food and set it down in front of her.

"Looks good," Hope said, lowering her face to the plate. "Smells good, too."

"For what it's worth, I appreciate what you did just now," he said in a low, careful voice.

"What did I do?"

Frank's face went tight. "You made a stand. About time somebody 'round here did that," he said in a hushed voice.

"Well, it weren't just me," Hope said.

Frank glanced back at the counter, caught Ruth's wary expression and seemed to shrink back from it. "Uh . . . better get back to it. You enjoy your meal, miss."

"I will," Hope said, frowning at the man's apparent lack of backbone as she bit into a strip of bacon.

The bald man nodded politely to Frank

73

as he approached her table. "Mind if I sit opposite?" he asked Hope.

She shrugged. "Not at all."

He cocked a brow. "I'm not gonna get scalding-hot coffee thrown in my face, am I? If so, I think I might wanna stay where I was."

"Not this time," Hope told him, eating another piece of bacon. "My urge to throw coffee around has passed."

"Good." The bald stranger pulled out a chair and sat down. "Hope you didn't mind me intervening on your behalf."

"I'm glad you did. I think I'd have been hard-pressed to take on the two of 'em on my own."

"Not so sure about that," the man said appraisingly. "I saw what you did with that whip of yours this afternoon. Catching that runaway. Nice work."

"You did? I didn't see nobody else around but that bounty hunter and the sheriff."

"I have a way of keeping myself unseen if I want to be," he said.

Hope broke off a piece of biscuit and ate it. "I didn't catch your name."

"Ethan Harper."

She swallowed hard. *Really?*

"Well . . . that's the same name I've had since before I can remember, so yeah, sure.

Do you not believe me?"

"No, no, nothing like that." Hope sat back. "It's just that there's a fair bit of reputation comes with that name of yours."

"Is there? First I've heard of it."

"Don't act like you aren't aware," Hope said. "Everyone knows Ethan Harper is one of the fastest guns out there. Particularly when it comes to the draw. Your skills with a gun are, well, legendary."

Ethan sighed. "Trouble with legends is they tend to be blown out of proportion. I can shoot, sure. And I can hit what I shoot at. But I'm not sure that makes my talents *legendary* by any stretch of the imagination," he said with obvious distaste. As if the suggestion of notoriety were anathema to him.

"Do you live here in Fortune's Cross?" Hope asked.

"No, no. I'm like you. Just traveling through."

"A fellow pilgrim. So you're here for the contest, then."

Ethan shook his head. "No. What makes you think that?"

"I just assumed . . ." Hope said, catching herself making the same irritating assumption people in Fortune's Cross had made

75

about her. "Sorry. I'm just as bad as they are."

"As who are?"

"The people around here. I've been asked a few times since riding into town if I was here for the contest. I guess they see the gun and think I must be. I'm guilty of thinking the same about you. I saw your two pistols at your hips. Thought you must be in town to show your quality."

"Not on this occasion," Ethan told her. "I'm just passing through. It's my own bad luck I'm here when that damn contest is taking place. But I guess I've gotta stop somewhere, and here's just as good as anywhere."

"Been here before?"

"Several times."

Hope sat forward. "What's this contest like?"

"Barbaric."

"I thought it must be."

"The man whose table you took always wins it."

"So I heard. It didn't much impress me then, and it don't impress me now."

"He wins every year. Bests everyone," Ethan said. "From what I know, he masquerades as some kind of businessman, but everyone knows he's a criminal. So that's quite an enemy you made tonight. He has a lot of clout."

"In case you forgot, we *both* made enemies of him tonight."

Ethan shrugged his shoulders. "I am no stranger to enemies. It's friends I fear."

That made her laugh. She reached across the tabletop and offered her hand. "I'm Hope Cassidy."

"Pleasure to meet you, Hope Cassidy."

"By the way, I don't always get into fights in little cafés."

Ethan sat with his elbow over the back of the chair next to him. "Oh, really? It looked like an occupational hazard."

"Well, it's not."

"So what *is* it you do, Hope?" Ethan asked.

Hope glanced about the café and lowered her voice. "I'm a bounty hunter."

"Not a low profession," Ethan told her. "Nothing to be ashamed about."

"I never said it was."

"Is your quarry in this town?" Ethan asked her.

Hope eyeballed him, her fork held in her hand. "I'm not here on business."

"You here for the contest?"

"Just to watch."

"I wish you were able to say that in a more

77

convincing manner," Ethan said with a smirk.

"Believe what you like," Hope said with a shrug of her shoulders.

"Tell you what I believe. I believe you're hunting a man, but he's not in town yet. But you're hanging around because you know he will be."

Now it was Hope's turn to smirk. "Why would you assume my hypothetical quarry would be a he?"

Ethan's head tilted to one side as he regarded her. "I made an assumption."

She set her fork down. "I need to be going," Hope said, wanting neither to confirm nor deny.

Ethan said, "Watch yourself out there."

Hope stood. "I can take care of myself," she said, stepping away. Then she stopped and turned back to him. "That said . . . thank you for stepping in there."

"Speak nothing of it. Just helping a lady out."

"Well, thank you anyway, pilgrim," Hope said, and left.

The town of Fortune's Cross took on a whole new persona in the dark. With the sound of the café behind her, Hope walked the deserted street on edge, her entire body tense, waiting for something to happen. Her eyes flitted from one shadow to the next, trying to adjust to the dark, to see if there was someone waiting to spring out at her. She made it as far as the saloon and went to walk in, lured by the warmth, the flow of lamplight and sounds of merriment, but she hesitated at the threshold. She shrank back into the cover of darkness, wondering if it was for the best. Could Barbosa and his men be waiting for her? Or somebody else associated with Barbosa? It was possible. Hope stepped down from the porch and made her way around the side of the building.

She looked up at the window of her room and made a quick assessment of the downpipe and the barrel it emptied into. She reckoned she could shimmy up the pipe and make it as far as her window, but was unsure if she'd left the window unlocked or not. That could pose a significant problem.

"Damn," she muttered, not knowing what to do. She heard the horses in the stable at the rear of the saloon and figured she could bed down in there if she ran out of ideas.

"Ma'am?" a familiar voice whispered from the shadows.

Hope looked for the source of the voice.

Jasper stepped into the pale moonlight

and made himself known. "It's just me," he said.

"What're you doing out here, Jasper?"

"Checking on the horses," the boy said, frowning at her. "What're you doin' out here, ma'am?"

"Trying to get to my room without being seen."

Jasper looked up at her window. "Because you don't want to be seen walking through?"

"Yes."

"Ah," Jasper said.

"Now I'm figuring I'll have to spend the night in the stable," Hope continued.

"No, ma'am," Jasper said, shaking his head. "No way. I can get you up there."

"How?"

Jasper had already begun to walk off. "Leave it with me." Without further word or explanation he was gone.

Hope folded her arms. "Damn kid," she grumbled, looking around to check if the coast was clear.

Moments later she heard her window slide up. Jasper appeared, leaning against the sill. He unraveled a length of rope until it coiled at her feet.

Hope looked around one more time before taking the rope in her arms. She looked up at Jasper. "You got it tied to something?"

80

"Yes, ma'am. Don't you worry."

Hope gripped the rope with both hands and gave it a pull. It was taut. She steadied one boot against the side of the building, then, using the rope as her anchor, lifted her other boot from the ground. It was hard work but she set to it, and before Hope knew it, she was nearly at her window. Jasper moved away as she clutched at the sill with one hand, then the other, kicking off with her boots to push herself through the opening. Panting from the exertion of the climb, she slid to the floor in a heap and remained there for a second.

"That took serious strength," Jasper said, untying the rope, then looping it up in his hands.

"I had an accident once. A bad one. I had to work hard at recovering from it. But I think I came back stronger than I'd been before."

Jasper extended a hand and helped her up. "What kinda accident?"

"The bad kind," Hope said, digging in her pocket and producing a dollar.

"I can't accept that."

But Hope insisted, pressing the money into his hand.

"Yes, you can, damn you, and you will."

Jasper averted his eyes. "Thank you,

ma'am."

"You've sure helped me out tonight, Jasper."

"Just glad to be of assistance," Jasper said.

"I'm glad you were, too."

"Well, good night, ma'am," Jasper said.

She watched the boy leave the room, shutting the door softly behind him. Hope locked the door, then crossed back over to the window and slid it shut. She put the little lock across and then worked her feet free of her boots.

Hope used some pillows to pad out the bed, to make it look as if someone were asleep beneath the sheets. Then she took to a chair in the corner, facing the door, ready to shoot anybody who dared come in.

There was something about Fortune's Cross that weighed on her. She could not help but feel a sense of unease about the town, and the impression that the townsfolk were under Barbosa's shadow. Living in fear and uncertainty. It wasn't right.

The only person to come to her aid back at the café had been a fellow pilgrim, she realized.

That spoke volumes.

Fortune's Cross was a town strangled by fear.

CHAPTER THREE

"Morning," Burt said as Hope came down the stairs.

Her back was a little stiff from sleeping upright in the chair, but she'd otherwise had one of the best night's sleep she'd ever had. No one had so much as approached her door, and with the lights out, she'd sunk into the softness of the chair and not stirred until dawn.

"I got a pot of coffee on the make if you're up for some."

"That sounds perfect," Hope said.

She took a seat at one of the tables by the window so she could see the townsfolk coming and going — and monitor who was coming into the saloon. It was presently deserted, but she knew that could change in an instant. Burt brought out the coffee and sat opposite her.

"Thank you," Hope said. She took a sip. It was just right. "Mm, good."

"Glad to hear it," Burt said, blowing across the top of his own cup. "I always start the day with a pot of black coffee. Sets me up real fine."

"A whole pot?"

"Sometimes," Burt said. "This line of work ain't for the kinda folk like to sleep in, if you know what I mean. Bar work is for the birds. That's what I think anyway."

"I guess it has to be that way," Hope said. She glanced around. "It's strange in here like this. So quiet. It could be a church. It has that air to it."

"It is a place of worship to some," Burt said contemplatively. "Anyway, come tonight, it'll be a whole different kettle of fish around here. You'll see."

Hope sipped her coffee. "The quiet before the storm, huh?"

"That's about right," Burt agreed.

He sat facing the street, looking out at the people going about their business, as if nothing ever happened in Fortune's Cross. As if a contest was not about to take place that would result in five people being killed.

"What happens when the shooting starts? I mean, what do you townsfolk do?" Hope asked.

"They lock themselves away, pray it ends soon. And if things go south, they get the hell out of town. As for me, I'll be right here serving drinks, just like always."

"Even if there's a chance you might catch a bullet?"

Burt looked at her. "Every bartender gets shot eventually."

She had not realized all town meetings took place in the only church in Fortune's Cross. Sheriff Travis Maxwell oversaw the proceedings and ensured they didn't get out of hand — at least, that was what was *meant* to happen. The pairing of contestants was apparently made at random to begin with. As the players fell, one by one, the contest whittled down to a final duel between the two remaining shootists.

Each gunslinger arrived accompanied not by a posse or a gang, but by the bluster of their own egos. They were coming to Fortune's Cross to die or be the last shootist standing. There was no second place, no silver medal. Any contestant knew how it was to be — either you won or you lost. And to lose meant death, simple as that.

Hope was on the front porch of the saloon when Ethan Harper sidled by.

"Hey," he said around the thin cigarillo he was smoking.

"Pilgrim," Hope said. She inclined her

head toward the steady stream of people making their way to the church. "Guess it's gettin' going."

Ethan followed her gaze down the street. "Looks that way. They start early in this town," he said, turning back to her. "You going along?"

"Wasn't planning to."

"I don't mind playing at being your chaperone if you like. Not that you need one."

She fixed him with a stern expression. "No, I do not. I'm more than capable of holding my own. But I'll take you up on your offer. Now that I see everyone heading to the church, I am curious to see what takes place."

"Then let's go so you don't miss it," Ethan said, offering his arm.

She brushed past him, grinning. "I can walk unaided."

They headed for the church.

"A strong, independent woman," Ethan said, chuckling to himself.

Hope looked at him. "What's so funny?"

"Nothing."

"Spit it out."

"I was just thinking, this town doesn't know what's hit it yet."

"How so?"

Ethan pitched the dog end of his cigarillo

away, out onto the muddy slush. "You're not here to participate in that godforsaken contest. You're here to kill a man."

"According to *you*. Like I said last night at the café, you made an assumption under your own steam."

"You didn't need to confirm a thing. It's obvious."

Hope rolled her eyes. "There you go again with your assumptions, pilgrim."

"When you do whatever it is you're gonna do, there'll be a world of trouble falling on you. Especially here. Do you realize that?"

Hope stopped walking. "How many times I gotta say, I can take care of myself. I appreciate the advice, but this is my business."

"My apologies," Ethan said, holding up his hands, as if Hope had him at gunpoint. "You're right. It's your own affair."

Now it was her turn to snigger.

"Go on," Ethan said, lowering his hands. "Tell me the joke."

"An understanding man," Hope said. "Now, there's a contradiction in terms if ever there was one. I'm not convinced those two words go together, pilgrim."

The church was packed to the rafters. The stage at the front had been cleared and a row of six chairs arranged with a good deal of distance between them, ensuring the participants in the contest weren't bunched together.

Sheriff Travis Maxwell called for quiet. "Easy now, folks. Or you'll struggle to hear anything. That's better. Thank you."

There was a large chalkboard to the right with a table drawn on it. A local woman who worked at the feed store, Mrs. Samson, had been drafted in to do the lettering. She stood on a stool behind the sheriff so as to reach the topmost line of the table.

Maxwell turned to her. "Ready?"

Mrs. Samson nodded.

"Good," Maxwell said, clearing his throat.

When he spoke next, his voice was clearer, louder. It carried through the church, all the way to the back, where Hope and Ethan stood with a crowd of onlookers who, like them, arrived too late to get a good seat.

"In a moment we will introduce our contestants. I believe the sixth shootist has just arrived and is making his way to the church as I speak. But first, for those who don't know better, I'll take a moment to explain how this is going to work.

"There are six participants in this most deadly of contests. As the gladiators of old fought for the right to their freedom from slavery, these six gunslingers are here to

88

prove they are the greatest by eliminating their foes and staking a claim for fastest gun in the West. Gladiators by other means, other names . . . but gladiators nonetheless.

"Each shootist has contributed two thousand dollars to the prize money, totaling twelve thousand dollars."

The sheriff paused to let the grand sum of the prize money really sink in. Whoever won it would have enough money to do whatever they liked. Travel far away. Buy a place. Start a business. Have somebody killed. Have several people killed!

"A lot of money," Hope said.

Ethan nodded along. "Yeah . . . enough money to die for."

"Or kill for."

Sheriff Maxwell cleared his throat. Opened his arms. "To the victor, the spoils. Now it is time to reveal who will be participating in this year's contest of guns."

The church doors opened, letting in the cold.

Every head turned to watch the six combatants stride in and take their places up on the stage. Hope's body tensed as her eyes followed them. The fifth gunslinger to walk in didn't so much as glance in her direction, but Hope found herself unable to take her eyes off him. Only when he'd reached the stage and the sixth, and last, contestant walked in was she able to look away. Cyrus Barbosa did not have his henchmen with him this time — he did not need them. He was the largest of the shootists to take their seats up on the stage, but his size did not restrict his movements. He held himself with the grace of a man a third his size, although his considerable bulk barely fit in the chair that had been left for him.

"Starting on the right," Sheriff Maxwell said. "Miss Daiyu Wu. The daughter of immigrant railroad workers, Miss Wu manifests her own destiny in this land of opportunity and enterprise with her twin shooters."

Wu eyed the crowd, then pulled her pistols from their holsters and made them twirl on her fingers. With a theatrical flourish, she gave them one more spin on her forefingers, then dropped them into their holsters in one smooth movement.

"Thank you," Maxwell said. "Next up we have Sid Babcock, or 'Crazy' Sid Babcock as he's known around these parts. How's about you stand up, Sid, give the people a good look at you?"

Babcock was chewing tobacco and eyeballing the sheriff, his freckled face fixed in a scowl. He made a show of slowly getting to his feet, then spitting brown tobacco juice off the side of the stage. There were several murmurs of discontent from the crowd, but the sheriff was able to calm them before their reaction to Babcock's dirty habit escalated to something more.

"Now, now, ladies and gents. Calm yourselves. I don't think Mister Babcock meant much wrong by it."

Babcock grinned at the sheriff, showing rows of dingy brown teeth.

Maxwell watched the bandit resume his seat.

"Our third participant made his name in the war as part of a special unit tasked with infiltrating enemy camps and catching them with their britches down, so to speak. Some of you folks might recall reading about their shenanigans in the papers at the time. You'd be mistaken for thinkin' he's called Red on account of fiery hair, but he's no more ginger than I am. He's called Red because he was often covered, head to toe, with blood. And that's a true story, or so I'm told."

Red Nelson stood and bowed his head, smiling thinly at the gathered spectators before sitting back down.

Sheriff Maxwell looked at the woman next to Red Nelson. "The next shootist is a lady by the name of Renee Lane. Recall that shoot-out in Balboa Bridge a little over six months ago? The only survivor of that gunfight with the deadly Blue Viper Gang was — yes, you guess correctly — Miss Lane here."

Renee Lane stood, then promptly sat back down. She did not appear amused or impressed. Her lone pistol rested at her left hip, and her hand rested there absently, as if she expected an assassin to leap from the shadows at any moment.

"The next gunslinger of this competition has spent the last couple of years raising merry hell down South. Mister Lance Knox has finally agreed to take part in this here contest and put his reputation to the ultimate test," Maxwell said.

Knox did not stand or make any movement, other than to glance at the man next to him. He and Barbosa exchanged silent looks.

Hope got the distinct impression there was no love lost between Knox and Barbosa. For her own part, it was hard to look at Knox, to see him looking older, more rugged. Knowing that he'd ended her father's life and left her for dead. Knowing he and Puck Cosby had brought her whole world crashing down on her that one fateful day — she'd spent too long imagining how it would be when she avenged her father's death. And as she looked upon him, sat smugly up on the stage — in a place of worship no less! — Hope felt her blood boil with fury.

Ethan's hand fell to her wrist. He was looking at her, brow creased, face tight. "You look like you're about to kill somebody," he said, moving his hand away.

Hope eased up. Remembered to breathe to calm herself. She needed a clear head. She needed to do what she'd come to Fortune's Cross to do. Rage could fall on you like a thick curtain, obscuring your purpose and your direction, but only if you allowed it to do so.

"I am about to kill somebody," Hope whispered, looking once more at Lance Knox.

Ethan followed her gaze. "Ah." The true meaning of her visit to Fortune's Cross had finally become apparent to him.

Sheriff Maxwell wound up the proceedings. "Last, but certainly not least, we have the reigning champion of this contest. No introduction is needed. You all know him by now. Allow me to present Cyrus Barbosa. Undisputed, sure, but will he remain undefeated? We shall see."

Barbosa got to his feet. He smiled at the

sheriff and then at the audience in turn. His eyes flicked toward Hope and Ethan, then away, as if they were no more important than anyone else. Their confrontation in the café the night before was seemingly forgotten.

Hope had no doubt that the man would hold a grudge for being belittled in public, and act upon it later down the line, but for now Barbosa had bigger fish to fry.

Her own gaze fell back upon Lance Knox. She could still hear his voice so close to her ear, speaking in little more than a whisper, the feeling of his breath tickling her skin enough to make her feel sick. *Killed him like a dog. Because that's what he was, a good-for-nothin' dog. When a dog got no use, you put it down. Just like we did your pop.*

She closed her eyes, the pain of that memory visceral and fresh as an open wound.

The sheriff was speaking. Hope opened her eyes again. Barbosa had retaken his seat.

Maxwell said, "Now that we've met the players, let's see who is facin' who in the first round. As you all well know, the contest is fought out in the street, at dawn, high noon and dusk." He took his hat and carried it to his assistant. "Missus Samson was kind enough to write down all the names of the contestants earlier today, then fold them up so nobody can see what name is written on each bit of paper. Missus Samson will now drop these bits of paper into my hat. I'll reach in without lookin' and pick one. The first two names I pick will fight tomorrow at dawn. The next two at high noon, and so on. The combatants on the second day will be decided by coin toss. That's the way it's always been done."

Mrs. Samson dropped the six folded bits of paper into the hollow of his upturned hat. The crowd collectively held their breath as Sheriff Maxwell lowered his hand into the hat and removed one of the bits of paper.

He unfolded it and read the name written there in Mrs. Samson's curling script.

"Renee Lane."

Maxwell took another piece of paper. Unfolded it. Read it out, then held it up for all to see.

"Crazy Sid Babcock."

Mrs. Samson chalked their names onto the board. When she was done, Sheriff Maxwell repeated the process.

"Lance Knox."

Hope swallowed.

The sheriff unfolded the fourth piece of paper.

"Red Nelson." Maxwell turned to the contestants. "That means that with only two names left, Daiyu Wu will compete against Cyrus Barbosa."

On the board were written *Renee Lane* and *Sid Babcock* in the dawn column for the first day, *Lance Knox* and *Red Nelson* competing at high noon and, in the dusk column, *Daiyu Wu* and *Cyrus Barbosa*.

A day of killing, Hope thought with distaste. *Such disrespect for life.*

As the chatter among the audience rose in volume, Ethan turned to Hope. "It's Knox, isn't it?"

Hope looked at the man on the stage. She felt in control, but at the same time, she could not look away.

"Yes," she said.

"You'd better hope he makes it through the first round. Or this whole thing will be a waste of time."

Hope said, "He won't make it to the first round."

CHAPTER FOUR

As everyone filed out of the church, Barbosa announced in his thunderous voice that he would be buying drinks at the saloon for all who wished to celebrate the start of the contest. There were some cheers from the crowd, but Hope noted most people were hurrying home to get prepared for the following day's proceedings. There would be shooting and there would be dead bodies in the street. The townsfolk would either hole themselves up behind boarded windows and bolted doors or leave town altogether. Gunslinging was one thing, but getting caught in the cross fire, when you were doing little more than minding your own business, was another. To stand someone down had an element of honor to it that not even Hope Cassidy could deny. As senseless as it seemed, there was reasoning behind it. But to die by accident, from a bullet punching through your wall, was the definition of unfair. Folk who knowingly put themselves in harm's way like that were willful fodder to a game of chance.

The gaggle of people in the street steadily thinned out. Those heading home broke in various directions, while those making their way to the saloon continued in one large group. Hope saw Lance Knox walking away and knew her moment had come.

"Get out of here," she said to Ethan.

"What?"

"Go!"

Ethan continued walking, without so much as a sideward glance. He knew what she was about to do — and that no matter what he might say to her, Hope's mind was set.

Hope pulled her bullwhip free. She drew a breath. "Lance Knox!" she yelled.

He stopped walking. Began to turn around.

"I've been waiting a long time for this!"

Before he could face her fully, Hope flicked the bullwhip out. The tail caught Knox around the throat and wrapped itself around him. Hope gave the whip a good hard pull, yanking Knox forward. He lost his footing and fell to his knees in the cold mud. He reached up, hands clawing at the length of whip around his neck and successfully pulling it free. Hope snapped the whip, the tail slashing his face open like a knife.

Knox cried out, clutching at his face.

Hope walked steadily toward him. The other contestants and assorted onlookers stopped in their tracks to watch what was happening, the faces of the unsuspecting townsfolk frozen in stunned disbelief.

"You don't recognize me, do you?"

"I don't care who you are!" Knox spat, getting to his feet. "I'll kill you!"

"My father was Tobias Cassidy, and eight years ago, you and Puck Cosby killed him in cold blood. Then you tried to kill me," Hope said, fixing the whip back in place. She left her hand hanging over her holster. "Probably thought you did kill me. But I lived. I survived. And the only thing that kept me going all this time was the thought of catching up with the two of you."

"Cosby's dead," Knox said.

Hope kept her eyes fixed on his. "I know. It was me killed him. Now I am going to kill you, too. Right here, right now."

Sheriff Maxwell approached. "Hey, now, I think we can find a peaceful alternative to this —"

"Back off!" Hope snapped.

The sheriff stopped moving.

Barbosa stood on the sidelines. He whistled, a single shrill sound. "This ain't the way we do things, Travis."

"I know," Maxwell replied. "Can't you see I'm tryin' to deal with the situation?"

Knox's patience had run out. "I ain't got time for this," he said, reaching for his gun.

"No!" Maxwell shouted.

Hope drew first. She didn't hesitate in pulling the trigger. The report of her gun echoed through the town like a thunderbolt, loud and sharp. The gunshot sent Knox's sidearm flying up into the air with the clang of lead striking metal.

Knox looked at her in shock. He took an uncertain step back. Raised his hands in apparent surrender.

"I don't know what's going on here, Miss Cassidy, but I want you to rethink this," Sheriff Maxwell said in an even, calm voice she couldn't help but listen to. "You can still walk away. Get on your horse. Leave town."

"I swore that once I found him, I wouldn't rest until he was in the ground and that's what's happening."

Knox shook his head. "Have some mercy."

"Mercy?" Hope asked. "Did you show my father mercy? Were you going to show *me* any mercy that night after you'd both had your fun? I don't think so. We both know how that would've ended. This has been eight years coming for you, Lance Knox."

With two quick retorts of her pistol, Hope shot Knox through the palms of his hands. He looked at them in horror, turning them over in shock and disbelief. His hands had been rendered useless, torn to shreds, blood running down his wrists and over his clothes. Then the pain seemed to hit.

Knox howled, gaping in horror at what Hope had done to them. "My hands! My damn hands!"

Hope stepped in close to him until she was little more than an arm's length away. She touched his forehead with the end of her pistol. "This is for my father," she said, and pulled the trigger before anyone could stop her.

The bullet exploded out the back of his head, taking the mushy pink contents of his skull with it. He fell back and landed with an audible squelch in the cold, wet mud, his body jerking involuntarily, then growing still.

The sheriff pulled his own gun and leveled it at her. "Damn you, that's enough. Toss your shooter on the ground and put your hands up. You're under arrest!"

Hope let her gun fall to the mud in the

street. Maxwell wasted no time pulling her hands down to the small of her back, pinning her by the wrists and clapping her in irons. He collected her gun.

"Sorry," Hope said.

"Too late for that now."

"It had to be done."

"You sure as hell ain't made this easy. When you said you had dealings with somebody in town, I didn't expect you to go shootin' 'em down dead in the street for all to see."

"I didn't expect you to understand," she said.

Maxwell steered her away, heading for the sheriff's office. He lowered his voice as they left the crowd behind. "Are you crazy?"

She didn't answer him.

"I suggest when I get you to a cell, you start explaining yourself. Because by the time Barbosa is done stirring up the town, they're gonna want to see you hang or use you for target practice."

Sheriff Travis Maxwell took down Hope's particulars, her full name and anything else she could tell him about herself, then showed her to an empty cell. He instructed her to stand inside while he rolled the barred door closed and locked it shut.

"Get as close to the bars as possible so I can unlock your irons," he instructed her. Hope held out her shackled wrists and Maxwell reached through to unlock the cuffs. "There we are."

Hope worked at her wrists. The cuffs had bitten into her skin, leaving red rings.

"Thought you had a fella in here already," Hope said, looking at the two empty cells next to hers. "The one Katie Roper brought in."

"You mean, the man you helped wrangle when he cut loose?" Maxwell said. "He got sent on his way this morning, first light. So I seem to have lost one occupant and gained another."

There was considerable noise outside, and it was getting louder as each moment passed.

"What is that?" Hope asked.

Maxwell looked toward the front of the building, weighing up his options. "They're waitin' on a verdict."

Hope sat down on the bare cot the other side of the cell. "It'll be what it'll be."

"I'll go out there, talk to them, tell them all to be on their way," Maxwell told her.

She watched the sheriff go, heard him open the door to the sheriff's office, then address the crowd outside. She did not hear

103

what he promised them, not that she desired to know. There was a part of her that feared the crowd, feared what was coming. But mainly she felt a great sense of calm wash over her. Fate would decide what happened next. She had never been more aware than she was in that moment that she was fate's instrument.

When the sheriff returned a good twenty minutes later, he looked flustered by his exchange with the crowd. Maxwell removed his hat and tossed it onto a peg on the wall. He walked to his desk, opened the bottom drawer and retrieved a flask of whiskey, then dragged a chair into the corridor and sat in front of her cell, sipping the whiskey, deep in thought.

"So? Am I to hang for killing Knox?"

"They were a tough crowd," he said. "But I got them to calm down for now. Sent them on their way."

"No pound of flesh yet, then."

"Not for the minute," Maxwell said, taking a sip of his whiskey. "But you've spilled blood today, and the other contestants are after some in return. I think it's high time you explain yourself, Miss Cassidy. I want you to tell me why in the hell you shot that man dead when he was defenseless, no less."

"He was only defenseless when I shot the

gun he pulled on me out of his hands."

Maxwell jabbed a finger in her direction. "I don't have no time for nitpicking. The wolves are at the door, Miss Cassidy, and I need to understand why this situation has blown up the way it has, out of nowhere."

"As I said, it's a long story."

"Then you'd best begin it," Sheriff Maxwell told her. "In the saloon you told me you had business to settle with a man in town. And do you remember me telling you I didn't want any additional bloodshed? That was only yesterday I had that conversation with you. And here you are in a cell for murdering a man in the street."

Hope ran her fingers through her hair. She felt strangely naked without her gun at her side. She wondered how long it had been since she last took it off — and realized that she hadn't for years. Only to sleep, and then it would be right next to her, mere inches away. Ready to grab at the slightest sound of something, or someone, approaching.

"I have to start at the beginning. I have to start with the death of my father. Well, not his death . . . his murder. His slaughter."

The sheriff pushed the cork in the whiskey bottle and set it down on the floor next to his chair. "Go on."

Hope drew a deep breath. Had she ever

spoken about any of this? Only to Elijah. But she had no need to mention him, at least not to the sheriff. Elijah had gotten her back on her feet. Elijah had been the second man to teach her how to live. She looked the sheriff in the eye. Then she told him why she had come to Fortune's Cross to kill Lance Knox.

CHAPTER FIVE

When Hope Cassidy finished the tale, Sheriff Travis Maxwell handed his half bottle of whiskey to her through the bars of the cell. His demeanor toward her had softened noticeably through the telling of the tale.

"Here you are. I think you could use a nip of this."

"Thanks," Hope said, accepting the booze.

"You said it was a long story," Maxwell said, eyes heavy. "You weren't kidding, were you?"

"No," Hope said, drinking some of the whiskey.

The sheriff got to his feet.

Hope looked up at him. "Where are you going?"

"After the story you just told me? I've got a body to examine."

Maxwell collected his hat and stepped outside into the crisp air. Earlier there had been a crowd of men waiting in the street, outraged by what they'd witnessed happen to Knox, and eager for blood. But now the street was empty. The sheriff was able to go about his business unhindered by a mob. Lance Knox remained where he'd fallen, though his body had been covered with a dirty sheet.

At the sight of the sheriff emerging from his office, Cyrus Barbosa appeared on the front porch of the saloon and waved him over.

I'd die a happy man if I didn't have to appease him every time he lays eyes on me, Maxwell thought, forcing something akin to a smile onto his face. "Cyrus."

The rotund gunslinger thudded down the steps of the porch. "Well? You got to the bottom of this mess, Sheriff?"

"I'm about to."

"You are?"

Maxwell nodded. "I believe so, yes."

"I gotta see this," Barbosa said in a mocking tone.

Maxwell walked over to the body of Lance Knox and hunkered down in the muddy slush. It squelched up his boots as he pulled the sheet back and searched the man's body, lifting one arm and then the other.

"What're you lookin' for there, Sheriff?"

Barbosa asked.

"I'll know it when I see it," Maxwell said.

Barbosa laughed. "I think it's clear to everyone but you what killed Knox. You can tell by lookin' at what's left of his head."

"I'm not looking for cause of death, Cyrus. Aaahhh," he said as he found what he'd been looking for.

Barbosa scowled at him. " 'Aaahhh' what?"

"This," Maxwell said. He lifted Knox's arm to show Barbosa the tattoo of a black scorpion on his wrist. "Right where she said it would be." He repositioned Knox's arm at his side and pulled the sheet back up over what was left of the man's head.

Barbosa looked strangely unsettled by the sheriff's revelation. "I don't see what this has to do with anything. Shootin' a fella down in the street like that. She ain't in the contest. She had no cause. It was an act of cold-blooded murder, is what it was. I say it can't stand, Travis."

Maxwell stood. "Well, there's the rub. It weren't as cold-blooded as you think. The lady had a legitimate reason to gun this man down, in my opinion."

"And what might that be? Because he had a tattoo?" Barbosa scoffed.

The sheriff folded his arms in front of his

chest. "No. Because this was one of the men killed her pop. And she says she's been lookin' high and low for him all this time. Eventually tracked him down here, when she heard through the grapevine Knox would be takin' part in the contest. Makes the whole thing a little complicated, don't it?"

Barbosa looked down at the awkward shape of Knox beneath the sheet. "In your opinion," he said, his gaze lifting to meet the sheriff's.

"What's that supposed to mean?"

"Well, it's your personal take on things, ain't it? It's not the view of the law. If we're followin' the law here in Fortune's Cross, then murder is murder, whether it was committed out of vengeance or not. Am I right?"

"Well . . ." Maxwell tried and failed to think of a rebuttal to what Barbosa had just said. "I reckon so."

Barbosa stood with his thumbs hooked into the belt of his pants, breath blowing like hot steam as he spoke. "The folks assembled for this contest have a lot of money invested. And they ain't happy one of the participants got himself killed before the contest got goin'. Now you stand there and tell me you understand that woman's motivation. Well, that's down to you, Sheriff.

Like I done told you, that's your personal opinion. But in the meantime, the law has to be upheld. That woman should hang for shooting Knox dead like that."

"I'm not hanging anyone," Maxwell said.

Barbosa did not attempt to disguise his consternation at the sheriff's attitude. "You're not the only one can throw a rope around her neck, Travis."

"What're you saying?"

Barbosa stepped in close. "I'm sayin', if you ain't willing to see things done, we'll see to it ourselves."

"Is that a threat?" Maxwell asked.

"Not a threat," Barbosa said. He ran a hand over the lower portion of his round, pudgy face. "I'd say it's a certainty. If you won't wield the powers of the law, then I'm afraid me and a couple of the other fellas stand ready and willing to do so. We'll lynch that murderess and make her pay for killing Lance Knox."

Maxwell took a step back. "You wouldn't dare!"

Barbosa said, "Wouldn't I?"

"Do you have any respect for the rule of law at all, Cyrus?" Maxwell asked.

" 'Wrest once the law to your authority,' " Barbosa quoted. " 'To do a great right, do a little wrong.' "

"It does no good to kill that woman."

"Then what do you propose?"

Twenty minutes later, Maxwell had arranged for Lance Knox's body to be removed from the street, on account of the trauma it might cause the townsfolk who'd been under the impression there wouldn't be any shooting, or dead bodies, until the following day.

He returned to the sheriff's office and removed his hat. Maxwell knew Hope Cassidy was waiting to hear what he had to say. The sheriff almost couldn't believe the way Barbosa had threatened him. But Maxwell knew he was powerless to stop him from lynching the woman. What good was one man against so many? Barbosa had men at his disposal. What did Maxwell have? A gun and a tin star. That was about the extent of it.

He felt powerless. Ineffectual. And for all intents and purposes, he *was* powerless. Mob rule would see Barbosa gather up an army of people to storm the sheriff's office and take control. They'd wrench Cassidy from her cell and see to it her life was ended — without any pretense of a fair trial or a defense. But there was a way out, a single chance at keeping her neck free of a noose

112

and Maxwell hoped she could see the right of it.

Maxwell dreaded the look of disappointment when he told her the alternative. She would see that he was weak, that he was diminished by mob rule. She would see through him as surely as if he were made of paper.

Every contest, he prayed that Barbosa ate a bullet. And every year, the son of a bitch survived to the end. Barbosa won each time and took all the money, all the glory. It would take a rogue element to upset the course of things.

Sheriff Travis Maxwell wondered if Hope Cassidy might be what he'd been hoping for.

He walked down the corridor toward her cell. Cassidy was lying on the cot, hands folded on her chest as she stared up at the ceiling. She looked peaceful, at rest, as if consigned to her fate — whatever shape her fate ended up taking.

Hope sat up as he approached, eager to hear what he had to say. "So?"

The sheriff did not sit in the chair he'd dragged there earlier. He remained standing to break the news, tell her the choice she had to make. Was it really a choice if there was no other way?

"I'm gonna put it simple. Tell you straight. That's the only way it can be, d'you understand?"

"Just spit it out."

"I told Barbosa your reasons for killin' Knox, but he ain't interested in the whys and the wherefores of the situation. Far as he sees it, you owe the house now. Given half a chance, he'll have you strung up by sundown. Not a lot I can do about it if he forms a mob and storms in here."

"You're one man," Hope agreed, to his surprise. "You can't fight a dozen by yourself."

He struggled to find his words at first. "So, you see how it is. There's just one way out of this, but you won't like it."

"A way out of this?"

Maxwell nodded. "Yeah. Barbosa made me an offer to bring to you."

"*Offer?* What offer?"

"If you take Knox's place in the contest, Barbosa'll let it slide. Because the way he sees it, he's gonna win this thing and you'll get what's comin' to you. You'll be dead, and he'll be the victor," he explained. "That is, of course, unless you win."

"I didn't come here to kill people I've got no quarrel with," Hope told him.

"I know that. But this is your only chance.

114

Either you hang, or you compete in this contest to live. It's one or the other. There ain't no ifs or buts about it."

Hope walked away. There was a tiny slit of a window at the top of the wall in front of her, bars across it. The cold air wafted in, stirring some of her hair.

"Fine." She turned back. "Tell him I'll do it."

"You will?"

"Yes. These aren't innocent people I'm going up against. They're all killers, just like me. Am I right?"

The sheriff sighed. "You sure about playing this game of his?"

"I am."

"Then you should tell him yourself." Maxwell unlocked the door to her cell and slid it back on its runners. "Lord, it's about time Barbosa caught the losing end of this contest," he said, handing her the half-filled bottle of whiskey. He watched as she took a good, long swallow of the amber liquid, wiping at her mouth with the back of her hand.

"Let me ask you something," Hope said, handing the bottle back. "What is it, exactly, Barbosa does here?"

"I can't rightly say," Sheriff Maxwell said, scratching his jaw line. "He's got his fingers in a lot of pies. Different businesses. He's got land here and there, and lemme tell you, that man's always on the lookout for more. Far as I'm aware, his business dealings is all legitimate. But as to what exactly he does, well, that's for the birds."

"He has business interests in Fortune's Cross?"

"Some, I think. I know he's after the café down the street. Been eyeing it up for years. Ruth and Frank have declined his offers so far . . . but that don't mean they'll turn him down forever. Eventually he'll get his own way, and it'll be another bit of this fine town he owns."

Hope wouldn't have gone so far as to call Fortune's Cross a fine town, but she kept her opinion to herself. "Can I ask you something else, Sheriff?"

"Shoot."

"Would you allow this contest if Barbosa was dead?"

"No. I'd make this town a nice, quiet place to live again. Bring the townsfolk some peace."

Hope Cassidy collected her hat and slipped it back onto her head. "That's all I needed to hear."

Sheriff Maxwell walked out onto the main street of Fortune's Cross. He understood that the death of Lance Knox was a headache for Barbosa because the contest took months to wrangle together — each time shootists came to town to compete, five gunslingers who couldn't easily be replaced were killed. Especially at short notice. Every year the pool of talent grew ever shallower. With Knox out of the picture, Cyrus Barbosa might have had to cancel the contest entirely. That had never happened before.

Maxwell felt like a fulcrum sometimes, balancing the desire to do his duty with the need to play politics and keep Barbosa and his kind satisfied. It was not a part he enjoyed playing. It wasn't a part he'd ever imagined for himself. But this was the life he had come to know. It hurt, letting go of his principles, but if he was anything, he was a survivor. Nobody made old bones poking bears with a stick. Sometimes it was best to treat the bear like a friend. It was all about knowing when to leave well enough alone.

When he escorted Hope across the street to the saloon for her meeting with Barbosa, he half expected somebody to come at them. But it seemed that witnessing Cassidy blast Knox's brain matter across the street was giving folk pause.

The lady bounty hunter was on the porch

117

leaning against the railing, having a smoke. Maxwell could hear Barbosa and the rest inside.

The bounty hunter raised a hand in greeting to them both. "Howdy, howdy."

"Miss Roper," Maxwell said.

Roper looked at Hope appraisingly. "If it ain't the stone-cold killer. There I was thinkin' you were the quiet type."

"I used to be, years ago," Hope said.

"But not anymore, I take it."

"No," Hope said. "Joining the festivities?"

"Me? No. Uh-uh. I was gonna have one last drink, then make my move outta here. But I wanted to speak with you a moment first. If the sheriff here don't mind, that is."

Maxwell shifted on his feet. "Matter of fact, can this wait a moment? We have a matter to clear up first. This young lady is still under arrest."

Roper lifted her cigarette. Bowed her head a little. "I'll be right out here."

Maxwell opened the saloon doors for Hope and she stepped inside. The air was thick with smoke, the voices of the patrons raised in revelry. Burt looked rushed off his feet behind the bar. As Hope followed Sheriff Maxwell across the saloon, the voices trailed away until they fell completely silent.

"Two hits of whiskey, Burt, if you please," Maxwell said.

The bartender smiled and did as he was asked.

"I'll get these," Hope said.

"No, no —"

Hope shook her head. "I insist."

"Much obliged." Maxwell sank his shot of whiskey. He turned in time to see Barbosa ambling toward them. "Here he comes," he mumbled.

Hope gave a discreet nod to indicate she'd heard him.

Barbosa's hand fell to the bar top next to Hope. "Is there any of that whiskey going, Burt?"

Hope looked to the bartender. "Give the man a glass, will you?"

Burt nodded. "Sure," he said, setting a glass down in front of Barbosa. He filled it to the top with whiskey.

Barbosa lifted the glass and downed it in one without so much as a gasp. He regarded the empty vessel in his hand, then looked directly at Hope. "Takes a lot of guts to shoot a man dead in the street. In broad daylight, right in front of everyone."

"Does it?"

Barbosa put the glass down. "Yes."

Hope frowned. "So, you don't disapprove

— except so far as it affects your tournament? Or do you hold a grudge over last night?"

"I am not a petty man," Barbosa said with a shrug. "I'm sure the sheriff told you I have a lot of influence in this town. I hold my cards close to my chest, and I know how and when to play them, too. When you pulled that stunt in the café —"

"That wasn't a stunt," Hope said. "There's right and there's wrong. Simple as that."

Barbosa's eyes narrowed. "It was a stunt and you know it."

"You can think what you like. That's your prerogative," Hope said. "Where's this conversation going?"

" 'Life's but a walking shadow, a poor player that struts and frets his hour upon the stage, and then is heard no more: It is a tale told by an idiot, full of sound and fury, signifying nothing.' "

Hope frowned. "What in the hell is that supposed to mean?"

"You're not versed in Shakespeare, are you?"

"No. It sounds like you're speaking in riddles."

Barbosa sighed. "I feel it's only right that I expect blood in return for blood. You owe the house, girlie. The debt has to be paid. I take it the sheriff told you my offer?"

"He did."

"And what do you say to it?"

"I say, count me in."

Barbosa smiled thinly. "Reckon yourself a decent shot, do you?"

"I do okay."

"Good enough to go up against me?" Barbosa asked.

Hope shrugged. "Maybe. I guess we'll find out, won't we? Thing about being the best is, you end up with a big target on your back. You've won this contest so many times, Barbosa, the money no longer matters. Killing you is now the ultimate prize."

"Are you speaking for yourself?" Barbosa asked.

"Since I've been given the option of either dangling at the end of a rope or participating in your wretched contest, I reckon I *am* speaking for myself. If we're the last guns standing, I'll look forward to taking you down."

Barbosa grinned then. Big and wide, the sickly smile consumed his entire face. "And I look forward to seeing you try."

When they were outside again, Sheriff Maxwell removed his hat and ran his fingers through his hair. "Damn that was tense."

"Seemed pretty straightforward to me," Hope said.

A horse and cart rattled past, lanterns swinging from the back of it, and the two of them watched it go on its way.

"Leaving town while they still can?" Hope asked.

"Probably," Maxwell said. "He must like your spunk. You talk straight and to the point and Barbosa is the kinda fella appreciates that."

"Is that so? Well, there's no point in beating around the bush, is there?"

"I guess not. Feeling confident about your chances?" Maxwell asked.

Hope looked back at the saloon, at Katie Roper, who, having finished her smoke, was leaning against the railing, watching them converse. "Confident as I can be."

"Well, I should be heading back. Big day tomorrow. Try to get some decent shut-eye if you can."

"I will. Thanks, Sheriff," Hope said, heading back toward the saloon.

Katie Roper nodded toward the sheriff. "Night."

"Night," he said, walking off in the direction of his office.

Hope took a seat next to her. "You wanted to speak to me?"

122

"I heard you're taking part in the contest," Katie said.

"Not out of choice."

Katie said, "I heard that, too."

"What else have you heard?"

"That your father was killed by Black Scorpions."

Hope felt suddenly off-balance, as if all that she'd known before was just the tip of an iceberg and, for the first time, she was seeing just how far below the surface the ice descended.

"Wh-who?" she asked, the word slurring clumsily in her mouth.

"The outlaw gang. The Black Scorpions."

"I'm not sure who or what you're talking about."

"You've never heard of them?"

Hope shook her head. "No."

"It doesn't matter," Katie said.

"How would you know they were Black Scorpions?"

"I hear things," Katie said with a shrug. "A US marshal gets gunned down in cold blood? You'd better believe the wrong types of people hear about what happened. Most importantly, it don't take long for folk to know who pulled the trigger."

"Is that how you categorize yourself, as

one of the wrong types of people?" Hope asked.

"I used to be," Katie said. She walked across the porch until she was near the window, her face caught in the glow of the firelight from within. She jutted her chin. "Look at him."

Hope stood behind her. It was instantly clear who Katie was talking about. Barbosa stood entertaining the patrons of the saloon, no doubt buying them drinks, regaling them with tales of his escapades.

"Looks like the locals adore him."

"They fear him," Katie said. "Which is sometimes the same thing. He's got this whole town in his grip and they don't even feel him squeezing."

"I'm going to take him down," Hope said.

Katie took Hope's elbow and nudged her into the shadows. "Watch your step."

"What do you mean?"

"Those men who killed your father."

"What about them?"

"Are you operating under the assumption that your father's murder had something to do with him being a marshal?"

"That's what I've always thought."

Katie said, "Has it ever crossed your mind that it might've been more personal than that?"

124

"Of course it has."

"Listen, maybe it *was* just for being a marshal. Maybe they killed him in revenge for sending one of the gang to jail or he stopped them pulling off a job. I wouldn't know. But think about it. And watch yourself in Fortune's Cross. You don't have many friends here. Assume that enemies are all around because it's highly likely they are."

Hope thought back to that awful day.

"Puck Cosby, and this here is Lance Knox."

"You don't have to introduce yourselves. Not to me."

"We thought you might've forgotten, is all," Knox said, raising his arm to reveal a black tattoo of a scorpion on his wrist.

"There ain't no forgetting." Tobias breathed steadily, calmly.

It slowly dawned on Hope. The realization felt like a cold wave, working its way through her entire body. It was so obvious, so clear.

Katie was right. It *had* been personal.

"The men who killed my father . . . they had black scorpion tattoos. I remember now. I think they knew him somehow."

"That's what I heard, that there was some connection."

"Why are you telling me this?"

"Because I see a kindred spirit," Katie

125

said. "Listen to me. A life on the road, you hear a lot. Some of it true, some of it not so much. Let me ask you something. Does Barbosa know who you are?"

"As in, does he know I'm my father's daughter?"

"Yes."

"I don't think so. Unless the sheriff mentioned it to him."

"Be careful," Katie said. "From what I heard, Cyrus Barbosa had dealings with various outlaw gangs. But when it came to the Black Scorpions, it was more than that. He *ran* them. As in, he was their leader. He's not to be trusted."

Hope stood for a moment watching Barbosa through the window.

I wouldn't trust him as far as I could spit, she thought.

She turned back to say as much to Katie Roper, only to find that Katie had already left. Hope walked to the end of the porch and looked for her but could see no sign.

Evidently Katie Roper was not one for small talk . . . or goodbyes.

Jasper watched Hope climb the staircase. "Miss, you don't need my help tonight?"

"Not this time," Hope said. "Thanks, Jasper."

She went to her room, locked the door behind her and settled into the chair in the corner once more. Hope didn't think Barbosa would attempt anything now that she was a part of the contest, but she couldn't know for sure. So she slept as she had the night before, facing the door with her gun close to hand.

Her father lay on the ground, lay on the ground and stared into the dark chasm of the gun. He turned his head and looked at her, eyes focusing. He did not have to tell her that he loved her. He did not have time to say goodbye or offer any last wisdom.

There was just that one look.

One last connection between them.

The seconds became minutes, hours, days, an eternity. . . .

The trigger was pulled and the gun erupted. Hope flinched from the sound, squeezing her eyes shut. And in the darkness she fell, arms and legs windmilling, screaming for her father. But she screamed without sound. Nothing but silence issued from her mouth.

Hope did not hit water. She was not dragged along by the current. She just kept falling, and screaming

Hope jerked awake, covered in sweat, gun in her hand. Her finger sat up against the trigger, ready to fire with the slightest amount of additional pressure. It took her a moment to realize she was alone in the room, and that there was no threat to be found there.

Holstering her gun, Hope went to the window and opened it wide, allowing the ice-cold air to flood in, cooling her off. Any lingering fog from the nightmare blew away with it.

Hope looked up at the sky and saw the darkness, and the stars, and the cold white moon, and in that moment she thought of her father, and the endless void to which they were all committed, eventually.

The same void she'd sent Knox and Cosby to. Was it the right thing? She did not know. There was solace to be found in justice, and she'd always known that there would be no satisfaction in her father's killers getting their day in court. She had to bring the void to them, to ensure they met the infinite black with the same lack of compassion they'd shown her father.

That was justice, and it was as cold and pure as the air that chilled her skin.

Hope pulled the window closed, the nightmare's spell broken.

Her resolve just as strong as it had always been.

■ ■ ■ ■

PART TWO:
ONE OF THESE DAYS

■ ■ ■ ■

CHAPTER SIX

Eight Years Ago

Hope Cassidy fell through darkness. She plunged into the depths, the waterfall turning her over, slamming her against the rocks beneath the surface. Her right shoulder flared with pain from the impact. She cried out, expelling the contents of her lungs, leaving them burning. She was jostled to the side, against a large boulder. She braced her right hand against its smooth surface and pushed off, breaking the surface long enough to take several breaths before being sucked back under by the current.

The log she had lost hold of now rose up in front of her, and Hope hooked her arms around it. The log was kicked sideward, tossing Hope against the rocks again, crushing the delicate bones of both hands as the log rolled, then surged up to break the surface. Hope coughed up the water that had collected in her lungs. Her mouth tasted of silt and mud. The river pushed her along and she began to slip, her shoulder singing, the pain radiating throughout her entire body. In that moment, death seemed inevitable to her. She wondered if it might not be so bad to simply drown. Let herself go, slip beneath the water's surface and let it take her. It would at least put an end to the pain.

But then the log caught a current that took her to the left, close to a bank of reeds. The end of the log snagged against the reeds enough to slow it down. It turned around, one end still propelled by the flow of water, then got properly stuck. Hope pushed through the reeds, making for the shore, her feet finding purchase on the gritty mud of the riverbed. She stumbled up the incline, collapsing first to her knees, then forward onto her torso, finally spent.

She sobbed at the pain in her gut, in her shoulder, in her broken hands; at the feeling of being broken in ways that went beyond the physical. Broken inside, broken in her soul.

Then, exhausted, she closed her eyes and knew no more.

Hope found the chest under her parents' bed. She got down on her belly and attempted to reach it, the tips of her fingers just skirting the corroded iron handle by a fraction of an inch. If she could just reach the handle, she could pull the chest free of the bed and see what was inside. Hope wondered what she could use to gain purchase.

"What're you doing?"

Hope froze.

"Come on. Out of there," Tobias said, sternly. "This isn't a room you should be playing in."

"I just wanted to explore," Hope told him.

She got to her feet. Her father touched the soft mop of her hair. "I know, little one, but there's things in this room aren't for your eyes."

"What do you mean?"

"You wouldn't understand," her father said. "I have old guns in here. They're not something you can play with. They're not toys."

Maria stood at the bottom of the stairs and called up to them. "Dinner is ready. Are you coming down?"

"Just a minute," Tobias called back.

Hope blinked at him. "You keep guns under your bed?"

Tobias winced. "Among other things. Anyway, at your age you shouldn't have to worry about things like guns. Just stay out of this room."

He led her out and closed the door behind

him. Hope walked along the landing and down the stairs with her father.

"Pop?"

"Yes, Hope."

"Why do you have guns?"

"They're tools I use to do my job. But they have another purpose."

"What's that?"

"I also carry them to protect us," he said.

Hope frowned as he led her into the kitchen and they sat at the table. Maria stood in front of the stove, stirring a big pot of stew.

"From what?" Hope asked.

"Well, it's complicated. . . . There are bad people in this world. And I have guns so that I can scare them off if they try to hurt us. It shouldn't have to be that way, but unfortunately that's the way the world is."

She absorbed this information. "Do you kill the bad people?"

Maria turned to face them. "Hope, why would you say that?" she asked, looking directly at her husband. "Tobias, we shouldn't be talking about this. Especially at dinnertime."

"I know —" Tobias began, but Hope interrupted.

"Pop, you kill the birds."

Tobias looked at his wife, and then back to his daughter. "Yes, I do."

"Why?"

He reached out and took her little hand in his own. "You know very well why I do that, Hope. So that we can eat them. Where have all these questions come from?"

"Do you kill all the bad people, every time you catch 'em, Pop?"

"Not everyone is bad through and through. Sometimes good people find themselves gettin' caught up doing bad things. Not every criminal deserves to meet their justice at the end of a gun, or a rope. There's such a thing as second chances, Hope. Most of the people I arrest get sent to jail. And you know what? Most of 'em come out of jail wantin' to change their ways. Be better people than they was before. That tells me they ain't bad to the core. That tells me that, for the most part, people have the capacity to change. They just have to be given a chance."

Hope looked down at his huge hand holding hers. Her gaze shifted to the scarred area on the inside of his wrist.

"What's that?"

Tobias pulled his sleeve down over it. "Just an old scar. An accident I got into years ago."

"Did it hurt?"

"Many people got hurt. But I . . . Listen, why don't we go for a walk after dinner? I heard tell there was a peacock on the loose 'round

135

here somewhere," Tobias told her. "Old man Winslow said one of his got out and he ain't seen head nor tail of the thing since."

"If we find it, will there be a prize?" Hope asked, as Maria set a bowl of hot stew in front of her. She was sold on the prospect of catching sight of the elusive bird.

"There most certainly will," Tobias said.

Hope's eyes adjusted to the flickering light. She heard the crackle of a fire and knew she was somewhere warm and dry. She didn't move for a long time. She just lay where she was, unsure how to move, or if she even could. Her hands were covered with bandages and throbbed madly beneath their bindings. The same with the rest of her body — she felt as though she'd been trampled by an elephant.

She couldn't move either arm, or sit up, despite trying. Hope wondered how she could still be alive. She was coherent enough to realize that someone must have found her at the river's edge and taken her home. Whoever it was, they'd saved her life. But how and why were a mystery.

"Hello?" she asked aloud, her voice breaking.

At first no one answered. And then, out of the silence, a man said, "Don't try to move."

Hope swallowed. Her mouth and throat were terribly dry. "Who are you?"

A man stepped into view. He had lank gray hair that fell way down his back. He was bare chested, and painfully thin, but possessed of tightly wound cords of hard muscle. It did not surprise Hope that the man had been able to carry her from the riverbank to wherever his home happened to be. His scraggly beard was braided with beads and twine — it looked as if it hadn't been washed in weeks, if ever. He had the appearance of one who bathes in a pond.

"My name is Elijah," he said.

"Elijah," Hope repeated. She licked her cracked lips. "How long have I been here?"

"A long time," Elijah told her. "Days, maybe a week already."

She swallowed. "You don't know?"

"Time can be . . . strange for me," Elijah said, almost embarrassed by his admission. "The days and nights come and go. The seasons change. That is all I know. I have lived by myself for a long, long while. Perhaps too long."

"Am I your prisoner?"

Elijah recoiled, bearing an expression of horror at the suggestion. "No! Why would you ask such a thing?"

"You said not to move."

137

"Because you are hurt," Elijah said. "I don't think there is a part of you that wasn't damaged."

"I feel stiff all over," Hope said, already exhausted from the conversation alone. "Like I'm swollen."

"That's because you are. It's hard to tell what you look like," Elijah told her.

Hope swallowed. She wanted to see herself — and yet she would have given anything not to. "Where did you find me?"

Elijah carried a wooden bowl over and fed her small amounts of water, a spoonful at a time. "Down by the river. At first, I thought you were dead," he told her. "But then I saw that you were breathing. I knew I must help or you would die there in the mud. It's in my nature to help others. Sometimes it's a handicap."

"I got shot."

Elijah took the water away. "Twice. Luckily for you, they must have passed right through without hitting anything. I stitched you up best I could, but I'm not a natural when it comes to that kind of thing. At least you won't bleed out. That's the main thing. Your wounds will heal. The shoulder was tricky, though. I don't know if that will be like it was before."

Hope lifted her bandaged hands. "And these?"

"I did my best," Elijah said. He sat down next to the cot. The firelight caught one side of his face, illuminating the craggy terrain of his weathered features. "I have had some dealings with bones before. My own hands, as you can see, are riddled with arthritis, which makes fine work like sewing a challenge. But bones I understand. It's about getting them to set straight once they're broken. And I'm afraid that in your case, I had to do a lot of breaking to be sure they'd set the way they should."

"You did . . . what?"

Elijah looked away. "If I hadn't, your hands would never heal. That's the truth. I just hope I did 'em right. It's been a while."

The tears spilled from Hope's eyes and ran into her ears. "Will they go back?"

"Only time will tell. You're lucky I found you. It don't feel like that right now, I know, but one day you'll understand."

Hope had to close her eyes. Her vision was smeared from crying and she did not have hands with which to wipe at them. "How long until they heal?"

"I don't know."

She had no words available to herself in that moment to express the sadness, the rage, the fear coursing through her. All that she'd been subjected to, it just wasn't fair. What had she ever done to deserve what she'd experienced?

Elijah continued: "The healing isn't the worst part."

Hope opened her eyes. "What is?"

"Learning to use them again. When those bandages come off for good, you're gonna have two hands you can't use. And that shoulder of yours is gonna give you hell, too," he said, getting back to his feet. "But that comes later. You should rest now. Sleep helps the body heal. Sleep is nature's miracle."

"Who are you?" Hope asked.

"I told you, my name is Elijah."

She shook her head. "No, no. I know your name. But who *are* you?"

At first he seemed to consider answering her. "Another time, perhaps," Elijah said eventually, walking away.

Hope looked up into the darkness. Despite thinking she would not sleep — could not, given the news about the gunshot wounds, her broken hands — she swiftly succumbed to the exhaustion. Sleep enveloped her like a soft, warm blanket and Hope was all too happy to let it take her.

CHAPTER SEVEN

Dash Cassidy watched as his niece attempted to use the bullwhip to strike an empty whiskey bottle he'd positioned at the top of a fence post. He got well out of the way as Hope practiced bringing the whip around and then flicking it out.

"Takes practice, is all," he told her. "You'll fail a hundred times and get the hang of it just the once. But that's all you need, that first time. Once you hit the bottle with the end of that whip, you'll know just what to do."

"This is so hard," Hope said through gritted teeth as she gave it another try — the bullwhip made a sound like a thunderclap as it struck the base of the fence post. The empty whiskey bottle wobbled slightly but was otherwise undisturbed.

"Nothing in life is easy," Dash said.

Hope smirked. "You sound just like my pop."

"Do I?"

"A little."

Her uncle pulled a face. "I don't rightly know if I should be offended or not."

"It was just an observation," Hope said.

"Uh-huh." Dash folded his arms. "How is the old rascal anyway?"

"I haven't heard from him in over a month," Hope said, cracking the whip again. "He's up to his knees in work again."

"Your father has always been up to his knees in work. Up to his elbows sometimes," Dash said, grimacing as Hope failed to hit her target again. "Hey, rest that arm. Take a minute."

"What was he like when he was younger?"

Dash leaned against the fence and looked at the clouds crossing the horizon. "He was . . . trouble, I guess you could say."

Hope stood with her forearms against the fence, frowning. "Trouble?"

"Yeah. He went crazy, I think. Ran off, got himself into all kinds of things. I never asked about any of it — tell the truth, I didn't want to know, if that makes sense to you."

"I think so."

Her uncle sighed. "I hit the prairie and learned how to drive cattle, and then a bounty hunter I got to know took me under his wing. So I left the cattle business behind and threw myself into learning all I could from him. I guess it was my callin' because that's all I done since. All I know, really, is how to find people and collect the bounty on their good-for-nothin' heads."

"But Pop eventually became a marshal. That makes up for the trouble he got in, don't it?" Hope asked.

Dash hesitated. "I guess."

She looked at her uncle. "You don't think so?"

"I never said that."

"You didn't have to," Hope told him. "I could see it in your face."

Dash stuffed tobacco into a pipe. "Listen. There are some things a man does, he don't like to talk about." He lit the pipe and took a few good draws on it. "It won't make sense to you, being young and all. But one day it will. Don't think to try and ask your pop about the past; that man won't give nothin' up, Hope. My brother is a closed book if ever there was one."

Hope watched her uncle smoke. "Do you wish he'd followed your lead?"

"There was a time I got hung up on that," Dash said with a shrug. "But it is what it is. Folk might think I'm crazy for saying this, but I see the bounty huntin' game as kind of an idyllic life. I'm out in the open, traveling from here to there, seein' different parts of this good country along the way. And most times I get to be with nature, with my thoughts. Now and then I get some trouble from folk who don't take kindly to men and women of my profession, and I've a feeling that ain't going nowhere. But on the whole, it's a life of freedom and that's what I always wanted. If I weren't doing what I am, I'd be the other side of the law, hurtin' others and leavin' a trail of misery and destruction in my wake. That ain't good for nobody."

Hope looked at the gun on his hip. "But you still carry that."

Her uncle's eyebrows rose as he peered down at his sidearm. "Yeah, well, a man's got a right to protect himself, don't he?"

"Of course," Hope said. "What model is that? A Colt?"

"Colt Navy," Dash corrected her. "Best there is, in my opinion."

"Have much caused to fire it?"

He smiled. "What you're really asking is, have you ever shot someone, right?"

"Yes."

Dash looked away, his gaze focusing once again on the horizon. "A conversation for another time, perhaps. Now . . . how's about we do a bit more practicing with that bullwhip. I've gotta leave in the morning."

"You're not staying to see Pop?"

"Afraid not."

144

"He'll be disappointed he missed you again," Hope told him.

"No, he won't." Dash drew off the pipe, exhaling from his nostrils. "Don't worry. Me and your pop . . . we're used to missing each other."

When she woke again, Hope realized that she was not in a cabin, as she'd thought, but a cave of some kind. Above her she saw the uneven but smooth roof of the cave. There was daylight but it did not come from a window or door that was visible to her. The light was pale, and bright, and seemed to come from the end of a long tunnel. It played on the surface of the stone walls and floor. Where a fire still burned, Hope saw that the smoke wafted up into a cavity above it, from where, presumably, it could escape into the open air. However it worked, she was not affected by fumes — though she was affected in a positive fashion by the sumptuous smell of meat roasting over the flames. Her stomach gurgled at the thought of eating and she looked to see if Elijah was around, but she was completely alone.

The man was clearly some kind of hermit. Hiding out in a cave, far removed from society. She had heard of such people who renounced the trappings of contemporary life and turned instead to a life spent in the bosom of nature. It made sense to her that a man like Elijah could lose all track of time. If he'd been living in the middle of nowhere, alone for a long period, it was understandable he didn't know just how long she had been there. Society as she knew it was dominated by the ticking of the pocket watch, the chiming of the grandfather clock, the marking of days on a calendar — all to know how much time had elapsed, and how much more there was to come.

How much was left.

Hope heard footsteps down at the end of the tunnel; then Elijah appeared, carrying a bucket of water in each hand. They looked heavy, and the sinewy muscles in his arms stood out like ropes from the strain of carrying them, but he seemed to bear their weight with ease. His face was relaxed, and when he caught sight of Hope looking at him, he smiled.

"Good to see you are awake again," Elijah said, setting the buckets down. "If you're wondering about the buckets, I was going to clean your wounds today. I got the water from a stream not far from here. It's fresh as can be. Comes straight down from the mountain, so you can't get any fresher. It's good for you."

146

Hope said, "Was I out long this time?"

"Another day at least."

That shocked her. She had never slept an entire day away before. Not even when her mother died and she felt the burden of grief bearing down on her. It felt strange to lose time the way she had, to have entire days pass in an instant. But Hope could not deny she felt better than she had before. Her body had needed the rest, she realized.

Elijah knelt down next to her and began to unravel her wrappings. "This is going to hurt. But it must be done, or the wounds will get infected. I don't want to have to be cutting body parts off."

Panic rose in her chest. "Can that happen?"

"Yes."

"Have you seen it?"

Elijah's eyes flicked up to meet hers. "Yes."

As he pulled the rags free, she quickly averted her gaze. "I can't look at them."

"It's essential that you do."

"I can't."

"You have to accept what has happened," Elijah told her. "Look at your wounds or you'll never acknowledge them."

Hope swallowed. She did not want to look at the state of her hands, but knew Elijah was right. She had to see. She had to understand the shape she was in.

She looked.

Her hands were ruined. Swollen purple from bruising, with lacerations all over. They barely resembled hands anymore. *No wonder I can't move them,* Hope thought. Tears spilled from her eyes and she could look no longer.

"They appear worse than they are," Elijah told her as he began to gently bathe them. He had a balled-up rag that he dunked into the water, then dabbed at her wounds. "Eventually the swelling will subside, and they will heal. I had to manipulate several of your fingers to ensure they set correctly. It was not . . . a good experience."

"They don't feel like they should," Hope said. She winced as he washed them. "Damn, that's painful."

Elijah nodded. "I am being as careful as I can."

"I appreciate everything you're doing for me," Hope said, watching as he set to work on her other hand.

He held her wrist, studying the wounds on her hand as he moved it this way and that. The pain was intense. She wondered how well they would heal, or if they would even heal at all. How much did Elijah really know about healing? Or was he making it all up as he went along?

"Anyone else would've left me to die," Hope said.

"I am not like anyone else."

"No," she said, "I can see you're not."

Elijah retrieved a stubby section of log into which he'd carved a hollow to make a bowl. He stirred at something with a short fat stick, a paste he had concocted while she slept. Hope could smell its earthy, pungent aroma.

It did not smell good.

"What is that?"

"A remedy of mine," Elijah said, holding the log to his nose to inhale the intense stink wafting up from it. "Oh, yes, that's ready now."

As she looked on, Elijah washed the bandages in the bucket of water he'd been using to clean her hands. Then he wrung them out and washed them a second time in the other bucket. By the time he was done, they were not dripping with old blood or puss and were quite clean. He wrung them dry again, forcing every last drop of moisture from the old cloth, then pushed them into the log. He sat on the floor, set the log between his knees and got to work forcing the bandages into the poultice he'd made.

"I want the rags to absorb as much of this as I can."

"What will it do?"

"Should help you heal," Elijah said. "But I have to tell you, when these go on, it will feel like your hands are on fire."

"It'll hurt?"

"Very much so, yes. But I promise you, it works. It is worth the pain."

Worth the pain, Hope thought.

Was anything really worth the pain? She had lost everything. Her mother. Her father. Her home. She'd been shot, beaten up by the river and nearly drowned in the process. Her body was ruined and she could not see the light at the end of the tunnel. Hope couldn't even sit up or move about. She felt as though dying on the riverbank would have been preferable to how she was now.

"I'm scared," Hope said.

Elijah stopped working his hands. He looked at her, and she saw only kindness in his face — a desire to ease her suffering in the wise glisten of his big eyes.

"I know," he said.

One by one, he wound the strips of bandage around her hands. Whatever he'd pounded into the poultice worked instantly. Hope whimpered as the burning began, and then she cried in agony. But still, she did not recoil, did not pull her hands away from him. The scream that burst from her mouth was loud, and long, and when it eventually dwindled to a gargling sputter of agony, Hope lay where she was, whimpering and crying. Unable to go anywhere, unable to do anything but ride the pain.

"Here. Drink this," Elijah said.

Hope didn't look to see what it was. She simply parted her lips as Elijah pressed the neck of a bottle there and filled her mouth with liquid. It burned, but in a different way. When she swallowed it down, the fire in her throat and then in her chest was not painful, but pleasurable. It was brandy.

Hope looked at Elijah. "Where did you get that?"

"A man traded me last winter. One stag antler for that bottle of brandy. I thought it a fair trade at the time, since I have no use for an antler," he explained. "I was waiting for the right time to open it."

Elijah gave her some more, then took a long swig from the bottle himself.

"It helps," Hope told him.

Elijah considered the bottle in his hand. "It really does, doesn't it?"

"That's right," Hope said weakly.

She lay back, closing her eyes. She heard Elijah get up, walk away — he'd taken the buckets because she could hear the water swilling about inside.

"That's right," she said again, to herself. Then, in the silence and solitude of the cave, the fog of oblivion found her again.

CHAPTER EIGHT

The next day, Hope was able to sit. Painfully, slowly and only with Elijah's assistance, but she could manage it.

The act of sitting felt like a great accomplishment; it felt like winning. The day after, Elijah got her to her feet and led her outside to sit in the sunshine. It was a brisk day, with a hint of fall in the air, but to be alive and experience the kiss of the sun on her face felt like a gift to her. She should have died, but there she was, sitting on a rock, breathing the fresh air and taking stock of her surroundings. The cave was situated at the base of a mountain, with a valley of rich green hills beneath. There were woods, and a stream winding through them — Hope could see its surface glittering under the sun.

She wondered if the stream was in any way connected to the river that had carried her from the two killers who had butchered her father. The thought spoiled the feeling of euphoria she had been experiencing at simply being alive. When Elijah left her to go and check traps he had set in the trees below, Hope closed her eyes and remembered the water sucking her under, tossing her against rocks. She opened her eyes and looked down at her bandaged hands. The cost of surviving had been great. And Hope could not help but wonder if she would ever be as she was before — she guessed she wouldn't. The simple fact of watching her father die had seen to that. The thought of what those two men had done, and what they'd been about to do to her before she'd escaped, was enough to chill her blood. She looked for Elijah, wanting him to return so that she could go back inside. Suddenly, the world had grown very, very cold.

Days became weeks. The wrappings came off her hands. Elijah had changed them every few days, and whatever was in the concoction he'd made seemed to have worked wonders on them. They resembled actual hands again. They were still bruised purple, and the lacerations were scabbed over and unsightly, but Hope could recognize her hands for what they were, and that was a step in the right direction. The two gunshot wounds had closed nicely, though they would leave ugly scars when the skin there was done knitting together. Hope knew the pain in her ribs was something she'd have to continue living with until they healed in their own time. But even that had subsided some.

Elijah did not wait for her hands to heal further.

"Here. Take this," he said, extending a branch he'd fashioned into a walking stick for her. He'd cut all the sharp, stubby parts away and smoothed the surface.

Hope reached out to take it, then realized she couldn't open and close her right hand. When Elijah had told her she'd be left with two hands she couldn't use, he hadn't been exaggerating.

She looked at him in panic. "I . . . I can't."

"But you will," he said, squatting down in front of Hope, taking her right wrist and moving it toward the top of the walking stick. He used his fingers to gently pry Hope's own open enough so that he could wrap them around the top of the stick. The other side of the stick nestled smoothly against her palm. "Now try to squeeze it."

"I can't."

Elijah exhaled slowly. *"Try,"* he said, his voice like a low rumble.

155

Hope tried to will movement into her fingers but found they wouldn't do anything for her. Her digits remained where Elijah had put them, wrapped around the walking stick he'd made for her.

"They're not working!" she said in frustration. "I told you I can't do it!"

Elijah stood. "You can."

"I can't! You can see for yourself, my hand won't do anything."

"You're a failure."

Hope peered up at him. "What?"

"You're hopeless. I should have left you where I found you," Elijah said, scowling at her. "What a pitiful excuse you are, a worthless *nothing.* You'll never achieve anything because you're *weak,* just like your father."

Hope shook her head. "Stop. . . ."

"They shot him down like a dog. And when they find you, they'll do the same to you. Because the strong destroy the weak. That's the way it's always been, and that's how it will be for you. If your father could see you now, he'd be so ashamed, he'd probably be inclined to end your sorry existence himself."

Hope gripped the walking stick hard. She shot to her feet, pointing at him with her left hand. "I told you to stop!"

Elijah smiled.

Hope looked at her outstretched left arm. At her finger pointing toward Elijah. Then she looked at her right clutching the top of the walking stick so hard, her knuckles were turning white.

"I don't understand," she said, looking at Elijah in utter puzzlement, her voice barely a murmur. Her left arm fell to her side.

"I told you that you'd do it," Elijah said. "And now you have."

Hope swallowed. "I thought . . ." Her voice trailed off, as she lost the sense of what she had been about to say.

"The hard part has only begun. Holding a stick and pointing a finger is one thing. Actually using your hands to do something, well, that's another."

"I know."

Elijah smiled. "I regret saying those things to you. But I had to make you forget about your hands in order for you to just use them. I do not think your father would be ashamed of you. I never met him, but I think he'd be proud of you."

Hope slowly flexed her left hand. "I have to find the men who killed him."

Elijah sat on a nearby rock. "I understand wrath. It's in our nature to kill."

"Is that why you live out here on your own?"

Elijah looked down into the woods. "I have witnessed enough death to never want to be in its presence again. But that is my own path. Yours will take you from here, to stand before your father's killers and see him avenged. Of that, I have no doubt. In so many ways, your path is set as surely as my own."

Hope sat down, too. "Where does your path lead?"

"I came to the wilderness not just to *live* alone, but to *die* alone. That is what I wanted. Eventually sickness, old age or an accident of some kind will see to that."

Hope said, "It sounds awful lonely, Elijah."

"I have been with men as they died. I've held their hands. I've seen the light leave their eyes," he said. "Let me tell you, everyone dies alone in the end. I don't want anybody to witness my passing from this world. I want it to be as fleeting as the rain sweeping through the valley below."

Weeks later, Hope had regained enough dexterity in her fingers to peel an apple. She felt like a child who'd won a prize at a traveling fair.

Elijah led her down to the woods below, where he encouraged Hope to bathe in the stream that wound its way through the trees. The days were decidedly colder then, with a real nip in the air. But it was still warm enough to bathe. Hope watched as Elijah stripped out of his clothes, down to his long johns, and walked out to the middle of the stream. The water was up to his waist.

"It's not deep," he told her.

Hope hesitated, not wanting to strip out of her clothes in front of him. But it occurred to her that Elijah had undressed her at some point. He had tended to her wounds. He'd *bathed* her, which he couldn't have done if she had been fully clothed. She hadn't been molested then, so why would he do so now?

Elijah smiled. "You feel embarrassed."

"No. I . . ."

It wasn't just getting out of her clothes in front of him. It was the stream itself. The thought of wading into the running water filled her with dread — Hope's last experience with open water had not worked out well for her.

"If it helps, I will turn my back until you're in the water," Elijah said, turning around so that he couldn't see her.

Hope got out of her clothes. Down to her own undergarments. She could work at buttons now. Her fingers were clumsy, but she was able to do it. Hope braved the cool water, walking in until the water ran to her chest, concealing her breasts from view.

"I'm in," she said.

Elijah turned back around. "See? Not so bad, is it?"

"I guess not. Water's colder than I thought it'd be."

"Always is," Elijah said, dropping beneath the surface to wash his long gray hair. When he rose again, he looked something akin to clean for the first time since she'd met him. "I find bathing in open water so refreshing. Remember when I said it comes down from the mountain? I wasn't lying. This water could be running out of the heart of the world."

Hope couldn't deny it felt good just to let the water run around her. The current ran against her skin, washing all the dirt and dried blood away.

"The last time I was in open water wasn't so refreshing," Hope told him.

"True," Elijah said. "But you got into this stream without letting that get the better of you. Look how far you've come."

As Hope looked on, Elijah proceeded to swim upstream, gliding through the water with ease, his long gray hair fanning out behind him. Hope remained where she was.

She held her breath and ducked beneath the surface. The water filled her ears, muffling any sound but the hum of the stream itself. With her eyes closed, she could have been anywhere. She could have been in the darkness into which she'd fallen previously — a darkness she had risen from, very much alive and eager to enact vengeance.

By the time she walked out of the stream to get back into her clothes, Hope felt a sense of renewal she had never experienced before. The water had washed a lot of things away. She did not see Elijah for another half an hour. When he returned, he came bearing a catfish he'd caught and killed.

"That is repulsive," Hope said, looking at the slimy catfish with disgust. It was the ugliest thing she'd ever seen.

Elijah held it by the mouth, regarding his catch with pride. "No, it's good eating."

Another week brought with it another advancement in her recovery. Elijah presented her with an old revolver and a worn gun belt that had seen better days.

"What's that for?"

"You mentioned before that you're a crack shot with a pistol. I figured it's time you tested your new hands," Elijah said as he brewed coffee over the fire.

Hope snorted. "New hands," she said, looking down at them. *Butchered, more like,* she thought as she flexed her fingers and felt the stiffness there.

"You have mentioned to me that you could throw a bullwhip with precision. Well, unfortunately, I don't have one of those lying around. So you'll have to test your ability when you can get a new one."

"The men who killed my father took my weapons away from me," Hope said bitterly. She picked up the old revolver and turned it over in her hands. "This is yours?"

"Yes and no."

"What do you mean?"

Elijah moved the pot of coffee off the heat and filled two tin cups. "I did not come to the wilderness without protection. I brought a rifle and enough ammunition to last me a long while. But I've rarely used it. No, this I found on the body of a traveler who'd died in the woods. By the look of him, he'd been out there on the ground quite a while. The revolver was at his side. I took what I could use and buried the man beneath a tree. It seemed right. He had a box of bullets in his bag."

"Looks like it's seen a lot of action," Hope said.

Elijah nodded. "I thought so, too. But I

have no need for pistols. My days of shooting a pistol are long gone. A pistol is meant for fighting men and carrying one at my side would go against everything that compelled me to come out here in the first place."

"But you said you carry the rifle for protection," Hope said.

Elijah handed her a cup of coffee. "Bears," he said simply.

"Well, thank you for the gun. I didn't expect it."

Elijah wagged a finger. "Do not thank me too soon. You have yet to attempt firing it. First, it will need cleaning and oiling. That task will put your hands to the test. Then you have to try shooting at a target. That will test them further."

Hope's hand tightened around the gun. It hurt, but she was getting used to the pain in a way. It had become a companion on her road to recovery — she accepted it. Pain was with her and might be forever. But she was alive, and she had a purpose. And now she had a gun, she had a means, too.

After coffee, with the sun sinking in the sky and tinting the clouds a deep shade of sienna, Hope took aim with the revolver. She had spent hours taking it apart and cleaning every part of it, oiling it as she had been taught as a child and then reassembling it. Elijah had been right about her finding the task difficult. It was tougher than she'd expected it would be. Her hands now worked well enough, but coordinating her movements was still difficult. Her fingers lacked the finesse to manipulate small objects. Something so simple as working the brush into the cylinder became a frustrating experience as she struggled to guide the brush accurately, then rotate it to clean the dirt that had accumulated in there. By the time she was done with the revolver, her hands ached from the tips of her fingers to her wrists.

Elijah regarded the newly maintained revolver with appreciation. "You did well," he said, picking the gun up and rolling the chamber next to his ear with the palm of his hand. "Nice and smooth."

Now she stood at sunset with her arm extended, revolver cocked, aiming the weapon at the line of objects Elijah had assembled for her. They were arranged by size, and got progressively farther away. The largest was a sheet of bark Elijah had found somewhere. Farthest away, at least fifty feet from her, Elijah had set a pine cone on a rock.

"Just take your time," Elijah said.

Hope worked at controlling her breathing, just as her father had taught her. Steady lungs made steady hands, he'd always said. She knew it was a way of preventing fear from taking over.

Her aim was not true. She had trouble preventing the gun from wavering, no matter how hard she tried. Hope's hand felt weak, and with her arm extended, it felt as if she was bearing a great weight there with little to support her.

"It's so heavy," she gasped.

Elijah approached and gently pushed her arm down. "Relax. Give me the gun so you can rest that hand."

She reluctantly released her grip on the gun and Elijah took it away from her. Hope felt instant relief, not that she wanted to admit it. "Trying to aim with that thing is so hard," she told him.

"I knew it would be too heavy for you straightaway."

"You knew, but you still let me come down here to practice?" Hope asked. "What was the point if you knew I couldn't do it?"

"It's not important for me to know you can't do it straightaway. It's something you have to realize for yourself. Your expectations of what you can and can't do have to be realistic, Hope, or you'll never get to where you want to go. We have a lot of work to do before you fire this gun, but you might not have believed me without first attempting to take aim with it."

Hope winced as she flexed her gun hand. "What can I do?"

"It's a little something I got wounded soldiers to do when they were recovering. I call it 'holding rocks.' "

Elijah couldn't have hit the nail on the head any harder. The exercise was literally to *hold rocks*. For two weeks Hope did nothing but lift heavy rocks with her busted hands, carrying them from one place to another, for no reason other than to improve her ability to bear weight with her hands. Elijah would then have her spend ten minutes at a time holding a large rock with her arm outstretched, as if the rock in her hand were a gun. She did this so many times, her entire arm ached right up into her shoulder blade and down her back. But still she carried on trying, despite the pain and discomfort, and found that she was gradually able to hold the rock for longer periods. And her arm stopped moving. By the end of the two weeks, she was able to hold the rock dead still, and for as long as Elijah told her to. It hurt still, but as with the pain in her hands,

Hope grew to know that hurt and accept it.

"You're ready," Elijah said, returning the revolver to her.

They headed down the mountainside together, and Elijah arranged the targets once again, with the smaller items farther and farther away from her. This time when Hope raised the revolver, her arm was straight and did not move. She cocked the hammer back, took aim at the first target and fired without hesitation.

Just missed.

"Nearly," Elijah said, standing well back from her. "Try again."

Hope took a deep breath. In her head she heard her father's voice say, *'You are immovable.'* It calmed her, and this time when she pulled the trigger, she hit the sheet of bark dead center, blasting it to smithereens.

"I think you hit it," Elijah said.

Hope worked her shoulders looser and made short work of the other targets, destroying them in rapid succession, all the way to the end.

Hope took aim, squinting with one eye as she lined up her shot.

She fired.

The pine cone flew up into the sky, then fell into the canopy of the trees behind, startling several nesting birds that hadn't already gone to flight at the sound of the revolver firing in the first place.

Hope turned to look at Elijah. "So?"

His eyes shone. "You're ready."

"You saved me. Brought me back from the dead. Healed my hands. I don't know how to repay you," Hope said.

She went to hand the revolver back to him, but Elijah took a step back, shaking his head.

"It's yours."

"Really? I thought it was just to practice with."

"I always meant for you to have it. The gun's not much to look at, but I believe in fate."

"What do you mean?"

"Well, I think it was my fate to find you on the riverbank. That man died in these woods for a reason; I think he perished here so I'd find his gun. That gun is now in your hand because fate has put it there."

Hope looked down at the revolver. It had never seemed heavier. "You really think there's a reason for all that's happened?"

"I do."

She looked up. "I wish I could agree with you. But when my pop was killed in front of me, it seemed to me the world had no reason or meaning at all."

Elijah said, "Sometimes the people we lose, it's like we were meant to lose them, to give our lives real purpose."

"It'd be a pretty cruel world if that was the case."

"You don't think the world we live in is cruel?" Elijah asked.

Hope had to admit he had a point. There wasn't much she'd experienced that gave her a counterargument. The world was cruel, and hard, and the chips were stacked against you the moment you stepped one boot out the door. But still she found herself wanting to have her revenge.

"I think any world that takes a father from his daughter is a heartless one."

"Your father's loss has given you purpose, a reason to get better, and to face the world," Elijah said.

Hope looked back down at the gun. "Will it bring me peace, though?"

"That is something I cannot answer. Only time will tell," Elijah said. The hermit who had gifted her a second chance sighed heavily. "I hope for your sake that it does. Fulfill the oath you made to yourself. Then live your life. Once your father is avenged, promise me that you'll do that, Hope."

169

She slid the revolver into the gun belt around her hips. "I will. Once it's done."

Several days later, autumn came to the mountainside. The trees below began to shed leaves that had turned shades of gold and amber. The wind was cold and biting, and the sky seemed to have turned a perpetual shade of gray. Nights drew in, and the mornings were enlivened by glorious sunrises, the like of which Hope had never seen in her entire life.

"Soon it'll be time to move on," Elijah told her, watching the horizon for something — a sign, a hint of what might come. "In the winter I trap for furs, north of here."

"All winter?"

Elijah nodded. "I sell them in town when they're ready. I renounced society, but even I have need of things that only money can buy."

"Makes sense, I suppose."

"What will you do?" Elijah asked.

The question threw her. She hadn't given it much thought. She hadn't considered when the right time might be to leave him, to walk away from the kindly hermit who'd brought her back from the brink of death. He had given her so much, Hope didn't know if she'd ever be able to repay him.

"I . . . I don't know."

"You are welcome to join me, but it's a hard winter if you've never experienced it before. It isn't easy, or free of risk," Elijah told her.

Hope shook her head. "I don't think trapping is for me. I think I should head back to where I came from."

"Back to Eden's Ridge, was it?"

"That's right. My pop would have been buried without me. There'll be the house to deal with . . . lots to do."

"I understand," Elijah said, smiling thinly.

She woke one morning to find him gone. His things were gone from the cave. He had left her some food, some water, the box of bullets that he'd found with the gun and a skin to stave off the coolness of the season. Hope searched the woods below, and the entire valley, before accepting that Elijah had abandoned her to the same fate of which he'd spoken so acceptingly days before.

At first, his sudden abandonment of her didn't make a shred of sense. But then she reasoned that she'd made her plans clear to him. And he had made his own plans clear to her. He would head north.

Hope would somehow find her way south,

and head for home — if there was anything left of it.

CHAPTER NINE

At a dirt road traversed by riders on horseback and wagons heading in either direction, Hope was able to convince one of the wagons to stop and let her ride. The driver, a burly man with a thick white beard, made her sit in the back with the stores.

"Are you going anywhere near Eden's Ridge?"

"No," he said gruffly. The man looked her over and seemed to take pity on her. "Town limits, maybe."

The man hadn't given her a name to go by, and he did not speak to her the entire journey. Hope thought him unsociable for not wanting her to sit near him, or speak with him, until she considered how much she smelled, and how disheveled she looked in the same clothes she'd been wearing when Elijah yanked her from the muddy riverbank. She sat in the back of the wagon, clutching the fur Elijah had left her, and realized she was lucky anyone had bothered to stop for her at all.

The man stopped only once, to relieve himself at the side of the road. He drove all night and Hope did not sleep. She hugged her knees and watched the stars. Her stomach turned at the thought of returning home, of facing her father's grave, and the burned-out remains of their family home.

Family.

There hadn't been much of a family by the time sickness and murder were done with them. Her only relation now was her uncle Dash, a traveling cattleman. And Lord knew where he was at any given time. Hope wondered if Dash even knew about her father's murder, and dreaded the possibility of having to break the news to him herself.

As the sun's first light crept in over the distant hills, the man brought the wagon to a stop and instructed her to get out.

"You'll want this road," he said, nodding off to the left of the one they'd been traveling all night. "You're a couple of hours walk from Eden's Ridge. Unless you can get a lift from somebody, but doubt they get much traffic there and back."

"Thank you for letting me ride along."

The man regarded her with pity in his eyes.

God, I must look like death warmed up, Hope thought.

He reached into a bag and handed her some kind of fruitcake wrapped in cloth. "To keep you going."

"Thank you," Hope said.

She watched the wagon trundle on, then took to the road that would bear her home, picking at the cake he'd given her. She hadn't realized until she finished it that she'd been desperately hungry. And once the cake was gone, she wished there had been more, it had been so good. Several hours later, the sun by now high in the sky, Hope crested a rise and laid eyes on Eden's Ridge.

How the house still stood she did not know. It was a blackened husk, the roof collapsed and one of the bearing walls completely obliterated. There wasn't anything to salvage, anything to save. If her father had had any deeds or bonds, they'd surely been lost to the fire. The same for any money he might have squirreled away over the years.

Everything was lost.

Hope surveyed the land her parents had purchased and made into a home. *So this is all that's left. A piece of land. My sole inheritance, all I have in the world. And nothing to say that we were ever here,* she thought.

But of course, that was not true.

When Hope made her way to the town's cemetery, she came upon her family's lasting impression on the history of the town in the shape of her parent's graves. Her father was buried in a plot right next to her mother. There was no headstone, just a wooden cross with his name carved into it. Hope fell to her knees, overcome with fresh grief. The house had been burned down to the ground, and she would have to sell the land . . . but in the town's cemetery her parents would remain for all time. Whatever change might come to Eden's Ridge, they would bear witness to it in some way — they and the other permanent residents of the cemetery would be the only part of the town that would not be altered.

Tears spilled from her eyes.

Then a shadow fell over her. Hope turned to see a man with a wide-brimmed black hat. He removed the hat out of respect and laid a hand flat on his chest.

"I heard tell a woman had walked into town lookin' like she'd been lost to the wild, and I had to come find her. But I never figured it'd be you, Hope. Not in a thousand years," he said.

"Father?" Hope said, getting to her feet.

Father Flanagan's face was tight, his eyes pained as he took in her appearance. "My child, I never thought I would see you again. There was a big debate at town council as to whether we should allocate you a plot next to Tobias. Everybody was certain that some evil had befell you, as it had your father."

"They were going to give me an empty grave?"

"They were, yes," Flanagan said. "Yet here you stand before me. Living, breathing. Returned to us against all odds."

Wiping at her eyes, Hope laughed a little. "Resurrected, eh, Father?"

Flanagan placed his hands on her shoulders and slowly brought her in close to him, enfolding her in his arms. Hope had not realized just how much she had needed it, how much she had yearned for someone — anyone — to put their arms around her and treat her with tenderness.

"There, there, my child," Father Flanagan said as she wept against him. "You are home."

Flanagan saw to it that Hope could bathe and was given fresh clothes. He gave her a bed in the rectory. The bed was soft and warm and Hope slept until late morning

177

the next day. She felt fully refreshed at breakfast, at the town's café, fed plates of egg and bacon, washed down with strong black coffee that made her think of the coffee Elijah had made for her while she recuperated.

"You were hungry, I see," Flanagan said, sipping his own coffee with the restraint that was his hallmark.

The Father moved slow, talked slow, took everything at his own pace — and for whatever reason, it worked. He had a calming effect on everyone in his presence and carried with him an air of patience and serenity befitting a man of the cloth.

"Yes, thank you," Hope said, dabbing at her mouth.

She'd had several startled looks from other patrons of the café, but none of them had approached her, asking about what had happened. Hope did not know if the Father had had a quiet word with the people of the town about her return, perhaps warning them against overwhelming her with questions . . . or if they simply didn't know how to ask.

"I am curious. Will you tell me what you went through?" Flanagan asked, raising the subject of her absence for the first time.

Hope assumed that the Father had let her

rest before asking because her answers would hold far more clarity than if she'd been forced to answer while still exhausted from her journey home.

Hope told the priest about the men who'd killed her father, how they'd abducted her and how she'd jumped into a river and escaped by the skin of her teeth; she told him about Elijah, and how he had plucked her from the riverbank, half drowned and shot full of holes. She told him how Elijah had sewn up her wounds and fixed the busted ruins of her hands.

Father Flanagan nodded patiently along. "Quite an ordeal."

"If it weren't for Elijah, I'd have perished on the riverbank."

"He sounds like a very good man."

"He was."

Hope thought of the day Elijah had led her back to the river. She had felt no fear, no sense of ill intent on his part. She had known he simply wanted her to bathe and to feel refreshed. In a way it had been like a baptism, as if to symbolize that Hope had been born anew when Elijah saved her life.

"Can I ask you something?"

"Of course."

"Do you believe in second chances, Father?" Hope asked.

"I do."

"How about second chances for the wicked?"

"My child, the wicked are often the most in need of second chances, are they not?"

Hope shrugged. "I suppose," she said. "What about the men who killed my father?"

Father Flanagan sighed. "I am inclined to tell you that those men, in particular, would be worthy of a chance to repent their heinous crimes. That is as a man of the cloth."

"And if you weren't wearing that collar?" Hope asked.

Flanagan said, "Against my better angels . . . I confess that I might be tempted toward sin."

"To *revenge*, you mean," Hope said.

Flanagan nodded silently. "It's in any of us to desire revenge in these circumstances. But our belief in a higher power, a guiding force for good, steers us toward the correct path. And it is in faith that I find solace when the lure of sin entices the flesh."

"Well, Father, I intend on revenge," Hope said flatly. "And there isn't anything can be said that will stop me."

"I implore you to take the other road. There is little redemption to be found in

180

revenge, Hope Cassidy. The solace I find in faith, you will not find in acts of wrath against your fellow man. Only forgiveness and acceptance will ease the burden on your heart."

"You talk of other roads. But this is the only road upon which I wish to travel, Father."

Flanagan reached across the table and took her hands in his. "Then I shall pray for you."

"Please do," Hope replied. "I'm going to need all the help I can get."

When they were done, Father Flanagan took her to visit the sheriff, Cliff Rayner. He'd worn the badge for a little over a year — since Ned Grissom retired.

Cliff told Hope what had happened in her absence. How her father had been buried and the house cleared of anything she might want if she ever returned.

"I have to admit, I thought you were dead," Cliff said. "I never thought we'd see you again. Yet here you are, livin' and breathin' against all expectation."

"I nearly didn't make it," Hope said, describing to the sheriff how she had leapt into the river, how she'd nearly died and how Elijah had saved her.

Cliff sat back in his chair and whistled through his teeth. "You're one lucky girl. That's all I can say."

"I know I am," Hope said, thinking to herself: *Does my luck at being alive balance against losing my mother, my father, my home and nearly dying in the process?* "I went to the house. It looked about ready to collapse in on itself."

"I daresay that's true. The fire was out of control by the time people reached it. There wasn't anything could be done," Cliff said. "And the sight of your poor father on the ground . . . Well, I can tell you, it disturbed a fair few of us, and that's the truth."

Father Flanagan cleared his throat. "We held a very respectful service for Tobias. Nearly the entire town turned out to pay their respects. He was a great man."

"Thank you," Hope said. "He was. Did my uncle attend?"

"We had no way of reaching him," Flanagan said.

Cliff got up, went to a locked cabinet. He took a set of keys from his belt and unlocked the cabinet doors, revealing guns and ammunition, and a cloth sack at the bottom. Cliff picked it up and handed it to Hope.

"That there's all we could salvage from the house. It weren't safe to go in there rootin' through everything, but I figured if there was anything worth saving for you, it was the right thing to do, and worth the risk."

Hope looked through the contents. There was a charred jewelry box that had belonged to her mother. Some bonds in a leather billfold, various coins. The deeds to the house and surrounding land in Eden's Ridge. Hope frowned as she came upon ownership papers for land in other towns.

"What is it?" Cliff asked. "Found something you didn't expect?"

"You could say that," Hope said, handing the sheriff the papers to look at.

Sheriff Rayner's eyebrows peaked. "Well, I'll be. . . . He never told you he owned all this land?"

"Not once."

Father Flanagan came to stand next to the sheriff and peered down at the papers. "Oh, my," he exclaimed.

Cliff handed them back to Hope. "Must've had a windfall at some point. No way he could have bought all that land on a marshal's salary. Did he have rich parents?"

"I don't know," Hope said, perplexed. "He never spoke of them."

"It would seem your father harbored a few secrets, my dear," Flanagan said.

Hope tucked the papers back into the billfold. "Yes, it would . . ." she said. "Did you find . . . Can I have his star?"

"His star? You mean his marshal's badge?"

Hope nodded.

The sheriff shook his head. "I'm afraid not. It wasn't on him. We looked for it, to fix it to his breast for the burial, but it couldn't be found."

Hope sighed. "Thank you," she said, not knowing what else to say.

She looked at the billfold in her hands. It seemed to Hope the simplest thing to do would be to sell the land in Eden's Ridge. She needed money, and there was nothing left for her beyond the husk of a house and a lot of bad memories. And yet there was a part of her that would have been saddened to let it go. Bidding the last shred of her former life goodbye.

But she knew that she must, if she was to move on.

There could be no more ties, not if she was to see her path of vengeance through to the end.

After a few weeks, a farmer purchased the land for a fair price. Hope had enough to board at the inn rather than sleep in Father Flanagan's rectory, and to purchase a new horse, tack, saddle and saddlebags. The same day she put in an order with the tailor for new clothes, including boots and work gloves to protect her hands from the cold. She did not purchase a new hat — Sheriff Rayner had saved her father's hat, and she wore it with pride.

Hope purchased supplies from the general store to last her a long while on the road. And she made a visit to the gunsmith to make the most important purchase of all. The old revolver had been a gift from Elijah, and she did not wish to part with it. But she felt that to commit sin — to fulfill her vow of vengeance against the men who had killed her father — she was in need of a brand-new weapon. It would not have made sense to many people, the desire she felt for something that signified her transition to the person she had now become, but it made perfect sense to Hope. It made sense in more ways than she could count.

The weapon had to be a Colt Navy.

The gunsmith, a man called Tulley, squinted at her from behind his thick glasses. "Why a navy, specifically?"

"It's what my uncle carries. Just seems a decent, reliable model."

"It'll cost you."

Hope couldn't keep her eyes off the

brand-new revolver that gleamed on top of the glass cabinet, polished to a high shine. "Money's not a problem. I have enough. I'll take ammo, too."

"How much?" Tulley asked.

Hope looked up at him. "How much have you got?"

Hope kept enough money for the road. The rest she put into an envelope along with a note for Father Flanagan and left it in the confessional for him to find.

Hope was not fond of goodbyes. And the way she saw it, she'd had enough goodbyes to last her a lifetime. Her mother. Her father. Elijah. Now the town and the towns-folk she'd known her entire life. She was bidding farewell to all of it in order to hit the road. To find the men who'd caused her so much pain, misery and hardship. Find them. Kill them. Send their black souls into the void and know that the world would be a far better place for it.

As she rode through town, the sun began to lift over the trees, cutting through the early-morning mist. She climbed the road out of town until she was looking down on Eden's Ridge, with the town's cemetery in the distance, almost lost to the haze.

Goodbye, she thought, turning around

and taking her horse to a gallop. The last time she turned back to look for home, it was gone.

CHAPTER TEN

A couple of months later, Hope found Dash in the town of Elam Hollow stumbling from a saloon in the late afternoon, attempting without success to light his pipe.

"Want help with that?"

He looked up. Did a double take as he took her in. "Hope? Is that you?" he asked, rubbing at his eyes. "What in the hell are you doing here?"

"I've been looking for you. I searched from town to town, asking everyone I could find for word on your whereabouts."

Dash pointed back at the saloon. "I was havin' myself a day off. You know, a card game with the old boys? If I'd known there'd be a family reunion, I'd have laid off the whiskey."

"Now we both know that's not exactly true, is it?"

Dash grinned foolishly. "A barefaced lie!"

Hope climbed down from the saddle and

went to him, enfolding her uncle in a warm embrace. "It's good to see you," she said, realizing it was perhaps the most genuine thing she'd said to anyone for weeks.

In truth, there hadn't been many substantial conversations. Once she knew Dash wasn't to be found in certain towns, she'd made short work of moving on to the next. She could not afford to linger, not with winter clasping the land in its iron grip.

"Good to see you, too," Dash said as she released him. He cast about. "Where's your pop?"

There it is, Hope thought. The happiness she'd felt being in his presence again swiftly dissipated. "I'm afraid I have bad news."

"Bad news . . ." Dash said. His eyes watered. "He's dead, isn't he?"

She nodded. "I'm sorry."

Her uncle turned and leaned against the rail closest to him. She figured her uncle didn't want her to see his face, to see the pain and sadness, to witness the tears. Hope went to him, rubbed his shoulders as the man wept for his brother.

In a couple of minutes, Dash turned back around. "How did he die?"

"I can't tell you out in the street. Is there somewhere we can go?"

Dash sat in stunned silence. He had a camp just outside of town. She remembered her uncle telling her how he preferred not to use hotels or boardinghouses. The beds were too soft, and the sleep too good, to notice an assailant approaching. Out in the open, light sleeping on hard ground, Dash found he was more alert. In his line of work, one could never be too careful.

Except when there was drink involved. In that instance, all caution was thrown to the wind, it seemed.

Hope brewed hot coffee on the fire to sober him up. She wanted him to understand what she had told him, not wake up the next day wondering if it'd all been a figment of his imagination, a misremembered moment of a drunken spree.

"Unlike you to travel with others," she said, noting the sleeping bags dotted around the camp beneath the same stretched canvas.

Dash looked up. He'd been staring into the dark swirl of his coffee, as if it held anything resembling an answer. "What's that?"

"Your camp. I said, it's unlike you to travel

190

with others. Where are they?"

"In town."

"Who are they?"

"Just a couple of like-minded souls I know from way back. They hit the bordello the second we got here. Ain't seen 'em since."

"Ever thought about settling in a town like this?"

"No. Why?"

"You don't grow tired, always traveling?"

"Hey, this is the land of the free, is it not? A man can come and go as he pleases."

"Of course."

Hope looked out at the darkened fields and prairie. "It is nice out here at times. No one around."

"Yeah, plenty of empty space out here," Dash said. His eyes shifted to the fire. "How did he die?"

Hope swallowed. She'd been looking for her uncle in order to tell him the news in person, and yet, faced with the inevitable question, she found herself dreading telling him what had happened.

"Hope?" Dash asked.

She realized he was no longer gazing into the flickering flames, but at her. So Hope set her own coffee down on the ground and began to tell him. Starting that afternoon, with her father praising her ability with a pistol and then a bullwhip. Dash laughed at Tobias calling the bullwhip a cat-o'-nine-tails. Then she described how they'd ridden home and seen the smoke.

She described how the two men shot and killed Tobias in front of her, then knocked her out. How she'd woken up on the back of a horse and gotten her hands free. Hope could almost taste the river in her mouth as she related leaping into the dark water and nearly drowning in the process. Dash winced when she told him how she'd been shot, how the bones in her hands were broken. Her uncle looked sober as a judge when she told him how she collapsed on the riverbank and wished for death.

Hope told Dash about Elijah. She told him about learning to use her hands again, and regaining the ability to shoot. And then about Elijah leaving her on her own because their paths diverged. "I vowed revenge on the two men who killed Pop," Hope said. "And Elijah knew there weren't nothing he could say would make me think different."

"Do you still feel that way?"

"I do."

"How will you go about finding them?" Dash asked.

Hope shrugged. "I'm not sure."

"I'll teach you how. And then I'll help you

192

search every corner of this land. Even if it takes months, or even years. Here," he said, rummaging around for a moment before producing a coiled-up bullwhip. "Take this."

"I can't."

"I said, take it," Dash said, pressing the whip into her hands. "I see you got a gun. But you're missing the whip. They took your weapons off you, I suppose?"

"They did."

Dash opened his hands. "Well, when you kill 'em and get your things back, you can hand that whip to me. Then it'll be done. You'll be finished with what you set out to do."

"Thank you."

"Where is my brother buried?"

"Up in Eden's Ridge cemetery. They buried him, because they thought I was dead, y'see. They held a service and everything. He wasn't just buried in a hole in the ground, then forgotten."

"Is he next to your mother?"

Hope nodded.

"That's good. It's what he would have wanted," Dash said. "I'm sorry, Hope. Sorry this happened to you."

"I just have to find them," Hope told him. She got up, walked out to where the firelight did not reach and stood in the darkness. "I have to find them and kill them."

After a moment, Dash asked, "Have you considered letting it go?"

"No."

Dash said, "Not until the deed is done, huh?"

"That's right."

"Just the answer I was expectin'." Her uncle moved up next to her, put his arm around her shoulders. "I'll teach you all I know. It ain't gonna be easy going, though, do you hear? Mine's a hard life, sometimes."

"I'm ready," Hope said.

But as she stared out at the night, she thought, *Ain't nothing been easy so far. . . .*

■ ■ ■ ■

Part Three:
A New World's
Crown

■ ■ ■ ■

CHAPTER ELEVEN

Sheriff Travis Maxwell strode into the street at dawn.

The audience for the first gunfight of the first round was limited to the contestants, their entourages and whoever was brave enough to bear witness to it. The rest of the town had either retreated deep within their homes, where the bullets hopefully would not reach them — or they'd left town entirely for the few days the contest would take to conclude as the bodies accumulated.

The sheriff watched as Renee Lane and Crazy Sid Babcock stepped down from the porch of the saloon and walked into the street to join him. Crazy Sid spat a gob full of tobacco juice out the side of his mouth, then wiped at the spittle dribbling down his chin with the palm of one hand.

Remaining on the saloon porch, Cyrus Barbosa stood with his thumbs tucked into the belt of his exceptionally large frame, chewing jerky, the eyes set into his fat head twinkling with mirth. Next to him, Red Nelson and Daiyu Wu observed the ritual of contestants meeting where the sheriff stood, then turning their backs to each other. As they walked away, the sheriff had just enough time to rejoin everyone else in front of the saloon, walking backward himself so as to keep track of how many paces Renee and Sid took.

"That'll do now. Stop where you are and turn around to face each other," Maxwell yelled.

Renee Lane turned to face Crazy Sid Babcock.

The gunslinger might have been grinning at her with his brown teeth on full display, but there wasn't anything approaching warmth or friendliness in the expression. Crazy Sid bore the gleeful look of a man about to have his fill of something — in stark contrast to Renee's expression, which remained passive, a blank slate.

Hope Cassidy stood watching at the other end of the saloon's porch, a hard knot forming in her stomach. This was not how she'd planned it. Yes, she had intended on tracking Knox down and executing him in . . . well, was it really considered to be "in cold blood" if her blood at the time had been anything but? If she had acted with the fires of vengeance burning in her veins? She did not know. All she could be sure of was that she had wanted to end Knox's life, then leave town. And in so doing, leave the past behind, too.

But here she was, on the porch of the local saloon, about to watch two gunslingers go toe to toe with their sidearms. One would walk away; the other would die. She hadn't truly grasped the reality of the contest until just now, experiencing it firsthand. Realizing she would be participating in the next round filled her with a sense of dread she struggled to suppress. Either she would be the one walking away, or she'd be shot and bleed out on the frozen street.

Hope looked at Barbosa and recoiled at the repugnant enjoyment he seemed to garner from the gunfire about to take place. She had never enjoyed shooting somebody. But she felt no internal conflict about whether or not she would shoot her opponent in the next round. Because they would certainly not hesitate to shoot her down dead — not just to save their own skin, but to reach the next round and get one step closer to fortune and glory. Yes, Hope was locked in to playing the game, and she would play it to win, to be the last gunman standing. Because if she didn't, she'd die.

The sky was a dull orange as the rising sun spilled from the horizon. Dawn had come.

"Contestants, stand ready. Do *not* release your weapons from their holsters until the church bell tolls," Sheriff Maxwell told Renee and Crazy Sid. "The bell will toll. Your weapons must be discharged by the time the bell tolls a fifth time."

Hope wondered if anyone had ever inquired what would happen if they failed to shoot. What if there was a stalemate?

Neither Renee nor Crazy Sid acknowledged Maxwell.

"Do you both understand?" the sheriff demanded.

Crazy Sid spat on the ground. "Yuh, chief. Got it."

"Crystal clear," Renee said, her face tight.

"All right, then," Maxwell said, taking a position up on the porch of the saloon.

The next minute creaked around, taking an age it seemed. Renee stared hard at Crazy Sid — Crazy Sid stared right back at her, his cruel gaze unflinching. Both contestants stood with their hands hovering above their weapons, ready to draw. Waiting for the bell to toll, for the signal to be given.

Hope looked down the street toward the church. She saw the bell swing back on its rope. Her head snapped back toward the players as the first toll of the heavy old bell rang out through the town.

Crazy Sid reached for his pistol.

Renee's hand was a blur as she pulled her own sidearm free of the holster.

Grimacing with his disgusting brown teeth, Crazy Sid was the first to fire. He brought his shooter up and depressed the trigger straightaway.

Instinctively Renee flinched to the right. At the same time, she fired at Crazy Sid.

His bullet whipped past her head, missing her skull by a hair. She'd flinched just enough for the shot to miss its mark. Crazy Sid was not so fortunate.

Before the sound of their gunshots had had time to echo through the town, Crazy Sid fell to his knees, hands clasping his throat. Blood pumped from behind his fingers, cascading out over his hands and running in torrents down his wrists. He struggled to draw a single breath of air.

Renee did not leave him to drown in his own blood.

The bell tolled again.

Renee aimed.

Fired.

The shot penetrated Crazy Sid's chest, exploding out the back of his torso in a spray of blood and bone. On the third toll of the bell, Crazy Sid's body slid back to the ice and mud with the thud of a sack of potatoes.

The few townsfolk there to watch, including the patrons of the saloon, stepped out into the street, clapping their hands, congratulating Renee Lane on her victory. Meanwhile, Crazy Sid's body was slowly hauled away, his boots dragging in the mud.

"Damn," Hope muttered under her breath. "The barbarity of it."

"Something to say?" Barbosa demanded.

She hadn't noticed him draw near. He was clapping his hands along with everyone else.

"I do hope you're not having second thoughts."

"You're dismissive. But I'll do better than you think," Hope retorted.

"Is that so?"

She leaned in as she walked past. "Count on it."

Hope checked in on her horse, grateful to Jasper for taking such good care of the beast.

"Thank you — so much. She looks the best I've ever seen her," Hope said, running her hand down the horse's smooth but muscular neck. "You've done a great job. She'll be well rested by the time I ride out of here."

"Do you think you will be?" Jasper asked.

Hope looked at the boy. "Will be what?"

"Ridin' out of here."

"Of course," Hope said, and resumed stroking her horse. "I don't intend on dying here."

"I hope it goes your way," Jasper said.

"You don't sound very optimistic about my chances, Jasper," Hope said. "Why? Is Barbosa that good?"

Jasper nodded slowly. "He always wins."

"Well, not this time," said a voice behind her.

Hope spun around, startled, hand already reaching for her pistol. "Who the —"

Ethan held his hands up. "Wait. Don't shoot," he said, smiling. "I come in peace."

Hope relaxed. "It's you."

"It's me," Ethan said.

Jasper gathered his things together. "I'll leave you to it," he said, hefting a bucket containing his tools and other items. He tipped his head toward Ethan as he went out toward the saloon. "Sir."

"Kid," Ethan said, lifting his hat and giving a single courteous bow of his shiny bald head.

Hope sat on a hay bale. She inhaled deeply, practically tasting the earthiness of the hay, the smell of the horses in their stables, the cold ozone of the winter air pushing through the gaps in the rafters above.

"So what can I do you for, pilgrim?" she asked.

"I came by, see how you were doing."

"Fine as can be, I guess. You know, given the circumstances."

Ethan produced a cigarillo. "Mind?"

"I don't. I think Burt might mind you setting light to his barn, though."

"Burt?"

"The barkeep."

"Ah," Ethan said, continuing to light the cigarillo anyway. "I'll be doubly careful. That way Burt won't get upset."

"Good."

"Nervous about taking your turn?" Ethan asked.

"Wouldn't you be?" Hope said. She shook her head. "I was naive."

"Naive?"

"I didn't have a care for the consequences. I only ever thought about killing him. I should have waited to kill him in private but . . ."

"Your blood was up."

"Yeah. Just seeing him in the flesh again, livin' and breathin' while my pop's buried six feet under. I just couldn't let it go."

"It's hard to switch that off. I know all too well," Ethan replied. "Once you found Knox, there wasn't anything would have ever been able to stop you killing him."

"True."

"Makes that line separating us from the darker side of humanity seem awful thin, don't it?"

"It really does."

Ethan drew on the cigarillo. "I didn't have time to ask what it was all about. You just mentioned your pop. I take it Knox killed him?"

"Yes. He and another man executed him right in front of me," Hope said, the words bitter in her mouth. "Then they kidnapped me and were taking me somewhere to do their worst to me, but I got away. I nearly died in the process, but I escaped. I'm still here."

"And you finally got him, eh?"

"I got 'em both." Hope flexed her left hand. It was aching — the cold air getting to her bones and joints, which had never truly healed properly in the years since Elijah had pulled her from the muddy riverbank. "It don't much feel like I got *anything,* though. I feel like there's stuff left undone, you know?"

"I too once sought revenge on a man. I got it, just like you," Ethan said. "And just like you, it did not make me feel very much better. I felt . . . well, I can't rightly say how I felt."

"Hollow?"

He snapped his fingers. "Yeah, that's it. *Hollow.*"

"I never gave much thought to what might come after it was done," Hope said. "Now I'm wondering how I'll feel if I survive this round of the contest. Because a part of me wonders if it might be best if I take a bullet."

Ethan shook his head. "No one wants you getting killed here today."

"No?"

The man she called pilgrim set her with a hard but earnest stare. "No."

"It's nice of you to say."

"Listen, I wanted to make an offer to you. I'm heading on out from here in a few days. I was gonna find someplace to set down roots. Quit my rambling ways and try to make it as a regular fella."

Hope pointed to the twin shiny pistols at his hips. "Give those up, too?"

"Potentially, yes," Ethan said. "Would you

be opposed to considering the same?"

"If I win the contest, you mean."

"Well, obviously," Ethan said. "You won't be considering much of anything if you're buried in the earth."

Hope stood. "Is this a . . . proposition, Ethan?"

"I guess."

"Have you ever had much trouble with being forward?"

"Not really," Ethan said.

Hope said, "I'll bet."

"My thinking was to settle in one of those towns that spring up around a railway station. Erect a saloon there, but build it right alongside the station house." Ethan looked back at the saloon through the open doors of the barn. "Bit like this place, to tell the truth."

"So folk can step straight off the train and hit the saloon?"

"Exactly. On a hot day, there'd be nothing better than a glass of your preferred refreshment while you wait for your train to arrive, or for when you've just stepped off a train and fancy wetting your whistle," Ethan said. "I mean, it's just a thought."

"One of those little towns, you could really put your mark on the place, I guess," Hope said.

Ethan finished the cigarillo, and pinched the end between his thumb and forefinger. "But I'd need a partner. I thought someone such as yourself might be interested."

Hope laughed. "I'm sorry. I think I got the wrong end of the stick. This isn't a . . . *romantic* proposition?"

She thought Ethan blushed then, but couldn't be sure. The light wasn't so great, and his complexion was tanned anyway, so it was hard to tell. But she was almost sure of it.

"I don't mean to offend," Ethan said.

"I'm not offended. I'm flattered. Your idea certainly has my interest. Not sure I want to spend the rest of my days serving drinks in a saloon, though. I might miss traveling from place to place. I used to hate being on that open road, but now I wonder how I'd get by without it," Hope said. "All that good, clean air. Watching the sun rise and set, and the mountains turning bloodred at the close of day . . . there's nothing like it."

"Can't argue there," Ethan said. "It's just an idea. I have some money behind me, and when you win this contest, you will, too. I sense a kindred spirit in you. Someone I can trust. And I'd like to feel you can trust me, too."

"I do," Hope said. "I don't know why. I'm

208

not a very trusting person. But for some reason, I do get the impression I can trust you."

"Well, I should leave you to it. I wanted to wish you luck against Nelson. Watch your step with him. He's got quite the reputation. Even *I've* heard of him."

"Is he good, then?"

"He's bloodthirsty."

Hope frowned. "Most men are."

CHAPTER TWELVE

Hope sat in a corner of the saloon, gathering her thoughts. She had to resist the temptation to check her pistol yet again to ensure it was fully loaded and ready to shoot. The gun was in fine condition. Cleaned and oiled. Fully loaded. Her hands did not ache as they usually did, as if they were aware that on this day, of all days, they were expected to perform for her without clumsiness or hesitation. Hope's hands would need to be an extension of her instincts, working so fast they were literally blurs to any onlooker who happened to see her reach for her sidearm.

Red Nelson pulled out a chair. "Care if I sit?"

"Do I get much choice?"

He sat across the table from her and said, "I love this."

"You love . . . *what* exactly?"

"This." Nelson opened his arms to indicate

the whole saloon, the town, all the world. "The moment before it happens. The panic and fear pulsating just beneath the surface, like feeling your heartbeat thumping in your veins. It's in the air."

"Is it?"

"You don't smell it?" Nelson asked.

Hope shrugged. "Can't say as I do. Feels the same in here as it usually does," she said.

"No, no, it's definitely there."

Hope rolled her shoulders back. "I'll take your word for it. What do you want, Mister Nelson?"

"Want?"

"Yes. What do you want?"

"To speak with you before we fire bullets at each other."

Hope laughed.

Red Nelson peered at her quizzically, head cocked to one side. "What's so funny?"

"You."

"Me?"

"You're afraid."

"I do not fear anything."

"You're afraid of shooting me dead."

"Pathetic!" Nelson scoffed. "Such rubbish coming from your mouth. Afraid of shooting you dead? Why would I be afraid of something I want?"

"Because it'll be pretty terrible for you to

step out on that street and face a woman," Hope said. "You're thinkin' that if I shoot you, and kill you, then you've died a shameful death. Because men are superior, aren't they? At the same time, you're wondering how you can shoot *me,* and kill *me,* and somehow make it seem like a fair fight. Because men who kill women are beasts."

"You have a venomous tongue," Red Nelson said. He folded his arms. "How much do you want?"

"For what?"

His eyes shifted to take in the other patrons of the saloon. He lowered his voice to barely a whisper. "How much to walk away?"

"Nothing, because it ain't happening. I'm fighting."

"Oh, you are? You talk big for a woman."

Hope leaned forward. "I'm going to shoot you dead, right out there, in the cold. Trust me, if I say I'm gonna do somethin' . . . I *do* it."

Nelson slammed his fist down on the table, then pointed a finger at her face. "There's a first time for everything. Just you remember that. See you out in the street!"

He stormed out of the saloon, furiously shoving through the swinging doors. They squealed on their hinges as they swung back and forth in his wake.

Burt McCoy set a glass down in front of her and filled it with whiskey.

Hope peered up at him. "Is that for me?"

"One for the road."

She lifted the glass to her lips, taking it in one go.

Burt collected the glass. "I think one will do. You need your wits about you."

"Agreed," Hope said, standing from the table. "I don't intend on getting bested by that pig, either."

"Good. I was hoping you wouldn't."

"Can I ask you something?"

Burt nodded. "Sure."

"You've lived here a long time. You've seen firsthand some of the things Barbosa is responsible for."

Burt inhaled deeply, as if hurt. "I have," he said.

"If you had the chance to put an end to whatever it is he's doing here in Fortune's Cross, tell me honestly, would you take it?"

Burt leaned in close. "You askin' if I'd lay everything on the line just to see that son of a gun buried six feet deep?"

"Yes."

"I reckon I would," Burt told her. "Listen now, I'll be rootin' for you." He carried the bottle and the glass back to the bar.

Hope checked the time. She had twenty minutes left until her showdown in the street, which was time enough. She left the saloon and headed to the general store. There she purchased cigarillos and a paper bag of peppermint candy, the red-and-white-striped kind she'd been fond of as far back as she could recall.

Hope located Ethan at the café drinking a cup of coffee. She sat down next to him at the counter and slid the cigarillos across to him.

"What are these for?" Ethan asked.

"A thank-you. For the other night," Hope told him.

Ethan pushed the cigarillos into his breast pocket. "Well, I never turn down a free smoke. Even if I do think the gift is unnecessary."

"Don't mention it. I wanted to do somethin' to say thank you," Hope said.

"Thought I'd come in here, have a cup of joe before I watch the contest," Ethan said. He blew across the surface of his coffee, hot steam billowing out away from him. "From the whiskey I can smell on your breath, you had yourself a little Dutch courage."

"Is it that noticeable?"

"In an establishment like this, it is," Ethan said with a grin.

Hope pushed one of the red-and-white candies into her mouth. "Better?" she asked after sucking on it a few seconds to release the taste and aroma.

"Only one way to find out."

Ethan pulled her in close to him, his lips inches from hers, and shielded them from view with his hat in his hand. They kissed, tentatively at first.

Afterward, Hope pulled back and studied his face. "Do you like peppermint?" she asked.

Ethan's eyes twinkled as he looked at her. He lowered his hat. "I guess I do now."

"That was . . . unexpected," Hope said, looking about to see if anyone had been paying attention.

"The best things are," Ethan said.

Hope had five minutes to spare. When she walked back up the street, she found Red Nelson pacing back and forth in front of the saloon, looking the most agitated she'd seen him. He glared at her but made no attempt to approach or speak with her.

Cyrus Barbosa was in the exact same spot he had been that morning at dawn when he'd watched Renee Lane and Crazy Sid Babcock face each other down. He smoked and watched her approach with what seemed like genuine amusement written on his face. As she drew near, Barbosa took a pocket watch on a chain from a pocket sewn into his waistcoat and made a show of checking the time.

"Not long until the bells ring for you both," he declared.

Next to him, Renee Lane and Daiyu Wu laughed along.

Hope nodded at Daiyu. "I'm not sure why you're laughing, Miss Wu."

Daiyu's face became suddenly serious.

Hope continued: "The man next to you will be laughing over your corpse come sundown."

Barbosa slid the pocket watch back into his waistcoat. "I believe Mister Nelson had the measure of your character."

"How so?"

"He came out here and exclaimed, 'That woman in there has one venomous tongue!' and now I'm partial to believin' it."

Hope said, "I've been called far worse."

Barbosa nodded. "I'll bet you have."

Sheriff Maxwell strode out of the saloon. He took his position in the middle of the street. "Contestants, please come and stand at the ready with me."

Hope and Nelson did as the sheriff instructed.

"Now listen to me. Same rules as before. You are not to release your weapons from their holsters until the church bell tolls," Sheriff Maxwell told them. "You must have discharged your weapons by the time the bell tolls a fifth time. Is that understood?"

"Makes sense to me," Nelson said.

"And me," Hope said.

"Good. Now walk apart. And best of luck to you both," Maxwell said, heading for the saloon porch while Hope and Nelson walked away from each other until they'd reached the required distance.

Hope swallowed hard against the fear threatening to take over. Her legs felt weak, and she imagined what it would look like if she collapsed in the street, succumbing to every instinct willing her to curl up in a ball. It took all she had to walk straight and true, to reach her mark and turn to face her opponent.

No, her enemy.

Because any man or woman she might face in the contest could not possibly be considered anything but a mortal enemy — they would try to shoot her down dead, and she must do the same unto them without a moment's hesitation.

Hope drew a stance, her legs apart, hand hovering just over her holster. She looked hard at Red Nelson. The man they'd described as painted head to toe in the blood of his enemies during the war. The man who was now her enemy as surely as she was his.

"One minute until the bell," Sheriff Maxwell declared.

Red Nelson smiled at her with sick determination. It was a smile that said, *You're about to find out what this is all really about.* A smile that said he was ready to pull his gun first. Aim first. Fire first. Stand over her as she breathed her last breath, the light in the sky becoming blindingly bright above her.

Sheriff Maxwell consulted his pocket watch. "Thirty seconds!"

On the porch of the saloon, Cyrus Barbosa bounded forward and stood with his hands gripping the rail so hard, his knuckles turned white from the strain.

The bell rang out.

The sound of the old church bell echoed throughout the town, vibrating off the buildings, trembling through the quiet stillness of the open spaces. It set the ground vibrating, and the bones of all who resided deep in the frozen soil at the Fortune's Cross Cemetery — the fallen and the forgotten, the old faces long since lost to oblivion. The church bell rattled the past and present in one. Shaping what was to come.

Hope pulled her gun.

Nelson's eyes widened in shock as Hope's hand yanked the pistol from her holster. He did the same, wrenching his gun free, bringing it up to fire at her. Something punched him in the chest, knocking him back.

Hope Cassidy's gun flashed again and another hard punch hit him in the chest, this time throwing him to the ground. As he fell, he pulled the trigger of his own gun, firing blind. Seconds later he was lying in the frozen mud, arms and legs numb, lungs filling with blood as he struggled to breathe, gasping and sucking at the air like a landed fish.

Nelson's gunshot scraped the top of Hope's right arm as it skimmed past. It hurt, but it wasn't the worst pain she'd ever felt. Not by any stretch of the imagination. Hope strode quickly over to Nelson, pistol in her hand.

"He won't let you win . . ." Nelson said, speaking in a gurgling voice swamped with blood. He had to swallow hard just to complete his sentence.

He looked off to the side, to the porch of the saloon, where Barbosa stood watching him die. He drew one more breath, then breathed no more. The blood ran from the side of his slack mouth, then oozed from both nostrils.

Hope knelt down, closed the man's eyes. It seemed the right thing to do, despite her distaste for him.

She looked to where Barbosa stood at the porch rail, studied the dour expression on his face and wondered if the dead man could have been right.

Barbosa seized the sheriff by the arm and pulled him inside the saloon.

"Hey! What's this all about?" Sheriff Maxwell demanded, trying to get himself loose of Barbosa's mighty grip.

Barbosa wheeled him about and forcefully launched him against the nearest wall. The sheriff crashed against the timbers, grimacing from the impact. Before he could do anything in response, Barbosa had him pinned, his revolver pressed against the sheriff's temple.

"All it takes is one pull of the trigger," Barbosa snarled.

"If you kill me now, Cyrus, it'll be done in cold blood," Maxwell warned him.

Barbosa grunted. "Tell me one damn murder that ain't."

"I'm the lawman."

"Yeah. For now. Until I decide you ain't

fit for the purpose," Barbosa sneered. "Is that what you want, Travis? You want to look for a new job?"

Sheriff Maxwell gulped and shook his head. "I don't understand; what's the problem?"

"You never said that girl was a Cassidy."

"So? Why would I?" Maxwell was clearly confused.

Barbosa let him go. The sheriff shrank back along the wall as Barbosa walked away, lost in reverie.

"They never told me Tobias had a daughter. If they had, I'd have been askin' 'em why they hadn't dealt with her, too. They must've took a chance she wouldn't grow up to avenge her father. . . . Well, here she is."

"I don't know who you're talkin' about, Cyrus," Maxwell said.

Barbosa turned around, gesticulating with his gun hand, waving the revolver about as if he'd forgotten it was there. "Hope Cassidy! Are you not listening?" he demanded, eyes wild, face red. "Lance Knox and Puck Cosby. They took out her father but left his daughter alive. Now she's here, in Fortune's Cross. In this damned contest! If Knox and Cosby weren't dead already, I'd tear them limb from limb with my bare hands!"

"You and them fellas rode together, did you?"

"We did," Barbosa said, looking at the gun in his hand and frowning at it, as if wondering how it had gotten there. He slid it into its holster and Sheriff Maxwell breathed a sigh of relief. "Now I'm the last one left."

"Last what?"

Barbosa's eyes met his. "The last Black Scorpion."

CHAPTER THIRTEEN

"Roll up that sleeve," Dr. Edith Bell, the resident physician in Fortune's Cross, told her.

Hope rolled her sleeve all the way to her shoulder. The blood from the cut had seeped through her shirt.

Dr. Bell peered at the laceration Red's bullet had left as it sliced through Hope's skin and exposed the flesh beneath to the biting cold. At least it hadn't penetrated her body, embedded itself in her flesh. The bullet had whizzed by and left a mere reminder. It could have been worse. A lot worse.

"You've got quite the scar there already, I see," Bell said.

Hope grimaced. "I'm no stranger to bullets, Doc."

"I can see that." Dr. Bell cleaned the wound, then attacked it with stitches.

Hope flinched at the sensation of the needle penetrating her skin, the catgut pulling the two sides of the cut together.

"Sorry. I know it hurts," Dr. Bell said.

"Some."

"It would've hurt a helluva lot more a few inches to the left," the doctor told her. "This is a stupid game you're playing here. I hope you know that."

"I do."

Dr. Bell set about dressing the newly stitched wound. "Tell me something."

"Ask away."

"Do you have a death wish, competing in a contest like this?"

"No," Hope said, then quickly added, "But I don't fear death."

"*Everyone* should fear death," Dr. Bell told her. She pulled the bandage tight and Hope winced from the sudden burst of pain. "It's the only way we learn."

Hope looked up and down the street. "Do you always do your doctoring outside in the freezing cold?"

"Only when I need to." Dr. Bell fixed the bandage in place. "You can roll your sleeve down now. We're done here."

"I don't know whether to thank you or not," Hope said.

Dr. Bell packed up her things. "I don't think it matters. By tomorrow you'll be joining that man there in the mud with a hole in your head, or your chest, or your gut. All my fine stitching will be for nothing."

"I'm hopin' that won't be the case," said Hope.

Dr. Bell scoffed and walked away.

Sheriff Travis Maxwell emerged from the saloon, looking shaken.

"Sheriff?" Hope said as she approached him. "Can I have a word?"

The sheriff looked at her, eyes unfocused. Then he blinked several times, as if he were seeing her for the first time. "Sorry?"

"I was askin' you if I could have a word."

"Oh. Right. A word . . . about what?"

Hope frowned at him. "Is everything all right?"

"Of course." Maxwell folded his arms. "Why wouldn't it be?"

"I just . . ." Hope decided midsentence to leave it. If there was something going on with him, it wasn't any of her concern. Her only problem right now was surviving the contest. "Never mind. I wanted to talk to you about Red Nelson's body."

"His . . . *body*?" Sheriff Maxwell looked at Red's corpse still lying where it had fallen in the mixture of slushy ice and mud that passed for the street.

"Yes."

"Yes? What about it?"

Hope looked at Red. "I want to pay for the man's funeral."

"His funeral?"

The man seems intent on repeating everything I say back to me, thought Hope. "It seems the right thing to do."

"We already cover the costs for all that," the sheriff told her. "We deduct it from the prize money. The same for any damage incurred. You know, stray bullets flyin' around and such. Occasionally there's a splintered door, a broken window. That kind of thing. Everything's taken care of."

"Oh."

"Is it sinking in that you just killed a man?"

Hope frowned at him. "This isn't my first rodeo, Sheriff. I've shot and killed men before. The way this world works, I doubt he'll be the last, either."

"Well, if you've any design on making it to the end, then he *definitely* won't be the last, will he?"

They both turned to watch as Daiyu Wu checked her weapon, brow furrowed in concentration, right there on the steps of the porch. She glanced up at them but did not bother to ask what they might have been looking at before returning to what she was doing.

"I know," Hope said softly. "I don't relish it. That's why I got to thinking about Red's funeral. I'm guessin' he don't have any family."

"What do you care if he does or doesn't?"

Hope didn't have an answer.

She ran a hand over her face, feeling suddenly tired of it all. Would it really be so bad to fetch her horse and ride the hell out of there? But she knew she could not do that. She couldn't walk away. Not only would Barbosa and his men run her down and hold her accountable for Lance Knox's murder . . . but there was more to it. There was a part of her, deep down inside, that just couldn't give in. She couldn't admit defeat so easily as that. Perhaps it came with the blood, the Cassidy family blood, coursing so strongly through her veins. The tenacity of her father and her uncle, now resident in her — as ingrained as the visceral instinct of a wolf to hunt and to kill. She could not walk away, because her business in Fortune's Cross was not finished. She had been directly challenged and she would wield her gun to the last because she was Tobias Cassidy's daughter.

"Can't make it right you killed him," Sheriff Maxwell told her. "Nothing can."

"What do you mean?"

"I mean, you gotta reconcile that with yourself," Maxwell. "No amount of actin' the Good Samaritan will do that for ya."

His words were sharp, but there was truth in them and Hope could not find cause to argue.

She sighed. "There's no good can be done here, is there? I've just got to survive this contest. Getting through this with my skin intact seems to be about all there is to it."

"Pretty much. I wish I had more to say on the subject, but it's what they call 'black and white.' It is what it is."

"Kill or be killed."

"Yep," Maxwell said, looking back at the saloon as Barbosa emerged with a clatter.

Hope followed his gaze. "What happened inside the saloon, Sheriff?"

"I don't know what you're talking about."

"The way you came out of there," Hope said, shaking her head. "Did something happen between you and Barbosa?"

The sheriff jutted his chin in the direction of his office. "Walk with me."

They passed Red Nelson, lying on his back in the half-frozen mud of the street. Barely a half hour ago, Hope had closed the man's eyes and now one of the locals was busily removing his belt, his boots, stripping the corpse of anything of value.

"Hey, Paulie, leave him be," Maxwell said.

The man looked up from looting the dead body. "Huh?"

"You heard me. Leave him be. A man should be buried in his own goddamn boots at least, even if he is goin' straight to the bad place."

The man squinted at him. "Damn it, Sheriff. None of this is any good to him. They're good boots. Plenty of life left in 'em."

"I can see that. But they're *his* boots. That's the bit you're forgetting, friend. Continue lootin' his corpse and I might have to add another corpse to the mix. Now shove off and let the man alone, huh?"

"I didn't mean nothin' by it," Paulie said. "But the cold weather's settling in. These boots I got now, they're no good. They got holes in 'em. My toes are frozen through, Sheriff."

Hope tossed a couple of coins at the man. Paulie caught them and examined their worth in the palms of his dirty hands. "This is a fair amount of money, lady."

"Sure is."

"What're you throwing it at me for?" Paulie asked.

"So you'll see the sense in buying some boots you can call your own."

Paulie dropped Nelson's legs and took off, clutching hold of his money tightly in his hand.

Maxwell chuckled lightly. "He won't go to no store."

"What d'you mean?"

"That money you gave him, it'll go across the counter at the saloon. Mark my words. Only one man is gonna benefit from that money, and that's Burt McCoy."

Hope watched Paulie as he hurried away. "D'you reckon so?"

"I *know* so. This town is full of men like Paulie. Down on his luck, sure. But men like that, they've been down on their luck for so many years, ain't nothin' gonna help 'em."

And sure enough, as Hope looked on, Paulie ran straight into the saloon.

The sheriff shut the door.

"Are you throwing me back in jail?" Hope asked jokingly.

"You should be so lucky," Maxwell said, inviting her to sit. "You'd be less certain of getting shot."

Hope remained standing. "Why don't you just tell me what I'm doing here?"

"As you like," Maxwell said. "I never thought to tell Barbosa your family name before. And when it left your lips earlier, he got a little . . . heated, you could say."

"Ah," Hope said. "So that's why you looked so ruffled."

"I made it clear before, but I think it stands to be repeated: I'm just one man here. Barbosa and his men could overpower me and . . ."

"No need to explain your position any further, Sheriff. I understand."

Hope found the sheriff weak, but it was weakness born of conditions that were beyond the man's control. He was just working a job when all was said and done. Just like the husband and wife who operated the café. Just like the blacksmith or the doctor or the owner of the feed store. Everyone was trying to keep their bread buttered best they could, utilizing whatever talents they had been blessed with to make ends meet. The sheriff played peacemaker for fifty-one weeks of the year. For one week only, he had to step aside and let the lunatics loose in the asylum. He probably thought it was a small price to pay. A small compromise in the name of security.

As far as Hope was concerned, any price was a price too steep when it came to letting go of your principles or forgetting your own integrity.

"Why did Barbosa react like that to my name?" Hope asked.

"I don't know, 'cept he seems familiar with the two fellas killed your pop," Maxwell told her. "Oh, there was something else."

"Go on."

"He said they used to be Black Scorpions. And so was he."

Hope was stunned. "He said *what*?"

"When you told me what happened to your father, you mentioned that those fellas were Black Scorpions."

"That's right."

"Well, Barbosa knew it," Maxwell said, "and then he said *he* was a Black Scorpion, the only one left. I thought you should know about it."

Hope walked to the window and looked out at the snow-covered town. "A Black Scorpion, just like the outlaws that killed my father."

"Oh, he also knew your father by name."

Hope turned around. "My father was a US marshal. He probably caused those outlaws a lot of headaches, maybe hunted 'em down at one time or another."

"More than likely."

"Will you keep this to yourself for now, Sheriff?" Hope asked.

Maxwell opened his arms. "Who am I

gonna tell? I'm nothing but a master of ceremonies once the contest rolls into town. There's no mistaking the real man in charge right now, is there?"

"No," Hope said, looking back up the street. From where she stood, she could just see Cyrus Barbosa's back as he stood against the rail, smoking and talking to the people around him. "No doubt," she said.

CHAPTER FOURTEEN

The sky burned crimson over Fortune's Cross, the sun's last fire glowing red in the furnace of the horizon and turning the snow pink. In places it was hard to tell what was blood and what was the reflection of the sunset.

"Hey," Ethan said, sidling up next to Hope. "I heard you got winged earlier."

"Yeah, I did," Hope said, flexing her right arm. "Same arm I got plugged in a few years ago. It's not too bad, though. I've had worse, by any account."

"That's good to hear."

"Where were you?"

"I thought I was gonna watch," Ethan said, "but when it came to it, I had to go for a walk instead. I heard the gunshots, though. I heard those loud and clear."

Hope studied his face. "Did you think I'd been killed, pilgrim?"

"I hate to admit, it might've crossed my mind."

"Really? That's how little you think of me? You were a fountain of positivity just before."

Ethan held his palms up. "Now, hold on a second. I never said that. I said it *crossed my mind,* which it did. But then it occurred to me you'd be difficult to kill. You have the look of someone who'll stop at nothing to get the job done."

"I think they call it 'determination,' and last time I checked, it weren't a crime," Hope said.

Ethan smiled. "I stand corrected. You have the look of somebody who is *determined.* Is that better?"

"A little."

The big oaf Barbosa had identified as Cotton at the café appeared on the porch. He glared at both Hope and Ethan.

Hope's hand drifted to her sidearm.

"The boss wants to see you," Cotton said. Ethan started forward and Cotton placed a hand on the gunslinger's chest. "Not you."

"You'd be a smart man to never do that again, friend," Ethan said. "I don't take kindly to folk touching me who don't have need to."

Cotton slowly removed his hand from

Ethan's chest. He looked directly at Hope. "Just the lady here."

"Looks like I've been summoned," she said to Ethan, then looked at Cotton. "Lead on."

She followed Cotton inside the busy saloon to a table positioned in a corner at the back, where privacy was afforded by the shadows and the fog of tobacco smoke that permeated the air she walked through.

Barbosa was sitting at the table dressed as if for a wedding. Hope had never seen a man so consistently well-dressed.

"What's the special occasion?" she asked.

Cotton hovered behind her until Barbosa gave him a nod of his head and he left them to their conversation. Barbosa poured two glasses of whiskey.

"I could be going into a box today. Every time I play this game, I'm sure to wear my best. Well, one of my best, at least."

"Do you really believe you're going to lose this round?" Hope asked.

Barbosa pushed the cork into the whiskey bottle. " 'All the world's a stage, and all the men and women merely players. They have their exits and their entrances. . . .' As I recall, you do not know Shakespeare, do you?"

"No. Is he good with a pistol?" Hope

236

asked, pulling up a chair and sitting on the opposite side of the table.

Barbosa's deep, hearty laughter surprised her — she hadn't been trying to be funny.

He wiped at his eyes. "Oh, my, I haven't laughed like that in a very long while."

"Is that drink for me?"

"It is," Barbosa said, pushing the glass toward her across the table. "I have something to discuss with you."

"Discuss away."

"It is the matter of your name."

"My name?"

"Yes."

"What of it?"

Barbosa pulled up his sleeve and offered her his exposed wrist, revealing the same tattoo of a black scorpion she'd seen before. "I knew a man once, an acquaintance. I suppose you could say we rode in a gang."

"The Black Scorpions."

"We disbanded a long, long time ago," Barbosa said, rolling his sleeve back down. "Tell me the truth: why are you here in Fortune's Cross?"

"I came here to kill Lance Knox because he and Puck Cosby murdered my father."

"You didn't come here to kill me?"

"No."

Barbosa lifted his glass and took a sip.

"But you would like to now, I'll bet."

"What makes you say that? I just told you, I didn't come to Fortune's Cross to kill you. I'd never heard of you before riding into town."

Barbosa shook his head. "Don't play around with me, young lady. Who told you that I was a Black Scorpion? The sheriff, I take it. . . ."

"As a matter of fact, no. A lady bounty hunter who was passing through town," Hope said.

Barbosa cocked an eyebrow. "Roper? She knew I was in the Black Scorpions?"

Hope fixed him with an icy stare. "She said you *ran* the Black Scorpions."

"She says a lot, it seems."

"So it's true?"

"Yes. A lifetime ago. As you can see, I've moved on to bigger and better things since then. I have many businesses — legitimate, I'll have you know — and many investments that provide me with a comfortable living. My past is what it is. The past."

"If you ran the gang back then, it stands to reason you ordered the murder of my father."

"Does it?"

"I'd say so, yeah," Hope said.

Barbosa drained the last of the whiskey in

his glass. "Now we come to the crux of the matter, do we not, Hope Cassidy? What do you intend on doing with this new state of enlightenment you find yourself in?"

"I plan on facing you down, if you survive this round," Hope told him. She reached slowly across the table and touched the middle of his forehead with the tip of her gloved index finger. "And I'll be punching a hole right about there. Y'know, to let the air in a bit."

Barbosa reached up slowly, and took hold of her finger with his hand. "You know, it's easy to sit there and judge a man from the comfortable vantage point of not having walked the same path." He let go of her finger. "I had men to lead, and someone has to make the tough calls, young lady. That's how it is. 'Uneasy lies the head that wears the crown.' That's all I can say. Until you've borne that burden yourself, you have no idea what you're talking about."

Hope stood. "I know that I watched my father killed before my eyes. I know what I saw, what I felt. Don't you dare sit there and tell me I have no idea what I'm talking about. I know all too well, Mister Barbosa."

She tossed the whiskey back in one go, swallowing it with abandon, then slammed the glass back down on the tabletop. Hope made to walk off, but Barbosa snapped his fingers. Cotton and Ed stepped in from the sides, blocking her exit. There was no getting *around* them, and no getting *through* them.

She turned back to face him.

The big man pushed his chair back and stood, straightening his jacket. "I have something to tell you. But it can wait until this round is finished. If I am successful, I will reveal all to you. If I am shot down dead, then the truth shall die with me."

Hope frowned. "The *truth*? I already know you wanted my father dead. I'd say I've got all the truth I need."

"There are many truths, and let me assure you, some of them can be rather . . . inconvenient. But you'll learn, Miss Cassidy. In time you'll learn."

"What're you talkin' about?" Hope asked. "Say it plain."

But Barbosa had no interest in speaking with her further. He motioned for Ed and Cotton to let Hope go and paid her no further mind. They parted for her to pass between them. Hope brushed past the two henchmen and left the saloon. She walked out onto the porch, the stony air a welcome relief from the smoke-filled interior of the saloon.

"Hey." Ethan looked at her with concern. "Are you all right?"

"Yes. No. I . . . I can't be sure."

"What happened in there?" Ethan said, looking through the opening at the top of the swinging doors. "Did he do something to you?"

"Not yet."

"So what happened?" Ethan asked again, turning his attention back to Hope.

"He just confirmed he was what Katie Roper said he was," Hope told Ethan. "And he confirmed something else."

"What?"

"He was in charge of an outlaw gang called the Black Scorpions, and he ordered my father's murder," Hope said.

"My own father was an outlaw," Ethan told her.

"Really?"

Ethan nodded. "He left that life behind. And when his gang caught up with him, he'd made a new life for himself. He had my ma, my brother and me."

"What happened?"

"He, uh . . ." Ethan said, awkwardly trying to find the words. He swallowed. "He killed them all. Only I survived."

"I'm sorry," Hope said. "I'm sorry that happened to you."

"It was a long time ago. I've made peace with it now."

"Does it get easier?" Hope asked, searching Ethan's face for something — anything — that might bring her some solace. She yearned for it.

But if Ethan had comfort to offer, he kept it to himself. "Time doesn't erase what people have done. We all answer for our sins eventually. It'll be no different for Barbosa in the end."

"But his reckoning won't come from a higher power." Hope pulled her pistol. Held it up. "It'll come from this."

In the bloodred light, Cyrus Barbosa and Daiyu Wu took up their positions at opposite ends of the street. Sheriff Maxwell gave them his oft-repeated instructions, then retreated to the relative safety of the saloon's long porch.

The bell had yet to toll. As Hope took up at the sheriff's elbow, she noted that there was still a full minute to go by his pocket watch. He'd positioned Barbosa and Wu well ahead of time.

"There a reason why they're out in that street already, eyeballing each other?" Hope whispered.

Maxwell didn't take his eyes off the timepiece. "Well, I happen to think it does a lot to a person, looking their opponent in the eye. Sometimes it unsettles folk."

"That's what you're hoping."

"Pure speculation on your part, Miss Cassidy."

"Just as I thought," Hope whispered, glancing up at the two contestants.

They looked like David and Goliath out there in the dying light — Daiyu's petite frame taking a stand against the vast barrel-like form of Cyrus Barbosa. The twin pistols at her sides looked too big for her, as if they were oversized and out of proportion. But Hope remembered Wu flinging her guns around on the stage back at the church, so she knew the other woman could handle herself. However, whether she could hold her own against a ruthless, coldhearted, experienced shootist like Barbosa was another matter entirely.

The pocket watch showed there was half a minute left.

Hope said, "Can I ask you something?"

"So long as you're quick. Bell's gonna ring any second now," Maxwell said.

"Apart from Cotton and Ed, how many men does Barbosa have in town?"

"Plenty. He has plenty. Why?"

"Just asking," Hope said, watching the

243

second hand of the pocket watch approach the number ten.

"At least another six men," the sheriff said. "They're sat in that saloon. You can tell 'em apart real easy."

"Oh, yeah? How so?"

The church bell rang out, loud and clear. Maxwell snapped his pocket watch shut. "They wear gray dusters."

"Gray dusters. Good to know," Hope said. "When did they arrive?"

"Last night."

"Thanks, Sheriff," she said, backing up, her eyes on the contestants in the street.

Now that she thought about it, when she'd been escorted into the saloon by Cotton, she had noticed an abundance of men in gray dusters within, but hadn't ascribed it any importance. Now it made sense.

"Don't mention it," Maxwell told her. "I mean it. Literally, don't tell a soul."

The bell rang out again. Then a third time. Neither Cyrus Barbosa or Daiyu Wu moved an inch. They could have been statues out there in the fading sunlight, monuments to the possibilities and limitations of violence. One seeking to defend a legacy of inflicting pain and death, the other intent on staking a claim of her own.

Ethan stood with his arms braced against

the porch railing, a cigarillo pinched between his lips.

The church bell sounded a fourth time.

Daiyu Wu was the first to flinch. She pulled her guns free, hands a blur.

But Barbosa was quicker.

He whipped his gun out of its holster, shot Wu in the stomach. Thumbed the hammer back and shot her again without a second's pause, blasting a hole straight through her heart. Wu didn't get to fire a single shot. She fell on her side, dead before she landed in the frosted mud.

Ethan removed the cigarillo from his mouth. "Damn," he said.

Now that Sheriff Maxwell had pointed out as much to her, Hope noticed the gray dusters on the men who emerged from within the saloon, clapping their hands and hollering.

Beaming with pride at his own accomplishment, their employer raised his hands.

Another figure emerged from the saloon, pushing through the men in dusters. Renee Lane stood at the railing and took in the sight of Daiyu Wu dead in the street, and Cyrus Barbosa triumphantly gesticulating to his men about his victory over her.

"Come to have a look at his handiwork for yourself?" Hope asked.

Renee's expression was hard and unreadable. "I knew the minute his men emptied out of the saloon that he'd won. I'm not surprised."

"No?"

Renee looked at her. "Daiyu was never as good as she liked to think."

"It's just the three of us now," Hope said.

"And the next round is decided on a coin toss," Renee told her. "It won't bring me much joy to kill you. It really won't. But I cannot say the same about the prospect of killing that devil over there."

"I hope it don't come to that," she said, remembering that the configuration of combatants on the first day had been decided by the sheriff pulling names from a hat. Now they would be chosen at the toss of a coin.

"It is what it is," Renee said. She scowled at Ethan, as if his presence there next to Hope brought her displeasure. "Chance will decide the matchup. And then it's down to us."

Hope looked at the slumped form of Daiyu Wu out in the street, and at the fresh blood pooling out beneath her. The doctor who'd seen to Hope's wound, Dr. Bell, knelt next to Daiyu and felt for a pulse. She lowered her head and then stood, walking away with her hopes of having a patient to save dashed.

Barbosa came to the steps of the saloon and said, "Let's not waste time. Sheriff, do you have that coin available?"

"I do."

"Then let us head inside and see how tomorrow's matches will play out, shall we?"

Maxwell said, "You don't want to celebrate your win with your men, Cyrus?"

"There'll be plenty of time for that later," Barbosa said, his eyes flicking over to where Hope, Renee and Ethan were stood. "For now, we have matters to attend to."

"That means *us*," Renee said, following Barbosa inside, pushing through the swinging doors after him.

Ethan made to follow Hope inside, but she stopped him. "You don't have to come along."

"I insist," he said, momentarily taking her hand.

So Hope found the solace she'd been hoping for earlier. It was there; it'd just taken its time to be presented to her. She realized Ethan Harper was as much of a closed book as she was.

And there wasn't anything wrong with that.

"Okay," she said finally, and the two of them walked in together.

CHAPTER FIFTEEN

Hope's eyes skimmed over the faces of the people crammed into the saloon — she and Renee were the only women in attendance. That figured. The world Hope knew was populated almost exclusively by men. And even when she was around women, it was men who ran everything. There wasn't anything she could do to change that.

The sheriff hadn't been lying. Now that the gray dusters had been pointed out to her, Barbosa's men stuck out like sore thumbs to her. Cotton and Ed stood down at the far end of the bar, propping up the counter, much to Burt's annoyance as he attempted to wipe the top down with a rag. She stood with Renee and Barbosa as the only combatants left in the contest, and together they watched as the sheriff addressed the crowd. Finally he flipped a coin up into the air and caught it, then put it on the back of his other hand.

249

"If there were no women left at this stage, I'd have the men pulling straws to figure who's fightin' who. But since we have more women than men, it makes sense to decide if one of 'em will be fighting Barbosa, or if they'll be going up against each other. So this coin toss decides if it's woman against woman, or woman against man."

Hope rolled her eyes. It seemed an incredibly convoluted way of choosing the combatants this time around, but she didn't say anything in protest. It didn't matter much to her how it played out. She had no intention of losing, no matter whom she stood against.

The sheriff got ready to reveal the result of the coin toss. He seemed to be a good man, for the most part; he was just caught up in a situation he couldn't escape from. Maxwell wasn't the first man Hope had seen in that predicament and she doubted he'd be the last.

"Heads it's the women against each other. Tails it's one of 'em against the reigning champion."

"Come on, Travis, put us out of our misery," Barbosa said.

The sheriff lifted his hand. "Tails."

Barbosa looked at Hope and Renee with obvious relish. "Well, ladies, looks like you both get your shot at the title."

Maxwell said, "This toss decides which of you will face Barbosa in the morning." He flipped the coin up into the air. It turned and turned; then he caught it. "Heads it's Renee Lane. Tails it's Hope Cassidy."

He lifted his hand and looked at the result of the coin toss.

"Well?" Barbosa demanded.

"Heads. The next contest will be between Cyrus Barbosa and Renee Lane, with Hope Cassidy automatically in the final. She will stand against the victor."

The crowd cheered. Barbosa extended his big thick hand to Renee. "However it plays out, best of luck, eh?"

Renee reluctantly shook the man's hand. "Same to you," she mumbled.

Then Barbosa lifted her hand into the air, to loud hollers from his men and the towns-folk who'd gathered in the saloon to watch.

Then Barbosa turned to Hope. The mask of congeniality he'd been wearing since kill-ing Daiyu Wu finally slipped. It melted from his face, revealing itself as the facade it had been all along. "And you, young lady, will make your stand against the victor of tomor-row morning's contest, eh?"

"Looks like that's the case," Hope said.

"Yes. Now, I promised you some truth,

did I not?" Barbosa asked.

The crowd quieted to hear the exchange.

"You did."

Barbosa reached inside his suit jacket, producing a creased wanted poster yellowed with age. He held it out for her to take. "I've carried this a long time."

"What's that?"

"All the truth you need."

Hope took the poster and looked at it. The illustration, an artist's imagined scene, consisted of six men lined up in front of what looked like the burning wreckage of a train carriage. The flames licked out of the smashed, shattered windows, and black smoke filled the sky. But the carnage of the fire didn't seem to bother the men stood before it — it seemed to Hope they were responsible for it. Barbosa stood front and center. Not a trace of gray in his hair and not as fat around the belly, but undeniably a younger version of the man who'd just given her the wanted poster. Next to him, to his left, stood Lance Knox and Puck Cosby. Again, many years younger than the men she knew — the men who'd burned her home to the ground, murdered her father and kidnapped her. Nor were they the same men she'd caught up with eventually and killed in the name of reciprocity.

The men in the illustration had youth on their side. To Barbosa's right stood three more men. She didn't recognize the man at Barbosa's elbow, or the one at the very end, but the man in the middle of the three was instantly recognizable.

Her realization must have registered on her face because Barbosa began to chuckle.

"Yes, that's right. You ain't seeing things. That's your pop right there with us in that there picture. See him standing all proud the way he is? That's how I remember him. I'm the last of 'em left. Survival of the fittest, that's what it is."

Hope looked up at Barbosa. There were tears in her eyes; she couldn't help it. But it wasn't from sorrow. The tears that spilled from the corners of her eyes and down her cheeks came from a place of anger, of outrage at what he had revealed to her. "This can't be real."

Barbosa reached out, took the wanted poster back from her and regarded it himself. "This was a long time ago. But I remember that day clear as anything. We forced a train to stop and took everything they had. It made all the papers of the day. It was a big deal. There were so many witness statements, the artist was able to do a pretty good likeness of us, in my opinion.

It's close to how we used to look back then . . . or at least, how I remember us looking. D'you know, there were people inside that burning carriage? We locked the doors an' set the thing ablaze," Barbosa said, glancing up at her to gauge her reaction to what he was saying. He saw how emotional, how shocked she was at the revelation — and it gave him great pleasure to witness the raw hurt in her eyes. "They were railroad agents. We stood out there in the hot sun and listened to their screams as they burned. They didn't last long. I can tell you that. They didn't last long at all. That's the way it was back then. We didn't even wear masks. In a way, we wanted folk to know it was us."

"You're trying to convince me my father was a Black Scorpion. . . ."

"You've seen it for yourself," Barbosa said, smacking the folded-up wanted poster on the back of his hand. "This right here is the hard proof, silly girl!"

Hope backed up. She shook her head in disbelief. "No . . . no, it can't be true."

"But it is."

"Tobias Cassidy was a US marshal. He was a good, decent, honest man. He was the best man I've ever known," Hope said, fighting the emotions rising within her. Try-

254

ing to keep a handle on things, stop herself from losing grip of reality. "He wasn't like you."

"Your father was *just* like me," Barbosa said, closing in on her. His eyes burned with intensity. " 'Cept when he left us. When he turned his back on all we were doing. When he tried to turn us in to the law, stab us all in the back. I swore to him then that I'd track him down, show him once and for all that the Black Scorpions weren't something you could just walk away from. It took some time, but we got him in the end. Cosby and Knox got him good. They made him pay. I heard he begged for death. . . ."

Hope pulled her gun.

One of Barbosa's men in gray dusters stepped in, took hold of her arm and pinned it to her side so she couldn't raise it. Hope tried to fight him off but he was too strong. Ethan came to her aid, tried to intervene on her behalf.

Barbosa drew his pistol. "Ease up there, stranger. This ain't your business."

"I say it is," Ethan growled, eyeing up the competition, taking stock of the men around him.

Hope didn't know him well enough to guess his every move, but she reckoned Ethan would be figuring out how many of

Barbosa's men he could kill before he got shot full of holes himself.

Not enough to make a difference.

Hope knew that, and she knew *Ethan* knew that, too.

Barbosa walked up to Ethan and pistol-whipped him across the head, knocking him to the floor. Immediately, two of the dusters fell on him and wrestled his weapons away from him. They pinned his arms behind his back and restrained him so he couldn't cause any more trouble for their boss.

"Thanks, boys," Barbosa said, turning his attention back to Hope. "When he left, Tobias turned the law on us. He weren't just a no-good, dirty deserter. He was a damned turncoat, too. Set us all on the run. Then he had the gall to remake himself as a *lawman.* That's why it took us so many years to find the son of a gun. Last thing I expected was to find him workin' as a marshal. Almost couldn't believe it myself. But then, I sat back and had a good think about it and came to the realization what your pop done was a stroke of genius."

"You had no need to kill him. Why couldn't you leave him alone?"

Barbosa holstered his pistol. "Because loyalty is everything," he said, and took hold of Hope's right shoulder with his left hand.

He slugged her in the stomach with his right, knocking the air out of her. Hope immediately doubled over in agony. Barbosa took a step back and, while she was still bent forward, swung his knee up into her face.

Hope toppled over, barely drawing enough breath to groan in agony.

The saloon was silent.

She could have heard a pin drop.

Barbosa addressed the gathered men. "I have decided that tomorrow's contests will not go as planned. I will still face off against Renee Lane at dawn. I have no quarrel with her. Miss Lane came to Fortune's Cross to face me out in that street, and that's just what she'll get. All right, Renee?"

"Yes," she said. "That's what I came here for. It's all the same to me."

"Just as I thought. But I am going to shake things up a little bit. Miss Cassidy will no longer automatically face the victor of that round in the final. No, no, no, no, no," he said, clucking his tongue. "She will, instead, face off against her new pal here. They will take to the street at noon and we'll all see how they fare, having no choice but to kill each other. And at dusk, the victors of the morning and the afternoon rounds will show their quality in return for the ultimate prize."

The announcement was met with lots of cheering, whooping and raucous approval on behalf of the men in the saloon.

Hope slowly got to her feet, then stood up straight. There was blood running from her nose. When she touched her fingertips to her top lip, they came away wet with crimson.

Barbosa snapped his fingers at Sheriff Maxwell. "Travis, throw those two in a cell until tomorrow morning. I don't want them given an opportunity to run away in the night. Especially when this young lady is the daughter of a rat. A low-life, treacherous, disloyal rat who got everything he had coming to him."

Ethan strained against the men holding him in place. "You won't get away with this! I will kill you, do you hear?"

"You'll have to make it through the second round against your friend before you do," Barbosa said with a wink. "I knew who you was the second you rode into town, *Ethan Harper.*"

Hope spat at Barbosa. The mouthful of bloody saliva splattered on the toe of the big man's boot.

He looked down at what she'd done. "I'll

let you have that one. After all, I did order those two reprobates to kill your pa. But you'd best toe the line, young lady, or you're gonna find yourself missing your trigger finger. You'll be needing that tomorrow when you kill Mister Harper."

"It's not gonna happen."

Barbosa grinned. "We'll see. It might be different when you're out there in that street."

"And if I refuse to compete?"

Barbosa stabbed at the air with his finger. "Then you'd better consider the expediency of blowing your own brains out, Miss Cassidy, and save me the trouble. Oh, here, before I forget. A little memento from the grave for you."

Barbosa produced a silver marshal's badge and tossed it at her. Hope managed to catch it, turned it over in her hand and stared at it in disbelief.

Barbosa continued: "Sheriff, take them to the jail and keep 'em there. Tomorrow I'm gonna ensure this girl gets to see her pop again in the afterlife."

When Hope looked up from staring at the badge in her hand, her eyes swam with angry tears. "You rotten son of a bitch!" she shouted, unable to contain the outburst of raw emotion. "You'll pay for this, Barbosa.

Do you hear me? You'll pay for this!"

"Enough." Barbosa waved his hand at Maxwell. "I said, get 'em both out of my sight! Do it before I end this right here right now."

The cell door slammed shut.

The sheriff stood with his hands braced against the bars, head hung, visibly fighting shame and regret. "I never wanted any of this," he groaned. He looked up. "But neither of you made it easy."

"He just admitted to everyone in that saloon that he was an outlaw," Ethan said. "You should be heading across that street to arrest him."

Maxwell looked up. "Should I?"

"Yes!"

"Fair enough. Let me ask you, me and what army?"

"What use is the law if you can't wield it?"

"You tell me," Maxwell said.

Ethan groaned as he positioned a cigarillo between his lips and lit it.

"That's really the first thing you do?" Hope asked.

"Of course. What else would I do? Anyhow, we're both in a bad predicament here."

"Talk about statin' the obvious."

"It had to be said."

Hope sat on the edge of her own cot. "He's gonna make us face each other out there in the street tomorrow. Either I kill you, or you'll have to kill me."

"What if we both refuse to do either of those things?" Ethan asked, exhaling smoke from his nostrils.

Sheriff Maxwell stepped away from the bars. "He'll kill you both himself."

"Then the answer is simple. We have to kill him first," Ethan said.

Hope shook her head. "How do you reckon we do that? He has half a dozen men around him now. We'd be dead before we got as far as lining up the shot."

"Where there's a will, there's a way," Ethan said.

"If you say so."

Ethan stepped forward, pushed himself up against the bars separating their cells. "Hope, don't lose your namesake, okay? Because that's all we got."

"It's hard not to." Hope held her head in her hands. "The past eight years have been about my pop, about avenging his death. . . . Now I'm questioning if he has a right to be avenged at all."

"He was your pop, wasn't he?"

"Yes."

"Then you're on the right path. And there's just one last name to deal with," Ethan said. "Cyrus Barbosa."

Hope knew that Ethan spoke a lot of sense. There was an undeniable truth to his words that she couldn't ignore. She looked first to Ethan, and then to the haggard form of the beleaguered sheriff.

"Are you ready for a change, Maxwell?"

"I don't know if I can."

"Of course you can."

"It ain't that easy."

"Nothing is," Hope said.

Her statement rested between them for a moment. The sheriff sighed. "What do you have in mind? I'm not saying yes. I'm just gonna listen, then make my mind up."

"Can you get Burt over here to listen to this? Jasper, too."

"Burt the barkeep? What on earth for?" Maxwell asked, frowning.

Hope said, "Everything will be made clear. But I promise you, if what I've got in mind succeeds, the town of Fortune's Cross will be all the better for it."

"I don't know . . ." the sheriff said, uncertain.

Hope got up, walked to the bars. "Sheriff, it's time for you to get on with the job. Are you with us, or are you with Barbosa?"

262

"Well, I ain't with him. That's for sure."

"And you already said you'd listen to what I have to say before making your mind up, correct?" Hope asked.

"Yes."

"Then just give me a chance."

"All right, then." Maxwell set his hat on his head. "I'll go tell Burt to rustle up some food. That way he has an excuse to bring it across."

"Good," Hope said, watching the sheriff leave.

Ethan spoke, his voice full of gravel. "I know what you're planning on doing. It won't be easy. We could wind up getting killed. In fact, we could wind up getting innocent townsfolk killed, too."

"This is our only chance at getting out of this in one piece. We must take it. You know it and I know it."

"Hope . . . you're asking these people to take an awful big risk on our behalf," Ethan said.

She turned around. "I know," she said, pushing her hair back with her fingers. "But what choice do we have? We're straight out of options."

"I'm with you. Of course I am. I just hope this pays off," Ethan said, returning to his own cot. "For everyone's sakes."

"Me, too," Hope said.

And in the silence that replaced their conversation, it came as a surprise to find no doubt or fear waiting. Barbosa had sanctioned the murder of her father. He was just as culpable for Tobias Cassidy's death as Lance Knox and Puck Cosby. Ridding the town of Fortune's Cross of a monster like Cyrus Barbosa fell not just on her shoulders or Ethan's, but on those of all who cowered in his shadow.

It was time to show them the light.

■ ■ ■ ■

PART FOUR:
COLLECTOR
OF SOULS

■ ■ ■ ■

CHAPTER SIXTEEN

Six Years Ago

Hope eventually tracked Puck Cosby two thousand miles to a town called New Devon on the East Coast. Little more than a fishing settlement to begin with, New Devon had grown into a modest-sized town in its own right. It had been built right up to the beach, and whenever the wind picked up, it whipped the sand up off the beach and blew it everywhere. Up the main street, gathering in the corners of the window frames, at the foot of the steps to the church — wherever Hope looked, she saw evidence of the fine powdery substance. New Devon wasn't much of a place, not in comparison to many of the towns she'd seen on her travels, but the addition of the sea air and the gulls made it unique in her eyes. Hope had never seen the ocean before; it was wildly different from anything she could have imagined. She had not realized that as the tide came in, the water's edge would work farther and farther up the beach. And when the tide ran out, it left vast stretches of smooth silvery sand behind. She'd walked on the beach and watched as gulls dove from above, scooping up the worms as they worked their way to the surface of the wet sand. With the wind blowing her hair back, and a little bit of sun on her face, Hope had been able to close her eyes and feel something akin to peace, as if peace were a state of being that could be reached by simply finding herself present at the right time, in the right place. Somehow the sea offered possibility. Renewal. It was always washing in and remaking whatever it touched. Hope wondered whether, if she lay right there on the beach and let the tide roll over her, she might be remade by it. Might begin again.

Not yet, she reminded herself. *There will be a time for that . . . but it ain't yet.*

The journey had been long, and she could not afford to give up now. She'd come so far to find Lance Knox and Puck Cosby. If there was still a ways to go, then Hope knew she had to push on. The tide would wait for her.

She did not know if Puck Cosby happened to reside in New Devon or not, but she knew for sure that he frequented the place.

If she was ever going to catch him, it would be there. From what she knew of his recent movements, Cosby was now a fisherman going by the name of Pat Benchley. The beach directly adjacent to the town was mostly given over to fishing boats and their assorted rigs.

There was no representative of the law in town; New Devon was without a sheriff. The townsfolk had never seen much point in appointing a lawman when they had Captain Quinn.

Quinn had been overseeing the harbor, such as it was, for the better part of a decade. In truth, the harbor consisted of the beach and the two timber groins that had been built out into the water and were now covered in a thick coating of slimy green from exposure to the sea. So there wasn't a hell of a lot to oversee in that regard. But where Quinn earned his esteem was in his astute, seasoned management of the fishermen themselves. When Hope presented herself to him, Quinn was in the throes of trying to quell an argument that had broken out between two fishermen. Apparently, one of the fishermen had collected a crab cage that belonged to the other. How they told the difference between one crab cage and another was beyond Hope's comprehension. All the cages looked identical. But the two men either side of Captain Quinn seemed to know the difference and that was all that mattered.

The captain stood with his hands on their chests, holding them apart as they yelled at each other, eyes wild, spittle flying from their bearded mouths.

"Now, boys," Quinn said, "can't we find some kind of —"

The man on his left shook his head quickly. "No, he is a thief," he said in an Irish accent. "I watched him pull it up out of the water with me own eyes. Brazen, he was."

Hope thought, *Whose eyes would you watch it with but your own?*

"Liar!" the man on the right snapped. "It's my cage and he knows it. The scoundrel must have seen me drop it."

Captain Quinn had clearly had enough. He grabbed both men by the collar and, with one flex of his muscular arms, pulled them both in close to him. "That's enough, both of you!" he growled. "I have told you more than once to carve your names on your cages so we can settle these disputes nice and easy in future. I swear, I catch you landing the other's cage one more time, I'm going to belt you." Quinn looked at the man

270

on his right. "And I done told you before but you don't ever listen. If you got a dispute, you come see me first and I'll settle it. We can't be fightin' and arguin' amongst ourselves all the darn time."

Earl sagged in Quinn's viselike grip. "Right you are."

"I hear you," Seamus said, looking away.

Quinn let them both go. "Damnation, lads. Get your gear off this ever-lovin' beach."

The captain turned and got his first look at Hope. At the sight of a lady, his entire demeanor seemed to change. He smiled, his flinty blue eyes twinkling from within his lined and weathered face.

"Afternoon, miss. And how can I be of assistance to you?"

"I asked around in town. Everyone said I should come find you, Captain Quinn."

"Oh? And why would that be?"

Hope pushed the hair out of her eyes. "They told me you're as good as the law around here."

"It's been said." Quinn's smile faltered as his eyes flicked first to her sidearm, and then to the coiled-up bullwhip the other side. The shift in his attention was so quick as to be barely perceptible — but Hope caught it. "Why?"

"Is there somewhere we can talk privately?" Hope asked.

"I got an office at the back of the local watering hole serves me for matters like this, if that's not disagreeable to you."

"Why would it be disagreeable?"

"Well," Quinn said, his smile returning, "you bein' a woman and all."

Hope folded her arms. "Well, that depends."

"On what?"

"If this *watering hole* serves beer of some kind."

"A woman after my own heart." Quinn offered her his arm. "Believe me, I can do better than that."

The rum was strong, so dark as to be almost entirely black, and it had an aromatic sweetness that for some reason reminded Hope of burned sugar. The dark liquid held a little fire on the way down, but not in the same way whiskey did. The rum was not so rough.

"Is this what all you fishermen drink?" Hope asked, watching as the barkeep refilled her glass.

"For the most part," Quinn said, tossing his own glass of rum back in one go. "Smooth, isn't it?"

"It is," Hope admitted. "I can see why you

272

prefer it to whiskey."

Quinn slammed his palm down on the bar top. "Whiskey? Bah! Devil's water. Gut rot, they call it in some places. This is the real stuff right here. Nectar for the soul it is, and I'll challenge anyone to tell me different. It's been rum has kept many a man goin' when he's out there on that merciless cold sea. It has a way of eatin' at you, all that wind and rain and swell."

Quinn's words reminded Hope of what her father had told her about the whiskey he always carried. The very day he died, he'd said something similar.

"Let me tell you something. There's been times the only thing keeping me going is a toot from that flask. Especially when I'm tracking some murderer down or chasing the tail of a bandit. The ride gets lonely. It can eat at you sometimes, get right under your skin. A man's gotta have his vices," her father had told her.

The memory of what she said in response came back to her then and Hope instantly felt a pang of regret.

"I guess you would know all about that," she'd said.

How she wished that she could return to that day and snatch those words back.

Six years later the wound left by Tobias's

murder was still raw. The pain had kept her going in much the same way a nip from his flask had kept her pop going when times were tough. It had given her the strength to ride from town to town, all over the land, gradually drawing closer and closer to the men who'd shot her father down like a dog.

"You look adrift," Quinn said, breaking her reverie and bringing her back to the moment.

"I'm sorry. I got to thinking about something."

Quinn chuckled a little. "Thought the rum had done you in there for a moment."

"I can hold my own," Hope said with a thin smile. "Anyway, the reason I came here is I'm tracking a man by the name of Puck Cosby."

"Afraid I don't know anyone of that name," the captain said.

"How about Pat Benchley?"

The captain sat back straight in his chair. "Pat . . . I know a Pat. What of him?"

"Pat Benchley is really Puck Cosby. He can't use his real name for reasons I'll make clear in a moment," Hope said.

The captain nodded. "Right you are. Go on."

"Can I ask how long he has been in New Devon?"

"Well, he comes and goes like most of 'em. Takes a room up at the inn. A lot of the boys do that. Rent a room when they get back. Why? What're you tracking him for?" Quinn asked. "Is the man in trouble?"

"He is, yes."

"How can you be sure that Puck and Pat are the same man? Have you proof?"

Hope did not answer straightaway. She produced a rolled-up wanted poster and laid it out flat on the table for the captain to see. "This is Puck Cosby. Does he look like the Pat Benchley you are familiar with?"

Quinn's face said it all. "Well, I'll be damned . . ." he said, reading the list of Cosby's many crimes. "Wanted for murder?"

"I'm afraid so."

"You some kind of bounty hunter, then?"

"On occasion," Hope said, rolling the wanted poster back up. "But this one's personal."

"Personal? How so?"

"Puck Cosby killed someone very close to me. It's taken me a long time to find him, let me tell you. What with him using different names everywhere he goes, there were times on the trail when I wondered if I ever would. But here I am," Hope said.

"Here you are," Quinn repeated, voice

275

sounding distant for the first time since they'd met. "So what're your plans for him? I mean, what's your intent?"

"My intent? Well, I suppose my intent is retribution."

"I see," Quinn said. "Ordinarily, I would object to anybody — law or otherwise — riding into New Devon with such a purpose in mind. There ain't been a killing here in this town for a long while, for as far back as I can remember anyway. But if it's justified, well, then I reckon that's a case of what's sauce for the goose is sauce for the gander. . . ."

"I've not heard that one," Hope said.

Quinn winked at her. "You learn something new every day, am I right?"

"So where is Cosby now?"

"Out at sea, I'd imagine. I believe he's doing a stint on old man Bernstein's boat the last few weeks. The *Wayward Sue*. She's due back tomorrow evening, depending on the weather. But we can check in at the inn, if you like, see if he's there."

"You don't mind?"

"Not in the slightest. I've done my fair share today," Quinn said, getting up and stretching. "Besides, I figure you might need some help with him. He ain't a small fella, is he?"

"Not from what I remember," Hope said, feeling the acid rise in her throat at the memory of Puck Cosby standing next to her home as it went up in flames. "But that was a while ago."

"They say a woman scorned never forgets," Captain Quinn quipped, stepping around the table to get to the door.

Hope rolled her eyes. "Isn't the saying 'Hell hath no fury like a woman scorned'?"

The captain held the door to the pub open for her. "I'll be damned if I know. Only thing I'm sure of is, any woman I've had dealings with has been able to recall every failing on my part, no matter how long ago. And to me, that's a special kind of talent."

"Have you ever stopped to consider that it's not because women have a good memory, but that men would prefer us to be a hell of a lot more forgiving of their misdeeds?" Hope suggested.

The captain seemed taken aback. "I never thought of it that way," he said.

I rest my case, Hope thought.

The world was ruled by men, only they broke most of the rules. Occasionally, women like her got a chance at settling the score. Sometimes, for justice to be served, you had to fire the guns of wrath. Perhaps the captain was right. Women didn't forget.

Well, Hope thought, *we seem to be given a lot to remember.* Would avenging her father allow her to forget and move on? The two men who had murdered her father had assumed she died that night at the river. In a way, she had. She'd been shot, nearly drowned, beaten against the rocks. A girl had leapt into the river that night, and a broken woman had emerged. Neither Puck Cosby nor Lance Knox would have expected her to come after them with anything approaching the desire for revenge that burned so fiercely in her veins. A part of her hoped beyond hope that killing them would quiet the firestorm in her veins. But she knew deep down that the memory would never be fully dismissed. She'd carry it with her for the rest of her life, see her father killed, over and over, until she herself drew her last breath. But once she put Knox and Cosby in the ground, the memory would no longer be so painful.

Hope looked back at the pub, noticing the name — *The Albatross* — painted in cracked white lettering above the door.

"She's selling up, you know," the captain said.

"Who is?"

"Caroline, who served us a minute ago. It was her old man's place, but he went down

278

on the *Santero*. Whole ship pulled under without a trace. Can you imagine? Anyway, she can't run the place on her own. So it's a matter of time before she sells up, mark my words. Somebody ought to swoop in an' buy the place. If I had the money, I'd do it myself. Place could be a gold mine for the right owner."

CHAPTER SEVENTEEN

The majority of towns Hope had been in hadn't had anything approaching an inn or a guesthouse. They just weren't big enough to attract visitors needing rooms at an inn; instead, they had saloons or bars with a few rooms for rent on the floor above. Over the years she had stayed in a couple of inns like the Crow's Nest, though: two floors, white-washed throughout, offering baths and hot meals. The Crow's Nest was just a little rougher around the edges, Hope thought, than the inns she'd bedded down in.

"Ain't nothing special," Captain Quinn said. "Gotta remember, it's a home for sailors. Barely an inn at all, really, when I think about it. We're a rambunctious lot, I suppose. The place has got a bit beaten up around the edges over the years. In fact, I'm surprised none of the tenants have gone to bed with a lit match and sent the whole place up in flames."

"You stay here?" Hope asked.

Quinn shook his head. "No! I wouldn't wanna pay good money to rent a room here with this bunch of scallywags."

The captain led her inside the house. He didn't bother with the bell at the front desk, just walked on through toward a wide staircase that led to the next floor. Then the captain spun around as if he had forgotten something. He went behind the desk and retrieved one of the sets of keys from a hanger on the wall.

"Won't be gettin' far without a key, will we?"

"You have permission to go letting yourself into their rooms?" Hope asked as they climbed the stairs.

Quinn scoffed. "Permission? If he ain't in his room, he won't even know we've been there, will he?"

"He might realize it when he comes home."

"Only if we move his particulars, and I don't plan on doing that. Do you?"

"I guess not," Hope said.

The walls on the way up were marked and scuffed. Some sections had been damaged, presumably by drunk or frustrated guests. Holes punched in the wall, larger holes kicked in by boots.

"Rambunctious," Hope said, quoting the captain's word back at him.

He shrugged. "I run the *harbor*. I don't run the *men*. Especially when they're at home doin' what they do best."

"And what's that?"

"Drinkin'."

Hope followed Quinn down a corridor to a door at the far end. He knocked hard and sharp on the worn wood. They waited for a response from within. Quinn took the key and moved toward the lock.

"Knock again," Hope told him.

The captain peered at her. "He ain't here."

"What if he's stone-cold drunk in there?" Hope suggested.

Quinn accepted her point and hammered his fist on the door, then listened for any sign of life. "Happy?"

"I am now."

He slid the key into the lock and opened the door to Puck Cosby's room. It was larger than Hope had expected it to be. There was a bed, a table with a solitary chair, a dresser. It was dirty, and the smell that rose to meet them left little to the imagination. It was so strong, it almost took Hope's breath away.

"It smells like he up and died in here."

"I must be accustomed to the stink of

fishermen," the captain said, sniffing the air to little effect. "Is it that bad?"

Hope couldn't help but pull a face. "It's rancid," she said, moving among the detritus of Cosby's life.

The empty bottles everywhere. The grime that seemed to cover every surface. In many ways, the room was typical of a man who went to sea for weeks at a time. There were no belongings of a personal nature. Nothing to say who the occupant of the room was. Only that he stayed there whenever he wasn't out at sea.

"There's nothing to be learned here."

"Let's go," Quinn said. He followed her back out into the hall and locked the door after them.

An old woman stood at the top of the staircase. She squinted at them, as if trying to make them out. "Who's that down there? What're you doing?"

"It's all right. I'm bringing it back," Quinn said with a wave of the room key.

"Whoever you are, I don't permit my boarders to bring women to their rooms," she said.

"Who's that?" Hope asked.

"It's Wren. She runs the place."

"She doesn't seem to know you."

Quinn laughed. "She does. Trouble is,

she's blind as a bat."

They drew nearer and the old woman's face relaxed as soon as she recognized the captain. "Oh, it's you. I thought I knew that voice."

"I just had to check something out," he said, handing her the key.

She turned it over in her liver-spotted hands. "Ah. Mister Benchley's room. He ain't paid what he owes the past month. I told him, he'd better get me my money or I'd be throwing him out onto the street."

"Not one to mince your words, are you, Wren?" Quinn said.

"Can't afford to in my line of work," she said, eyeing Hope. "And who's the lady friend?"

"A bounty hunter," Quinn answered before Hope could say anything different. "Turns out, your tenant has a price on his head."

"Oh, I wish you'd have said," Wren told them, making her way down the staircase with one frail hand gripping the railing. "I'd have shot him myself and called for a marshal."

"I don't doubt it," Quinn said with a hearty laugh as he assisted Wren in navigating the stairs, Hope in tow.

When they reached the desk, Wren collapsed into a rocking chair positioned to the side of it. She sounded exhausted from the exertion of mounting the stairs to see what they were up to.

"Benchley's working right now, is he?" Hope asked her.

"On the *Wayward Sue,*" Wren said. "She's due back tonight."

Hope didn't attempt to hide her pleasure at that news. "Tonight? You're sure?"

"That's what he said."

Hope looked to Quinn. "You said tomorrow night."

"That's what I thought," the captain said.

The old woman shook her head. "He said he'd be back on Thursday and he was gonna pay me what's owed straightaway. Minute he walks through that door, apparently. Well, it's Thursday sure enough, but I won't wait here in this rocking chair with bated breath."

"I should wait down at the beach," Hope said.

Wren lifted a bony finger. "I hope there ain't nothin' brewin' here is gonna cost me my money what he owes."

"Absolutely not," Hope said, heading outside.

"Take care, Wren," Captain Quinn told the old woman, and followed in Hope's wake.

"I saw it on the wanted poster about the price on Cosby's head," said Quinn that night. "What I don't understand is why you're not cashing in on it."

"It wouldn't be right. I didn't come looking for him for the bounty," Hope said. "But by all means, when I've done what I have to do, you're welcome to claim for him."

"Truthfully?"

"You have my word," Hope said. "Help me get at him, and you can have the body. That bounty's a pretty penny. Might be enough you could find yourself another line of work."

The captain bellowed laughter. "I'd surely die. My life has always been the sea. Fair weather and foul, you'll find me here at the shore. Ain't nothing better. Give this up? To do what?"

"There's more to life," Hope began to say.

Quinn took her by the arm. "I'm a man of influence here, you understand? I run this miserable little town. Anywhere else, I'd be a nobody. I don't wanna live someplace I can't be known to one and all. Can't think of anything worse."

The captain smiled. "When you've done what you've gotta do, I'll take the body and claim the bounty. I figure Wren could use some of it to make that blasted inn a little more habitable."

"And the rest?" Hope asked.

The captain held out the sides of his threadbare coat. "A new one of these, I reckon. If this old thing gets any more holes, I'm gonna be the next body getting carted out of here."

It sure was windy. They passed rum between them to stave off the cold. Hope liked the captain. He was the sort of man anyone could get on with. He didn't set her on edge the way a lot of men had a way of doing. Hope didn't sense that the captain had an agenda, a falseness behind his smiles. He was a trustworthy man, or so he seemed, she thought. All she had was her own judgment — and when all was said and done, it was the only thing that mattered.

In addition to Captain Quinn, she liked New Devon. She almost wanted to remain, but the town had little to offer her in terms of earning her daily bread. And besides, Puck Cosby was but one half of the hellish task she had set for herself. Hope knew she would never know peace while either of those men was drawing a breath. But perhaps she might return someday.

"There it is," Quinn said, handing Hope the eyeglass.

She found the lanterns of the *Wayward*

Sue rocking back and forth on the dark water as it coasted in to shore.

The captain continued: "She'll moor up out there and they'll come aboard in a rowboat."

Hope lowered the eyeglass. "Will there be others with him?"

"I'd imagine so. Why do you think I stuck by your side until now? If the boys who're with Puck take it upon themselves to defend him, you're gonna need an extra set of hands."

"I appreciate it," Hope told him. "Are you always this helpful?"

"Afraid not."

"Really think the other fishermen might back his corner?"

Quinn shrugged. "Hard to tell. They trust me, but folk act in strange ways sometimes."

Time ticked on as Hope and Captain Quinn monitored the mooring of the *Wayward Sue* from their vantage point on the beach. Then they watched the smaller rowboat get lowered down to the water, and the men clambering down into it. They fixed a lantern in place, then pushed themselves away from the keel of the larger ship.

"How many men on there?" Hope asked.

Quinn squinted into the eyeglass. "I'd say half a dozen. It's murky, though. Can barely see my own hand inches from my face."

The minutes moved at a glacial pace matched only by the sluggishness of the rowboat itself. But eventually the little boat glided up onto the sand and the men disembarked.

"There they are," Quinn said. "Come on."

Hope followed him across the beach, unclipping her holster to allow her to pull the gun free without hesitation. She noted that the captain had not lit so much as a match to announce their presence to the fishermen as they talked amongst themselves on the sand, a couple of them sharing a smoke. He preferred to emerge out of the dark and catch them off guard, it seemed.

"Evenin', gents!" the captain said.

The six fishermen jumped at the sudden noise. Quinn was barely visible in the dim light afforded by the lantern attached to the boat. The moon peeked out from behind the clouds, affording a little more illumination — and the men noticed Hope's presence straightaway.

"Who's that, then?" one of the men said. He was the smallest of them, with hardened features and a scraggly beard that resembled seaweed clinging to his jawline.

"It's me."

"Who's *me*?"

"Quinn, you dolt," the captain said, stepping in closer to the circle of illumination.

The other man seemed to relax at the sight of him. "Oh, the good captain himself. Well, that's all right, then, ain't it?"

"I reckon so," Quinn said pleasantly.

"Something up?" Don asked.

Quinn scanned the faces of the men until he settled on the angular features of the man he'd come to know as Pat Benchley. "That you, Pat?"

"It is," he said, stepping forward.

Quinn turned to Hope. "That him for sure?"

Puck Cosby squinted at Hope as she came into the light. At first, he didn't seem to recognize her. Then his eyes widened, and familiarity dawned across his face. "No . . ."

"Yes," she said.

Puck dashed away, turning on his heels to make a quick escape. He pushed through the other men, ensuring that neither Hope nor the captain had a clear shot at him. Hope forced her way between them until she could just see him running away across the dark sand. It was no use trying to get a good clean shot with such poor visibility. Besides, she wasn't ready to kill him yet.

Hope took her bullwhip in her hand and flung it out, the tail catching Cosby by the ankles. She pulled hard on it, tripping him up. Captain Quinn ran over to Puck and pinned him to the spot.

Hope coiled the bullwhip back up in her hands as she walked over to them.

"That was a sure hand if ever I saw one," Quinn said.

"Turn him over," Hope said.

Quinn did as she asked.

Puck was red in the face. He scowled at her in temper. "You —"

Hope took her pistol and flipped it around. She leaned over Puck Cosby and said, "Any of this familiar to you?"

Then she smashed him in the head with the butt of her weapon. He sagged under Quinn's grip, his eyes rolling over white.

The captain let him flop to the sand. "You don't mess about, do you?"

"I don't make it a habit." Hope holstered her shooter. She looked back at Puck Cosby's shipmates. "Reckon they'll help get him to my horse?"

"I think they might."

Hope looked down at Puck Cosby. "I've never seen a more pathetic excuse for a man in my entire life."

"He's a yellabelly all right," Quinn said. He whistled toward the fishermen and beckoned them over.

Hope looked once more at Cosby. A dribble of blood ran from the spot where she'd struck him — not that it mattered. His fate had become an inevitability. A little hurt along the way made no difference at all.

CHAPTER EIGHTEEN

Puck Cosby opened his eyes to find himself confronted with the dawn of a new day. The clouds looked as though they were aflame, peeling away across a sky of silver, kissed by the red glow of the sun as it broke on the horizon. He sat up and instantly regretted it. Puck had to sit holding his head for a moment to regain some semblance of equilibrium. He got to his feet, took stock of his surroundings — he was in a clearing, surrounded by thick trees that had grown close together. There were also several stumps of felled trees nearby and, on one, a strategically placed revolver.

Puck put one foot in front of the other and staggered over to the revolver. It was old and heavy, but well cared for. Cleaned and oiled by someone who respected its firepower.

He'd never expected to see Hope Cassidy again. When she'd leapt into the rushing black water, he'd been certain that she would drown. Especially after they shot at her. One of those bullets had to have found their mark. Puck was sure of it. And besides, he'd never heard anything about her after that.

Yet last night she'd stood before him in the dim glow of the lamplight and Puck had felt the years peel away like thin paper. As if he were standing before her on the night she watched them gun her father down. When she'd looked up at them, and the burning house had been reflected in her tear-glazed eyes.

Puck's immediate response to the unexpected return of the past had been to get up and run. Clearly he hadn't run fast enough. He turned a slow circle, revolver cocked in his hand as he looked for signs of Hope Cassidy in the trees. Puck's vision was dangerously blurred and he tried desperately to clear it, rubbing at his eyes with his free hand.

"I don't know what kinda game this is!" Puck shouted, unsure of what to say to her exactly. He raised the pistol over his head and let off a couple of shots. "But whatever it is, I ain't playin' by your rules!"

The echoes of his gunshots finally faded to silence. Puck watched the trees for movement, knowing she had to be out there somewhere observing him.

The hit on the head she'd dealt him with the butt of her gun seemed to have damaged his vision for good, because he didn't see her until she stepped clear of the trees and raised her pistol. The first shot flipped him around as it bit into his shoulder and exploded out the other side. Puck fired blindly in the general direction of his aggressor until squeezing the trigger served only to produce an empty click.

He tossed the gun aside.

The second shot exploded through his kneecap.

Puck screamed. It spilled from his mouth, high-pitched and hysterical, and his leg buckled immediately. He fell to the ground, the agony running up his leg in heavy waves. He whimpered, feeling each wave, tears spilling from his eyes. He lay on his side, unsure which gunshot wound hurt the most, eventually deciding that the bullet through the kneecap was the single most excruciating sensation he'd ever experienced.

Hope Cassidy walked casually toward him.

Not a single bullet he'd fired had found its mark.

"You know who I am," she said.

"Hope Cassidy," he gasped.

"That's right."

"Why am I here?" Puck demanded through gritted teeth. "Why?"

Whatever he said, it seemed to have no impact on the girl — not that she was a girl anymore. How many years had it been? He tried to think but couldn't come up with a number. However long it had been, the girl seemed to have aged beyond her years. There was a hardness to her that hadn't been there when they'd killed her pop. An edge that seemed to have developed over the course of whatever journey her life had taken her on.

"My father was Tobias Cassidy. An innocent man."

He scoffed at that.

"The whip and the gun," she said.

"What?"

"The whip and the gun that you took from me that night. I want to know what happened to them."

"We sold them."

The girl — no, the woman — shook her head in disgust. "You'll regret that."

To his dismay, she raised her pistol again. Aimed it straight at his chest. Puck knew what that meant. Knew it, but could not find the strength to accept it.

He tried to get away, scrambling backward, breathing hard and fast as his heart clattered in his chest. Hope Cassidy merely closed in, more determined than she had been seconds before.

More certain of what needed to be done.

It didn't matter that he had not accepted what was coming — because she had wholly accepted what she had to do to him.

She pulled the trigger, the bullet ripping through the center of his chest, blasting it inward.

Puck lay on the dirt, and in his last seconds, he managed to draw breath enough to say, "Your father was —" before Hope Cassidy shot him again, silencing him forever.

"You left him in that clearing, like we agreed?" Captain Quinn asked.

Hope nodded. "I did. Even rolled him up for you."

"Much appreciated. Sure I can't convince you to hang around a while longer?"

"Afraid not. My work's only half finished."

The captain smiled. "Sometimes a glass half full is better than havin' it completely empty. You ever stopped to consider that?"

"Can't say I have."

"Knowing that man's out there gives you

purpose, don't it?" Captain Quinn asked her.

"I guess it does."

"So what're you gonna do when that purpose is gone?"

Hope didn't have an answer.

They parted ways there in the rising light, the captain heading into the trees to the clearing where she'd left Puck Cosby's body. Hope climbed a rise and caught sight of New Devon, a flock of gulls swooping in over the town. The way they twisted and turned in the shafts of pale light made her think of the soul she had just claimed . . . and the soul she was to collect.

■ ■ ■ ■

Part Five:
The Guns
of Wrath

■ ■ ■ ■

CHAPTER NINETEEN

Since revealing to Hope Cassidy the truth about her father, Cyrus Barbosa had found that his history with Tobias lay heavy on his mind.

He'd never dreamed he'd want Tobias dead. But the man had betrayed the Black Scorpions by leaving — and then tried to turn them over to the law. He'd crossed a line and gone to a place from which there was no return. Barbosa could not let such betrayal stand.

Tobias had given no hint that he'd turn on the rest of the gang when he announced he was leaving.

He said, "Men in this line of work, they don't make old bones, Cyrus."

"Stupid men don't," Barbosa had told him. "Men like us, who have their wits about them, they prosper. You're makin' a big mistake, Tobias."

"It's my choice."

301

"You know you'll never truly be free of us, don't you? Can't walk away from a brotherhood and sever every bond."

Tobias looked away then. "I know. But this life ain't for me no more. I'm leaving, Cyrus. And I won't be back."

"What if I was to say no?"

"No?"

"You heard me. What if I was to tell you, 'No, you can't leave the Black Scorpions'?"

Tobias turned back to him.

Barbosa could see the steely resolve in the man's face. His decision was made, his path set. There'd be no changing it.

"I'd say you'd have to shoot me in the back to stop me walking away," Tobias declared.

Barbosa exhaled heavily. "It is what it is, then."

"It is," Tobias said.

The only tailor in Fortune's Cross was a lady called Margaret Hatchett. Some months before, Cyrus Barbosa had ordered a brand-new suit from her — paid in advance, in full, and made to fit his exaggerated size with ease. Hatchett measured him twice over to be sure, knowing his demanding nature, and his tendency to erupt with anger when things failed to go his way.

Hatchett assured him that if there were any issues when the suit arrived, she would alter it to fit him perfectly.

Barbosa checked himself out in the full-length mirror of her store, turning this way and that to admire the blue suit, and the accompanying crisp white shirt. " 'For the apparel oft proclaims the man,' " he said, a smile creeping across his face.

Hatchett stood with her hands on her hips, assessing him from the sidelines. "Can't say I know that saying."

"Do you know Shakespeare, Miss Hatchett?"

"Can't say I do. And it's 'missus,' I'll have you know."

Barbosa turned to look at her. "Is it, now? I did not take you for a married lady."

"Why not?"

"You don't have that . . . aura."

Margaret Hatchett chuckled to herself. "Strike you as a spinster, do I, Mister Barbosa?"

"You are casting aspersions I would not dare to," Barbosa said, turning his attention back to his own reflection. "That line 'For the apparel oft proclaims the man' is from a play called *Hamlet*. It's by William Shakespeare."

"I see. Sounds British."

303

"He was! It's part of a long piece of monologue spoken by Polonius," Barbosa explained. "His son, Laertes, is leaving for Paris and Polonius is giving him some advice."

"Here, try this," Hatchett said, handing Barbosa a dark blue necktie. "So what advice does he give him? This Polo-what-have-you fella."

"Polonius. The usual advice a father would give his son. Don't borrow money. Listen when spoken to. 'To thine ownself be true,' which literally means 'be true to yourself,' " he said, fixing the necktie in place. Barbosa regarded it for a moment. "Do you think it's too dark?"

"Perhaps. Try a lighter blue," Hatchett said, taking the necktie and handing him another.

He worked it around his fat neck. Tied it. Looked at it for a moment. "I think that works."

"Yes, it does. It's a splendid suit."

"Not too fancy. But it makes ordinary folk take notice. Tells 'em I'm a man with influence, don't you think?"

Hatchett nodded slowly. "It does. It says 'money.' "

"Well, it should. It cost enough!"

"True, true," she said. "But that fabric

and that workmanship don't come cheap. So, that speech you were talking about. You give that advice to your own son?"

Barbosa ran his hands down the front of his suit jacket. The cloth was so fine, so clean and smooth. "Lord knows where he is. We haven't seen each other in a long, long time."

"You don't speak?"

"I'm afraid not."

Hatchett brushed off his shoulders and checked the suit over once more. "What about your own father, then?"

"Missus Hatchett, you grow more inquisitive about people's private matters with every year that passes by."

"I just like talking to people," she said. "I've learned something new already today."

"And the day is only just beginning."

Barbosa had arranged to have Margaret Hatchett open her store for him before dawn so that he could wear his new suit at the contest. If he was going to catch an unlucky bullet, then he wanted to be wearing his finery. Mrs. Hatchett had told him only the evening before that the suit had arrived. A last-minute drop.

The tailor peered out at the darkness beyond the window. "I'm rarely out of bed this early."

"Only for special customers, eh?"

"You were telling me about your father," Hatchett said.

Barbosa said, "I think you'll find you were asking me about him. Truth is, it was he who introduced me to Shakespeare. He was a schoolteacher. When I was young, he inherited some money, bought himself a collection of the works of Shakespeare and devoted most of his time to deciphering them. He never once had the kind of conversation with me that Polonius has with Laertes. That much is for certain."

"Were you cut from the same cloth, you two?"

"No, no. We couldn't have been any more different. There's a line in *A Midsummer Night's Dream* that goes, 'I would my father look'd but with my eyes,' and that one line explains why we didn't get on all that well. He couldn't see the world through my eyes, and I couldn't see it through his."

"So you were both blind."

"Yes . . ." Barbosa said.

Hatchett looked him up and down. "Are you leaving that suit on?"

"As I said last night, I will be wearing it in the contest. The sun will be up soon. Not long now."

"You might die in that suit," the tailor said.

Barbosa shrugged. "Only way to go."

"You people are crazy, in my opinion," Hatchett said.

"I can't argue with you on that score," Barbosa said. "What do I owe you for the necktie?"

"It's a gift."

"Much obliged, Missus Hatchett."

The tailor sat on a comfy chair in the corner. "At some point you must've read all those books you said he had."

"I did. When he passed, those big Shakespeare volumes went to me. At first I didn't know what I was meant to do with them. But when I'd head out on the road, I used to take one with me and pick away at it to while away the time. Over time I found I wasn't just reading them to kill time, but I was gettin' from those books what my pop used to. I guess there's something imprinted in me that is a part of him, after all."

"Fascinating. You're a man of many facets," Hatchett said. She led Barbosa to the door and held it open for him.

He paused at the threshold. Cold wind blew into the store and Margaret Hatchett shivered all over. Barbosa was unfazed by the sudden chill.

"There's another speech from *A Midsummer Night's Dream* that goes, 'Your father should be as a god. One that composed your beauties. And one to whom you are but as a form in wax, by him imprinted and within his power to leave the figure or disfigure it.' "

Hatchett wrapped her arms around herself to hold in the warmth. "Does that mean you can never be anything but a version of your father? I'm not sure I agree with that. I've a lot of well-off customers who come by here throughout the year, and I'm sure their success wasn't always based on them following in their father's footsteps."

"I hope you're right," Barbosa said.

He walked out into the street and Margaret Hatchett shut the door behind him. She watched him go, then returned to her comfortable chair in the corner of the store, near the furnace. Hatchett wondered if Barbosa would survive the day — and she kicked herself for not charging him more for the suit. It might be the last she ever sold him.

Burt McCoy unlocked the saloon doors and let Barbosa in. "Mornin'," he said, taking in an eyeful of the fancy suit.

"And to you," the shootist said.

"Early for you, ain't it?" Burt asked.

Barbosa pulled up a chair at a table near

the window. "I'm in an early-risin' mood."

"I see."

"You got coffee on the go yet?"

Burt nodded once. "I do."

"I'll take it as it comes," Barbosa said, distractedly. He was looking out the window at the dark street, consumed with his own thoughts.

Burt said, "I'll be back shortly."

What's gotten into me? Barbosa asked himself, absently flexing his hands.

He'd insisted on having the suit ready for that morning. Why? Because he felt different. Of all the contests he had fought and won, eliminating his opponents with ease, this was the first time he had ever considered the possibility of his own defeat. The arrival of Tobias Cassidy's daughter in Fortune's Cross had unsettled him in ways he'd failed to admit to himself. But subconsciously he was preparing for the defeat he feared. A nice new suit. Talking about his father to Margaret Hatchett of all people. Admitting the existence of his son.

He hadn't thought about Kyle for years. He was a mistake left in the past. Barbosa had never been meant for fatherhood. He'd done too much horror to too many people, Even if he tried to raise a child in ignorance of his crimes, the temptation to drag Kyle to hell with him would've proven too great.

Barbosa had gotten used to the life he led. Was Hope Cassidy an omen of change? A part of him — a very small part — thought there was real danger that could be the case. But in order to stop him in his tracks, she had to outdraw him. And before that could happen, she had to stand before Ethan Harper and kill him in cold blood. She had to believe in the righteousness of her retribution so strongly that she would gun Ethan Harper down in the street and watch him breathe his last. Just to progress to the next round, the *last* round, where all would be decided once and for all.

No way but this, he thought, in mind of Othello's last words. *Hurl my soul from heaven!*

It was true what Barbosa had told Hatchett about his father's books. He had spent years working his way through them all. They'd been with him all over the place. From his earliest days getting in and out of scrapes, to what Barbosa considered his heyday, running the Black Scorpions. At night, when the other members of the gang would snore next to the fire, Barbosa would read from whichever volume he had taken with him that time.

In some way, the words, the act of reading, kept him from succumbing to the guilt of what the Black Scorpions were doing. It kept doubt out of his mind until he reached a point where doubt was not something that occurred to him.

After Tobias Cassidy informed him that he was leaving, Barbosa had felt such rage, such fury over it, because quitting was an admission of weakness. Where Barbosa had ceased to feel guilt or doubt over the crimes of the Black Scorpions, Tobias seemed to bear enough doubt for all of them. Barbosa realized later what he should have done. He should have marched Tobias out in front of the others. Held a gun to the back of his head and blown his brains out. When the opportunity came to find Tobias and punish him for leaving his brotherhood of outlaws, and turning on them, Barbosa leapt at the chance for vengeance.

Yet here I sit, consumed with doubt, my thoughts all in disarray.

A long while after, their numbers diminished, Barbosa's thoughts had turned to Tobias Cassidy. The man who'd left the Black Scorpions and sealed their collective fates. When Barbosa heard tell that Tobias had reimagined himself as some kind of lawman, he had dispatched Lance Knox and

Puck Cosby to find out if the rumors were true.

And if they were, to put a bullet in Tobias's head.

When they returned, his men told him what had taken place. How they had burned Cassidy's home to the ground. How they'd executed him.

"Here, boss," Lance had said, pressing the star of a marshal into Barbosa's palm.

Barbosa looked down at it in disbelief. "This his?"

"Damn straight," Lance said, chuckling.

Barbosa had closed his fist around the metal star. "Good work, boys."

Now all that lay in the past. The betrayal. The retribution. Knox and Cosby were maggot feed. But the one thing Barbosa could not shake was that neither man had mentioned Tobias's daughter.

Because they'd had no proof they killed her. They had known that if they told him about her, Barbosa would have asked for evidence that she'd leapt into the river and drowned in the current, succumbed to her gunshot wounds . . . or both. Either way, Barbosa would have expected them to pull her body from the water and be doubly sure she wouldn't come looking for him some-day, seeking vengeance.

As she was now.

So they'd kept that detail from him. And how he wished Cosby and Knox hadn't been killed so that he could have the pleasure of doing so himself for their sloppiness.

"Here's your coffee," Burt said, setting down a cup and breaking Barbosa out of his reverie.

Barbosa cleared his throat. "Thank you."

"Not long now, eh?"

"That's right," Barbosa said.

He'd never much cared for the bartender. He could tell the man did not like him, and in fairness to Burt McCoy, the feeling was mutual. They tolerated each other and that was about all.

The saloon doors opened and Renee Lane strode in. She pulled out a chair at Barbosa's table and cast a fierce look at the bartender. "Coffee," she said.

"Coming right up," McCoy said, shuffling off.

Renee dropped into the chair.

"Please. Take a seat," Barbosa said sarcastically.

"Don't worry. I will," Renee said. "It's pretty quiet in here, ain't it?"

"I'm not surprised, given the time."

She looked at him appraisingly. "Early riser, too, eh?"

"I've been known to beat the sunrise from time to time," Barbosa said. "Though not for a long while."

"That's right. You don't get your hands so dirty these days, from what I hear."

Burt returned with a cup of steaming-hot coffee for her.

"Much obliged, barkeep." She watched Burt go.

"Why so confrontational all of a sudden? You were much nicer to me before."

"Well, you're gonna try and kill me in a half hour or so. That has a way of changing things," Renee told him. "Not forgetting I'm gonna try and shoot you dead, too, of course."

"You don't rate your chances?"

"I don't let my ego get in front of me the way you do," Renee said.

Barbosa laughed. "You got true grit, Renee Lane! Damn. To come in here alone, and speak to me the way you are? Takes plenty of that grit I referred to. . . ."

"And you got yourself a fresh new suit to die in, I see."

He looked down at himself. "Yeah, well, why the hell not?"

"One last splurge," she said in a mocking tone that grated on him so much it made the hairs stand on end at the nape of his neck.

Renee had shed all pretense of civility. Before, perhaps, he had been a hypothetical opponent. Now he was the man about to try to shoot her down in the street. She had nothing but hatred for him. Barbosa could see it in her eyes. The hate made it easier to pull the trigger and live with witnessing what a bullet could do.

"You'll admire my suit in the end," Barbosa said. He got to his feet. "When I'm stood over you, watching you fade like the sun in the west."

Renee didn't say anything. She just looked up at him, eyes set hard.

"If you'll excuse me," Barbosa said.

He headed for the doors, their hinges squeaking as they swung back and forth in his wake. Outside, he lit a smoke and stood against the porch railing, watching the light enter the sky.

His men wandered over toward the saloon in their long gray dusters, greeting Barbosa before heading inside for coffee. The sheriff emerged from his office, breathing clouds of condensation into the frigid air as he made his way down the street toward the saloon.

"Morning," Sheriff Maxwell said when he reached the porch. He looked up at the sky.

"Looks like it's gonna snow again."

Barbosa glanced up, too. "Yeah, I'd say so. Is it time?"

The sheriff consulted his pocket watch. "We've got about fifteen minutes."

"There's a line in a play called *Macbeth*. Do you know *Macbeth*?"

Maxwell shook his head. "Can't say as I do."

"Well," Barbosa said, undeterred. "It goes, 'All our yesterdays have lighted fools the way to dusty death.' Hazard a guess what that means?"

The sheriff frowned. "Can't say I have a clue, Cyrus."

"Allow me to illuminate you," Barbosa said. "Shakespeare's basically saying, 'We all die someday.' It don't matter what's been done, what's been said or any of that. . . . We're all destined to walk the same damn path, and there ain't a thing you or I can do about it."

"Everyone dies, huh?"

"That's it."

Maxwell sighed. "So those two I've got in the cells. Is this your way of reconciling pitting them against each other the way you have?"

Barbosa cocked his head to one side, thrown by an unexpected challenge from the resident lawman of Fortune's Cross. "Excuse me?"

Sheriff Maxwell continued, " 'Cause it don't make it right. *None* of this is right. Not one damn bit of it."

"You listen to me," Barbosa snarled, jabbing the sheriff in the center of his chest with one massive meaty finger. "I gave that woman a chance to redeem herself after she killed a man in cold blood, right down the street. In full view of the damned church, of all places! Shot him down like a dog, didn't give him no chance at defending himself. Know what they call that? It's murder, Sheriff. It's all it will ever be. Straight-up murder. Those what saw it demand blood, and this is my way of giving it to them. That woman does as she's damn well told, or else I invite her to take the gun when it's handed to her and use it to stick a bullet in her own head. Don't rightly care which."

Maxwell backed up a step. "Every bet gets settled. Is that what you're saying?"

"Damn straight. There's a board down at the church, you'll remember, keeping score."

To Barbosa's surprise, the sheriff advanced on him. He got as close to him as he could with Barbosa's large stomach in the way.

"I *am* keeping score," Maxwell said, his

face flushed with anger. "You'd best believe that, Cyrus. I've had enough of sitting back. I ain't doin' it no more."

Barbosa remained on the spot for a moment, eyes fixed on Sheriff Maxwell's. Neither man wanting to either back off or be the one to take things further.

"When this contest is over, so are you," Barbosa said, his voice a low rumble of fury.

"We'll see about that," Maxwell said, turning on his heel and walking back toward the sheriff's office.

Barbosa clenched and unclenched his hands. It would've been so easy to draw on the man, kill him in the street like the dog he was.

Where would he be without me? Barbosa thought. *I've kept him in his job. I've made that man's life comfortable and this is how he repays me.*

He couldn't believe the gall of the man, standing there threatening him in front of all and sundry. Who did Travis think he was?

"Time for a change around here," Barbosa murmured, eyes narrowed as he watched the sheriff walk away. "Time these people were reminded who calls the shots."

"Talking to yourself?" Renee Lane said from the steps of the saloon.

Barbosa turned to look at her. He checked

his own timepiece. "It's time. Get down here and let's get this done."

"And the lawman?" Renee asked, mystified by the sudden change in proceedings.

Barbosa said, "To hell with the sheriff! I don't need no one to tell me a bell's ringing."

CHAPTER TWENTY

Hope watched the sheriff slam the door shut after himself. The man was practically vibrating with anger. Maxwell breathed hard and fast as he searched for his whiskey bottle, pulled the stopper free with his teeth, spat it to one side, then drank the firewater down without pause.

He gasped as he pulled the bottle from his lips, wiping his mouth on the back of his hand.

"You realize it's barely dawn, don't you?" Hope asked him.

"I know full well what time it is."

"A little early for whiskey, isn't it, Sheriff?"

He pointed at her. "Keep that kinda comment to yourself. I'm still the sheriff of this town. I deserve your respect. If I want to come in here and drown my sorrows, well, I got a right."

"I'm not arguing with you, or disrespecting you," Hope said. "It's just I haven't seen

you like this before. Has something happened?"

Ethan stood up in his cell and moved to
stand with his arms hooked around the
bars, listening to the exchange.

Maxwell's eyes flitted from Hope to
Ethan. "I threatened Barbosa."

"Really?"

The sheriff nodded slowly. "Really."

"What brought that on?" Hope asked.

Maxwell took another mouthful of the
whiskey. "I don't know. I had enough, I
guess? A man can only take so much. And
I've taken a lot off that man over the years.
Too much. I've stood aside for too long."

Ethan said, "How did Barbosa react to
that?"

"He told me I was done here."

"Ah," Ethan said. "I see."

"It's pretty clear what that means," Maxwell said, shaking his head. "Wanna know
what he said to me out there? He said,
'When this contest is over, so are you.' I
don't think it leaves a lot to interpretation,
do you?"

"Not really."

Maxwell drank more of the whiskey. "I'm
gonna have to see this through now. Gotta
make a stand someday."

The night before, Maxwell had managed

to get Burt McCoy and Jasper to the sheriff's office to hear Hope's plan, under the pretense that they were bringing food to the prisoners — a simple meal of potatoes and stewed pork. Not even Cyrus Barbosa would have denied them a hot meal the night before they were due to face each other in a duel.

There in the lamplight, everything had been made clear to them. It could work only one way, because they would have to face not only Cyrus Barbosa, but his men in gray dusters, too. So the plan relied upon participation — and up until that moment, the sheriff had not been wholly convinced by the chances of the plan working in their favor. But something had changed, it seemed. Confronted with Barbosa, the sheriff had finally stood his ground and pledged to act. And now he would have to see it through, regardless of any doubt he might have been feeling.

Paulie had arrived, walking sheepishly into the sheriff's office. "You asked after me?"

"Not me," Maxwell said, indicating Hope. "Her."

Paulie frowned at her. "Wait . . . Why should I help you?"

"You owe me, from before."

"I don't remember," Paulie said.

Hope fixed him with a cold, hard stare. "Yes, you do."

"What d'you need, then?"

Hope strode toward him. Handed him a folded map, one spot marked on it with blue ink. "I need you to ride out to this point and tell my uncle Dash it's time."

"I ain't got no horse."

Maxwell rolled his eyes. "Take mine, you dolt."

Paulie licked his lips. "Listen . . . I don't wanna get involved in nothing I shouldn't be. If this is gonna land me in hot water —"

A good bath wouldn't go amiss with you, my smelly friend, Hope thought. "It won't land you in anything. All I want you to do is ride out there, pass on a message. You can ride, can't you?"

"Sure. I won't even know who I'm looking for!"

The sheriff howled with laughter. "You stupid good-for-nothing, Paulie. There's only gonna be one fella camped out there. And if you ask him if his name is Dash, and he replies in the affirmative, well, then you know it's him, don't you?"

"I guess. So . . . what's the message?"

"Tell him, 'Time to come in from the cold.' He'll know what you mean," Hope had said.

Now, as Hope looked at the grandfather clock down past the cells, she could only hope that Paulie had done as she asked. "Those church bells will ring any second."

Maxwell followed her gaze. "Wonder who'll come out on top."

"If Renee kills him, we can rest easy," Hope said. "Things will change around here for sure. But if Barbosa wins . . . it's the plan or nothing."

Maxwell took one more swallow of the whiskey, then headed for the door.

Ethan said, "Where are you going?"

"I've gotta see who wins."

With him gone, Ethan said, "How do we know we can trust him?"

"I have a feeling for people. I know I can trust him to help us," Hope said.

"I don't know what makes you so sure."

Hope shrugged. "I guess, what choice does he have? Barbosa will run him out of town once this is done. He's gotta act. I know he doesn't want to, but he really has no choice."

"I hope you're right," Ethan said.

So do I, Hope thought.

Renee Lane took her position in the middle of the street, on the same spot where Red Nelson, Crazy Sid Babcock and Daiyu Wu had fallen. Her thoughts turned to the blood that must have been somewhere underfoot. She tried to brush it aside so she could focus on the task at hand. Down the street, Cyrus Barbosa stood in a wide-legged stance, hand hovering over the pistol at his hip.

Renee adopted a similar stance, though not so wide. She'd coated her hands in chalk dust before leaving the saloon — sweaty palms were a handicap when she faced somebody down. She could see the determination on Barbosa's face, the focus in the hard flints of his eyes. The man was big and round, which made him a better target to aim for. But his size also meant he could be easily, and foolishly, underestimated.

She knew that the moment the church bell rang out, she would have to draw. She'd have to release her pistol from the holster faster than Barbosa did, line up her shot and hope she'd beat him to the punch.

Renee considered what she'd do if she did outdraw Barbosa. She'd surely have to eliminate the men in gray dusters assembled on the porch of the saloon to observe the proceedings. And she'd have to slam a bullet through the foreheads of the reprobates Barbosa called Ed and Cotton. Her chances of surviving the day were not great — and yet, in that full knowledge, she was still in the street at the break of dawn, making her stand.

She did so through free will, and free will was all that mattered when it came down to it. Wasn't it the very ideal of the country she loved? That you could create your own destiny, and manifest it into being, through sheer will? Will, determination, hard work would achieve your dream.

Growing up in poverty, Renee had always known that to have anything in this life, she'd have to reach for it herself. No one had forced her to participate in the contest — she'd wanted to. Because the boons of winning far outweighed the risks of taking part, at least to her mind. With that money she could make a real difference. And with the notoriety that came with winning, Renee could hold her head up high and say she'd done something: she'd rid the world of a monster. Vanquished him.

The church bell swung. The heavy clang of the iron broke the morning with its force. Renee's hand slid around her gun. She pulled it free. Raised it. Saw the flash at the end of Barbosa's gun. She hadn't seen him so much as move, he was so remarkably quick.

Her eyes traced the bullet bursting from the end of Barbosa's gun in a fleeting cloud of white smoke. It sliced through the air, heading straight for her. There was no time to do anything. Not even flinch or shut her eyes. She simply watched the bullet come her way. Watched it get closer and closer, until it was mere inches away and not stopping.

The bullet drove into her forehead. Renee experienced a flash of blinding light, then felt the dark of endless night, cool as a veil of mist over water.

The monster had prevailed.

The church bell rang out, every resonant toll ominous and heavy with portent. Hope looked up as the door to the sheriff's office opened and Maxwell slowly walked inside. He closed the door behind him and removed his hat.

"Well?" she asked.

They'd hear the gunshots, of course. She'd felt them; now the uncertainty seemed to reverberate in her soul.

The sheriff ran a hand over his tired face. "Barbosa won."

"Damn," Hope said.

"Not the outcome we were hoping for," Ethan said behind her.

She sighed. "No, it's not."

"So we fight this out," Sheriff Maxwell said.

"If you're still with us. There's always time to pull out. Get away from here," Hope said. "There's no shame in it."

"No, I told you both, I'm in," Maxwell said.

Hope nodded slowly. "All right, then. I just hope Burt and Jasper took care of the rest."

"Guess we'll find out at noon," Ethan said.

Sheriff Maxwell spun around as the door to his office swung open and the unmistakable forms of Ed and Cotton piled in.

"What in the hell do you two want?" Maxwell demanded.

"We're here for the girl," Cotton said, pointing at Hope. "The boss wants to take her for breakfast."

"For breakfast?"

"That's what he told us," Ed said. He took the keys off the wall and unlocked Hope's cell. He stood to one side so she could pass. "Get moving."

Hope looked to Ethan for assurance but he had none to give. Clearly he didn't know what was happening any more than she did. Hope brushed past Ed and made for the rack next to the door. Cotton tried to get in her way.

"Can I at least get my coat? In case you hadn't noticed, it's damned cold out there with the snow and all," she said.

Cotton blinked. Stepped aside so she could get to the rack. Hope worked her arms into the sleeves and buttoned the coat closed.

"Done?" the big brute asked.

"Yes."

Ed joined them. "Let's go," he boomed.

Outside, Hope looked up the street and spotted the body of Renee Lane — arms and legs splayed out, blood spattering the fresh snow, like so many red rose petals thrown on white linen.

Ed and Cotton escorted her to the café, then they instructed her to head inside while they guarded the door.

Hope walked into the warmth and the welcoming smell of bacon frying. She spotted Barbosa at his table in the corner straightaway. He was dunking a thick doorstop of bread, slathered with butter, into the runny yolk of an egg.

Barbosa looked up as she approached. He gestured to the seat opposite. "Sit."

"What's this about?" Hope asked, not moving an inch at first.

"Breakfast. Will you sit?"

Though distrusting his motive, Hope pulled out the chair and slowly sat. Her stomach growled from hunger but she didn't let on that the smells of bacon and biscuits were making her ravenous.

"You just killed a woman. Left her body in the street," she said.

"Man. Woman. Dead is dead."

"Still . . ."

"Look, she knew how things would be," Barbosa said. "Like Wu did. Like everyone. If you want to be called the greatest gunslinger of them all, you enter this contest and you take your chances."

"Now there's only us left."

"And Ethan Harper."

"I don't know why you're dragging him into it," Hope said. "This should be between me and you. He's got nothing to do with it."

"The fact that you care what happens to the man is all the reason I need to make him a part of this," Barbosa said without so much as a flicker of emotion.

Ruth came to the table with a cup of coffee and a plate of bacon and eggs. "This is for you," she said nervously, setting them down in front of Hope, then heading off.

"I took the liberty of ordering for you," Barbosa said.

"I don't want it."

He stabbed at the air with his fork. "Don't be ungrateful. Eat it of your own volition, young lady, or I'll have Ed and Cotton force-feed you like an invalid. I despise wasted food."

Hope lifted her cutlery and began to eat the bacon. She felt a pang of guilt at the thought of Ethan stuck back in his cell while she sat in the warmth of the café, eating a hot breakfast. The mixture of grease and salt was enough to convince her to put her inhibitions to one side for the moment and just eat.

What if the plan fails? What if I end up dead in the street like Renee Lane? I'll regret not eating this breakfast and drinking this coffee.

"So what's this about?" she asked.

"I wanted you to know, I intended no malice in your father's murder."

"No? How do you figure that?" Hope said. "I watched your men kill him and I can assure you, there was plenty of malice involved."

"Well, that was not the intent, as I have said."

"Then why have him killed in the first place?" Hope demanded.

Barbosa sipped his coffee. "It was a matter of principle."

"Principle?"

"Yes. Tobias knew our code. He knew you cannot simply leave the Black Scorpions. Even when we split, we never *stopped* being Black Scorpions. Not by choice. Your father betrayed us. Running off the way he did, turning on his brothers . . . he shamed himself *and* us. I could not let that stand. You see, it wasn't only principle. It was honor."

"A man like you does not have honor," Hope told him. "You wouldn't know honor if it hit you in the face."

"That's your opinion."

"Damn right it is."

Barbosa looked past her, over her shoulder. "It's snowing again."

Hope turned briefly around in her seat to look. "And?"

"I always feel as though the snow is a promise of sorts. New beginnings. It covers up the dirt and the failures. It offers a fresh new canvas upon which we can start again."

Hope said, "Trouble with snow is, it melts. And what you covered up with it ends up exposed for all the world to see."

"Perhaps," he said. "Its reprieve is short-lived, I agree. Winter, being full of care, makes summer's welcome thrice more wished, more rare."

Hope put her knife and fork down. "What in the hell am I here for?"

"Tobias Cassidy chose to betray me. But you would be wrong to think I do not regret his murder, or wish that he was still my friend and business partner. I wish things had gone another way, but we're only offered a finite number of paths in this life. Your father chose his. And in so doing, he left me no option but to choose mine."

"You keep telling yourself that."

Barbosa said, "You weren't there. Hell, you probably weren't even *born*. What does a silly girl like you know about anything?"

"Why have you brought me here?"

"To make you an offer."

"An offer?"

"A chance to turn away, to choose freedom over avenging your father's death."

Hope frowned. "You're offering to let me go?"

"I'm offering to cut you loose on the condition that you abandon your foolish errand of vengeance," Barbosa said.

"No."

"You don't want to think it over?"

"I don't need to," Hope told him.

Barbosa shook his head in dismay. "You are condemning your friend to the same fate as you."

333

"Perhaps," Hope said, not wanting to give anything away.

Barbosa licked the egg yolk off his fork and set it down on his plate. Then he proceeded to run his tongue along the knife.

"By sundown, you'll be dead," she said. She raised the cup of coffee with one hand, while her other rested on the tabletop. Sipped at the dark, smoky brew.

"Funny. I was about to say the exact same thing," Barbosa spat.

In just two movements he grabbed her wrist with one hand, and with his other he plunged the knife into her hand, all the way through to the wood, pinning her hand to the table with a loud thud.

Hope screamed, the pain exploding in her hand like fire and sending hot electricity running up her arm into her shoulder. Barbosa gripped her wrist with his giant mallet of a fist, crushing it as he applied pressure. Then he suddenly let go and pulled the knife free.

Trembling all over from the shock of the attack, Hope tentatively cradled her hand. Barbosa regarded the bloodied surface of the knife, then set it down on his plate. Hope looked over at Ruth and Frank, in the vain hope they might come to her aid, but they simply cowered behind the counter, unwilling to step forward and interfere in what was taking place between them.

Barbosa cocked his head to one side. "I'm sorry. Was that your gun hand?"

Hope didn't say anything. She couldn't. It was all she could do to prevent herself from crying. She couldn't help screaming when he drove the knife in but she refused to weep in front of him.

Barbosa leaned forward across the table. His stale breath smelled like a latrine. "I think we're done here. Ed and Cotton will walk you back to your cell. Hope you're as good with your left as your right, now you're a southpaw. . . ."

Hope stood, holding her hand to her chest, blood running from the wound down the front of her coat. She spoke through bared teeth. "You've got egg on your shirt," she said, and headed for the door.

Barbosa looked down at his shirt. "Oh, hell," he said, dabbing at the dribble of orange yolk with a handkerchief. "It's soiled."

"What happened to you?" Sheriff Maxwell asked Hope as she walked into the sheriff's office cradling her bloody hand.

Ed and Cotton stood in the door, watching the sheriff go to her aid — neither of them attempting to help in any way.

"I can take care of this. I don't need to be babysat," Maxwell told them.

The colossal men headed off without a single word.

Maxwell examined Hope's wound. "This is gonna need sewing up," he said, steering her toward a chair next to the fire.

"He stabbed it all the way through," Hope said shakily. "The knife was stuck in the table."

"It's barbaric." The sheriff went to Ethan's cell and unlocked it for him. "I'm going to go fetch Edith to come take a look at this. Just stay put, will you?"

"We won't go anywhere," Ethan told him.

The sheriff headed out to fetch Dr. Bell.

Ethan gently examined Hope's hand. "Why did he do this, d'you reckon?"

"There was no need for it!" she exclaimed. "I gave him no reason to attack me. He just suddenly brought the knife down and pinned my hand to the table."

"Unprovoked?"

"Yes."

Ethan grimaced as he turned her hand over. "That's your gun hand, isn't it?"

Hope nodded.

"Dirty cheat," Ethan said. "Giving himself an unfair advantage."

"But it doesn't make sense."

"What doesn't?"

Hope swallowed. The pain was so intense, it had her feeling nauseous. She kept telling herself it would pass, to keep herself from vomiting. "He knows we're facing each other first. So if he really wanted me to reach the final round and face off against him . . . why is he handing you the advantage?"

Ethan remained cupping her wounded hand in his own. "Two reasons. First, because he knows I will not harm you. He knows I'll just stand there and let you shoot me dead if that's what has to happen. Secondly, he's seen how good you are with a gun, and so he's giving himself an unfair advantage when you face off against each other. You see, he's pretty certain as to how this is gonna play out."

"You really would do that? Just let me shoot you?" Hope asked.

Ethan said, "I'd sooner turn my guns on myself than do anything to hurt you, Hope."

The door opened and a flushed Dr. Bell rushed inside, followed by an out-of-breath Sheriff Maxwell.

"Damn, the woman can sprint," Maxwell said.

Ethan got out of the way as Dr. Bell set to

work examining Hope's wound. "I will need fresh water and the cleanest cloth you have available," she said, frowning at Hope's hand. "These scars . . . you've seen some trauma."

"That's an understatement, Doc," Hope snapped.

"You sure do like getting yourself hurt, don't you?"

"It's not like I set out to get hurt. But this town keeps drawing blood somehow."

Sheriff Maxwell and Ethan rustled up a bucket of fresh water for her, and the cleanest rag the sheriff had to hand. As the two men looked on, the doctor cleaned the wound, then ordered Maxwell to pour Hope a measure of something strong to help her cope with the pain of getting sewn up.

"I've got some whiskey," Maxwell said.

"That'll do," Dr. Bell said. "Just to take the edge off."

Hope accepted the glass of whiskey and downed it in one go.

"Another?" Maxwell asked her.

Hope shook her head. "No."

"Ready? You need to stay really still," Dr. Bell instructed her.

"I understand," Hope said through gritted teeth.

But once the needle began to drag the

338

catgut through her flesh, crisscrossing the wound in order to pull it closed, Hope found the pain steadily uncomfortable, until eventually it took all her self-control not to pull her hand free and run for the hills.

"You're doing really well," Dr. Bell said. "Not a single tear shed."

"Yet," Hope corrected her.

The doctor smiled thinly. "Yes. There's plenty of time for that. Not that it makes much difference."

"How do you figure that, Doc?"

"Come noon, you'll be dead. Both of you."

Hope looked from Sheriff Maxwell to Dr. Bell and to Ethan in turn. "I've been dead before," she said.

"I could never condone taking the life of another for sport," Dr. Bell said.

"That's easy to say when you've never been put in the situation!" Hope exclaimed. "For those in the contest, it's not a choice. It's a matter of self-preservation."

"Is that the case for you?" Dr. Bell asked.

Hope looked sharply at her. "No. It's not *just* self-preservation for me. It's something *more.*"

"Wrath," Ethan put in. "Well-earned wrath."

Hope raised one shoulder. "I guess so."

" 'Do not let the sun go down on your

339

anger,' " Dr. Bell said. "Do you know that one?"

"Sounds like something from the Bible."

"It is. Ephesians."

"Your point?" Hope asked.

The doctor finished up the stitches. "Don't let your vengeance, or whatever it is that's driving you — don't let it be the one thing anyone remembers about you. It matters how you leave this world. Don't let wrath define you."

"I'm already defined by it," Hope told her. "It's in my blood. It's who I am. The man responsible for this contest is the root cause of that."

"Perhaps by facing him, you can find peace," Dr. Bell said.

"I don't hold out much hope for that," Hope scoffed.

The doctor fixed her with a look that was far from impressed. "Maybe you should."

CHAPTER TWENTY-ONE

At a half hour to noon, Sheriff Maxwell presented Hope and Ethan with their pistols.

Ethan was surprised that he was being reunited with both guns. "Really?"

"Why not?" Maxwell asked. "You don't want them?"

"No, no, I *want* them. I just didn't imagine I'd *get* them, is all," Ethan said, happily slipping his twin shooters into the holsters at his hips.

"And there's this," Maxwell said, tossing Hope's bullwhip onto her cot. "Guess you'd want that, too."

"You guessed right," Hope said.

Maxwell crossed to the other side to check his own weapons.

Hope held her revolver uncertainly in her left hand.

Ethan studied her expression. "Are you going to be able to shoot that thing?"

341

"I can shoot with either hand," Hope replied, holstering the piece, "but it's been a while."

"No chance to practice, either," Ethan said.

Hope looked at her bandaged right hand. Blood had seeped through from the stitches, turning the white of the bandages a watery shade of pink. "Can I ask you something?"

"Me?"

"Well, there's nobody else here, Ethan."

"Okay, then, shoot. What do you want to know?"

Hope looked up. "Were you serious when you suggested we run a place together?"

"Well . . . I don't say things like that to everyone I cross paths with," Ethan said.

"In that case I have something to tell you."

"Go on."

Hope sat down. "I tracked Puck Cosby to a little town by the Atlantic Ocean. New Devon. He was there working on a fishing boat if you can believe that."

"Under a different name, I take it."

"Of course."

Ethan shook his head. "Damn."

"Anyway, there was a pub for sale there. The Albatross. I have some money. You see, after I recovered enough to find my way back to Eden's Ridge, I learned my father

342

owned property all over the place. Now, when I think about it, it makes a lot of sense. The money he stole when he was a Black Scorpion, he must've been investing in land. So as I traveled around, I found those plots and sold them off. Not all, but most of them. By the time I reached New Devon, I had enough to buy that pub outright. I had *more* than enough."

"You tellin' me you own a pub?"

"I do."

"Why didn't you mention this before?" Ethan asked.

"It wasn't the right time. I still had to decide what I wanted to do."

"Wish I'd been left all that land," Ethan said.

Hope sighed. As good as it had felt to wear fresh new clothes, and own new gear, it felt that way no longer. It didn't seem right, benefiting from her father's ill-gotten gains. After learning about her father's past, Hope had been wrestling with her own conscience. Tobias had taken his outlaw money and used it to buy land up and down the country. And then, years later, Hope had ridden from one location to another, selling them off and pocketing the proceeds.

Now she knew he'd stolen from people to buy that land. He'd hurt them. Possibly, he'd killed some of them, too.

It felt wrong to benefit from it somehow. It didn't sit easy with her; that was for sure. Hope had always thought of herself as straight as a yardstick. But her father's past could not be changed.

Ethan had been asking her something. Hope blinked. Looked at him. "Sorry?"

"I said, are you still deciding what to do with it?"

Hope smiled. "No. I've come to a decision. All this time I've had a local couple running the place for me. But I think I want to set down roots there and run it myself. And I was wondering if you wanted to run it with me."

"Well . . ."

"It's not so different to what you had in mind, after all," Hope said. "And we get along very well. It would work out, I think."

Ethan considered for a moment. "A pub by the sea?"

"Lots of sailors drinking lots of rum," Hope told him.

"Nice place, is it?"

Hope said, "Nothing happens there. Nothing at all."

"Sounds perfect," Ethan said.

They broke into laughter.

The sheriff came back, laden with a pistol

and a rifle. "Something funny? You're laughin' a lot for two people who're about to face down a butcher's army."

"It wouldn't make sense to you."

"I see . . ." Maxwell said. "Well, after all the talk, are you two ready for this?"

"Yes. What about you, Sheriff? Ready to prove you got grit?" Ethan asked him.

Maxwell patted the rifle. "I am."

"Won't Barbosa notice you carrying that?" Hope asked.

"I'm going to stash it before the gunfight gets goin'. I'll have it to fall back on," he said.

"Good idea," Ethan said.

"What're you going to do about additional ammo? Once you've emptied your chambers, that's it. You can't afford to walk out there with pockets full of bullets. Barbosa will check to make sure you've only got what you can fire."

"Well, we're relying on Burt and Jasper to have stashed ammo at the feed store. It just depends on whether or not they've been able to do that," Hope said. "If we turn up and the ammo ain't there . . ."

"We're sunk," Ethan said.

"I reckon you'll both find out shortly," Maxwell said, opening the door for them. The cold harsh wind rushed inside the sheriff's office, biting at their faces. "Let's get this done."

Cyrus Barbosa and his men spilled out of the saloon to watch them approach. Six men in gunmetal dusters and the two big lugs called Ed and Cotton. All of them filling up the porch of the saloon to watch the "show" their boss had put on for them.

"If I was of a weaker disposition, the sight of 'em would make me sick," Ethan said.

"Me, too," Hope said. "All it makes me want to do is kill them all."

"I know. But hold fast. You'll get your moment."

Maxwell did not walk with the swagger of a lawman, a man of authority in town, a man others were meant to look up to. He moved with a guarded rigidness that told Hope he was a man on the edge. Back at the sheriff's office, she'd asked him if he was ready to prove he had grit; now she wondered if he might turn out to be a huge liability to them in some way.

They stood before Barbosa and his men. Hope noted a dearth of actual townsfolk. Had they heard something? Or did they just figure it'd get nasty? With Barbosa so lacking in scruples, it went without saying that his men were of the same ilk.

A light snow shower began to fall as Barbosa stepped down from the porch. He looked up and snowflakes landed on his mustache, glittering among the wiry black and gray hairs.

Barbosa studied the three of them. "Sheriff, are they ready?"

"They are."

"Guns locked and loaded?"

Maxwell said, "That's the way we do this, ain't it?"

"You know it is," Barbosa said, his voice clipped with tension. He cocked an eyebrow. "What about her bullwhip? That really necessary?"

"She says it is."

Barbosa's gaze fell on the twin pistols at Ethan's hips. "And does Ethan Harper, the renowned marksman, really need the two shooters?"

"That's what he uses. You want me to take one away?"

Barbosa considered the suggestion, then shook his head. "No. Let's keep it interesting. It's all the same to me. A whip. Two guns. It ain't gonna change anything."

Sheriff Maxwell checked the time on his pocket watch. "First bell is gonna sound in a few minutes. Want me to do the honors with this one?"

"Like I done told you, Sheriff, your services are no longer required. Miss Cassidy. Mister Harper. You both know how this game is played. Refuse to shoot each other, I will kill you myself. Is that understood? Believe me when I tell you, I will not hesitate to do what must be done."

"I think we're already aware of that," Hope told him.

Barbosa smiled. "There's that sharp tongue of yours again. How's the hand?"

"This one?" Hope asked, raising her uninjured left hand. "*This one* is doing just fine."

Barbosa's smile fell. "Good."

Hope shared the briefest of looks with Ethan, then they took up their positions facing each other. She held a stance and looked straight ahead, but her eyes skirted to the right, taking in the positions of Barbosa's men, assessing which of them she'd have to hit first to make an impact.

Without shifting her position at all, Hope next looked to the left, spotting Jasper up on the roof of the feed store with an old rifle at the ready, just as they'd agreed. Sheriff Maxwell stood near the hitching posts in front of the saloon, looking like a coiled spring ready to fly.

The church bell rang out. Hope looked

forward, locked on Ethan's face. At any other time, the tension of the moment would have come from not knowing when the other shootist was going to draw and fire. But now the same tension came from waiting for the moment to shoot their mutual enemy.

Ethan and Hope were in absolute agreement that they had to act simultaneously or it wouldn't work. "Strike quick and keep movin' " was one of the things Ethan had said last night. After that, she lay awake on the cot and thought about her father's crimes.

It was enough to drive her crazy, and Hope came to realize that the only way she could reconcile the image of her father Barbosa had conjured was to treat them as two different men. There was Tobias Cassidy the outlaw, who ran with the Black Scorpions. And there was the celebrated and respected Marshal Tobias Cassidy. He had changed his ways. He had loved his family and taken care of them. He had done good in the world. That man was her pop.

The church bell rang a second time.

Hope swallowed.

Ethan's eyes flicked to his left, in the direction of Barbosa and his men.

It's time.

Hope gave the lightest, barely perceptible nod of her head.

Let's do it.

She pulled her pistol with her left hand. At the same time, Ethan yanked both silver shooters from their dual holsters. Hope and Ethan raised their weapons as if to fire at each other. At the same time the church bell rang again and both Hope and Ethan pivoted about to face the saloon.

Hope aimed at one of the men in gray dusters. Her shot punched through his chest and he stumbled into the others, head snapping back from the force of the hit.

Ethan fired both pistols at once. The shot from the gun in his left hand struck Ed, obliterating his face as the bullet smashed through his nose and blew his brains out the other side of his enormous skull. The shot from his right whizzed between two of Barbosa's men and splintered the timber behind them, shaking loose the icicles from the lip of the porch roof.

At the same time, Hope broke to her right, thumbing the hammer back on her pistol, while Ethan hurried to his left.

"Get at 'em!" Barbosa yelled in outrage as he hastily pulled his own weapon to fire at them. "Run these dogs down!"

Sheriff Maxwell took up a position at the

corner of the saloon and fired into Barbosa's men. Hope and Ethan followed suit. Barbosa and his men pulled back, not knowing which direction to go.

On the roof opposite, Jasper rose behind the fascia with the rifle in his hand and took aim. His shot clapped into the floorboards in front of Barbosa's feet.

"Inside!" Barbosa shouted, shoving past them to reach the cover afforded by the saloon.

One of the gray dusters returned fire on the sheriff. Maxwell ducked behind the corner and waited for the henchman to break his rhythm. In the gap between firing and lining up the next shot, the sheriff saw his opportunity. He moved with the agility of someone half his age. The gray duster tried to open fire on him but he was too late. The sheriff shot him through the throat. The man clutched at his windpipe with both gloved hands, choking as his dark red blood pumped freely from the open wound. It ran down the front of his clothes and he collapsed onto the porch as his comrades in arms took cover inside the saloon.

Hope and Ethan joined up outside the feed store. As if on cue, they heard the front door unlock. Burt McCoy appeared in the entrance, ushering them inside.

"I did not expect that," Hope said, taking in the sight of the feed store owners, Mr. and Mrs. Samson, bound and gagged on the floor. "Don't tell me they're loyal to Barbosa."

"Sorry to say they are," Burt said.

Hope looked down on them with pity. "You fools."

"Is he all right up there?" Burt asked, indicating the roof of the feed store where Jasper was positioned to provide covering fire.

"Seems to be. He let off one round to give us some cover but seems to be keeping his head down for now, which is for the best."

"Good. I'd hate to see anything bad happen to the kid," Burt told her. "I questioned lettin' him put himself in harm's way . . . but in the end I didn't have no choice. He's old enough to do what he's gonna do. It weren't about letting him because he always does what he wants."

"How does he know how to shoot?" Ethan asked. "I thought he just did odd jobs at the saloon for you."

Burt shrugged. "He didn't learn no shooting from me. There's a lot I don't know about Jasper. A lot he won't tell me, too. There ain't much I can do about that."

352

Hope moved to the front windows and, standing off to the side, watched the empty street. "They're all in the bar. Barbosa is planning his move. I'm afraid the saloon has taken a few hits," she told the barkeep.

He sighed. "Not the first time, or the last, I reckon. My days of runnin' that place are over now anyway. I was gonna pack up and quit Fortune's Cross for someplace else. Maybe go and visit my brother in Nebraska. For years he's been tellin' me to join him out there."

Hope said, "Maybe you should go do that. Sounds like it would be a good change of pace, Burt."

"Maybe."

Hope saw Maxwell running across the street toward them. "Here comes the sheriff."

Maxwell hurried through the door. "Damn," he said, short of breath.

"Are you okay?" Ethan asked, noting the blood splatter on the sheriff's clothes.

"Okay? I'm *great*."

Ethan exchanged looks with Hope. "You're . . . great?" he asked confusedly.

"Never better. It's been too long," Maxwell said. "I don't know what I was frettin' about. I've not seen any action in a long, long time. I feel like this is what I was meant to do. Burt, did you reach out to any of the men? Get any takers?"

The barkeep said, "I crapped out when it came to backup, but least I tried. You'll notice the town's more deserted even than yesterday. They left last night to get away from the carnage that was coming their way. Can't say I blame 'em if I'm honest."

"That's the trouble with folk. Quick enough to complain about something, but ask them to step up to fight for change and they chicken out."

"Guess it's just us, then," Hope said. She looked out the window again. "Ed's out of the equation. And by my count, two of his men in gray dusters."

"Are they Black Scorpions?" Ethan asked.

Hope pulled a face. "No, I think they're just Barbosa's lapdogs. I think the Black Scorpions are firmly in the past now."

"That leaves Cotton, four more men in dusters and Barbosa himself," Maxwell said. He came to stand near her at the window. "Wonder what they're cookin' up over there."

"We'll find out before too long," Ethan said. "I wonder if Paulie reached your uncle."

Hope had been wondering the exact same thing. They didn't have much hope of swinging things in their favor without him.

"I'm sure he'll turn up," she said, trying to sound reassuring, but she heard the note of uncertainty in her own voice at the same time.

Cyrus Barbosa had blood on his new suit. *A wiser man would take this to be a sign of things to come,* he thought. He looked out of the window at the empty street, watching for any sign of movement. Behind him, Cotton sat at a table, holding his head in his hands.

"What's the matter with you?"

Cotton looked up. "Ed's dead."

"And you're not. Nothing else matters," Barbosa said.

There were tears in Cotton's eyes. "Didn't you hear me? He's dead!"

"I know. A great shame." Barbosa turned back to his view of the street. " 'The waters swell . . . before a boisterous storm.' "

One of his men, a man called Russell, approached. He'd been in his employ for some time. "Do you see anyone out there?"

"Not yet. They must be in one of the buildings opposite."

"In the chaos, I didn't see where they ran off to," Russell said. "But the sheriff was there, too, at the sidelines."

"He'll be with 'em now."

"It's just the two of 'em, though, ain't it?" Russell asked. He turned around to look at the others. "There's six of us against three. No matter how you look at it, we got the advantage here, Cyrus."

"You don't know that. They could have people backing them. We can't go rushing over there."

"So what's the alternative? We sit here countin' our toes and wait for them to show?" Russell demanded.

Barbosa faced him. He did not raise his voice — he did not need to. The threat implicit in his words was more than enough. "We wait until I say it's time to move."

"As you like, Cyrus. I was just stating facts, is all."

"Go tell McCoy to get the men a drink. I need a moment to think."

Russell went to the bar and called for Burt. When the barkeep didn't show, Russell went to the other side and began to pour measures of whiskey into glasses himself.

I'm looking at them, and they're looking at me, Barbosa thought as he gazed at the stores across the street. *It makes sense they'd be in one of the buildings opposite because then they'll know how many of us there are and when we're coming.*

But which one? He had an idea to catch them with their britches down, but first he had to have an inkling as to what store they were holed up in. It would have helped to know exactly how many of them were in cahoots, too, but that wasn't something he had any say in.

There! He saw movement behind the windows of the feed store. It wasn't light refracted off the fresh snow covering the ground. He was sure it was the shape of somebody walking across the room. It could have been the husband or wife who ran the place. He couldn't go sending his men over there to kill them just in case — though in his younger years, he would've done just that.

How things changed.

As Barbosa watched the feed store, his eyes were drawn to a flash of movement up on the roof. Someone was up there. He saw the tip of a rifle pop up from behind the fascia, then disappear — as if a shooter up there had just shifted position to get comfortable. He had no idea who it could be, but it made him think the movement he'd seen from within the feed store might not have been the owners. In fact, he would have bet good money they were hog-tied and gagged to prevent them from causing any trouble.

Barbosa turned to face the four men in dusters. "You, get ready to hit the feed store. Looks like people inside, and one up on the roof with a rifle."

"Any sign of the sheriff?" Russell asked.

Barbosa shook his head. "No, but I'm betting he's in the feed store with them, because that's the kinda move I expect from a yellabelly, no-good coward like him." He paused, frowning at the vacant bar. "Where's McCoy?"

"I called him but he wouldn't come."

"Well, go get him," Barbosa snapped impatiently.

Russell told one of the men to go look out the back. He returned a moment later. "Ain't nobody out there."

"What? Check upstairs," Barbosa ordered.

The gray duster checked the rooms and descended the stairs with a joyless expression. "Place is empty."

"What does that mean?" Russell asked.

"It means the barkeep is with them," Barbosa said without waiting on an answer. "Lord knows why. Probably got the kid with him, too. They both should've kept their noses out of affairs that don't concern them. Oh, well, the reasons don't matter. They just signed their death warrants." His words dripped with malice.

Russell stepped forward. "How're we doing this?"

"I'll come to that," Barbosa said, holding up a finger as he turned his attention to grief-stricken Cotton. "Are you ready to get yourself some revenge on the one killed your partner, son?"

Cotton's eyes were pink at the edges. "I don't know which one did it."

"I do."

Cotton got to his feet. "Tell me."

"Ethan Harper."

"The bald one?"

Barbosa nodded. "I saw it happen," he said. "The same Ethan Harper who pinned Ed to the floor back at the café. Do you remember? The night Hope Cassidy bested you. Threw hot coffee in your face, then threw that right hook to the jaw."

"She did *not* best me."

"Well, considering you was out cold on the floor, I'd say she did. Must have been embarrassing. I mean, it was embarrassing enough for me."

Cotton's hands balled into fists of rage at his sides. "That's enough," he growled.

Barbosa didn't waste a second. He got up close to Cotton, eyeballing him to let the man know he was unmoved by threats or intimidation. Even coming from a man of Cotton's considerable size.

"Take your anger and turn it on those what killed Ed," he said, jabbing Cotton in the stomach. "Use that fire in your belly to make 'em pay, d'you understand?"

"Yes, boss," Cotton said.

Barbosa smiled. "Good boy. Now listen to me carefully. Here's what you're going to do. . . ."

Chapter Twenty-Two

"What're you packing?" Ethan asked, peering at the shotgun in Burt McCoy's hands.

The barkeep regarded the weapon. "This old thing? A twelve-gauge I've had since I was a young man. They used to call these 'messenger guns' on account of 'em being used to defend wagons and stagecoaches from bandits. It's been everywhere with me. Short range, mind, but sometimes that's what you need, you know? She's got plenty of stopping power and that's all that matters."

"There's been a few times I could've done with a good shotgun at my side," Ethan said.

"Well, now it will be," Burt said with a cheeky grin.

Ethan clapped him on the shoulder. "Good to hear it. Now, you empty both barrels of that shotgun through the front door when you hear me give the word. Got it?"

"Loud and clear, sonny."

Maxwell said, "Let's take up spots next to the windows. Smash a few panels so you've got a clear line of sight."

Hope flipped her pistol around and smashed several glass panes with the handle. "Burt, have you got that ammo?"

He shoved a handful of spare bullets at her.

"Thanks," she said, pushing them into her pockets.

Burt did the same for Ethan, then got into position, hunkered down on the floor behind the bottom half of the front door.

"Here they come!" Hope yelled, stepping away from the window.

The four men in gray dusters spilled from the saloon and fanned out into the street. They trudged through the snow with their weapons drawn, dusters billowing out behind them, grim faces locked in expressions of weariness and resignation to the task at hand.

Ethan took one window, Hope the other, with the sheriff next to her.

"Fire," Ethan told her.

Hope discharged her pistol out the window, in the general vicinity of the four men. Ethan edged out from behind the window frame and shot at the duster closest to him. His first shot winged the man, spun him about. Ethan shot at him again with his other pistol, but his shot went wide of the mark. The other three scattered, moving in different directions and firing back at the same time.

Hope pulled back as the bullets smashed into the front of the building, punching holes of daylight through the timbers. The rest of the window blew out in front of Ethan, causing him to wheel away from it, the shards of glass scattering everywhere. Burt remained where he'd been told to hide, but visibly jumped with each gunshot, twitching like a puppy scared by thunder.

The gray duster Ethan had winged reached the door.

"Now, Burt!" Ethan yelled.

Burt scooted backward as he unloaded both barrels of the shotgun into the door. The sound of the ancient weapon firing was deafening. Ethan saw the man fly backward like he'd been kicked by a horse's hind legs.

Burt scrambled to his feet and went for his ammo to reload. Hope looked up in time to see a man standing at the threshold of the back door. It took her a second to recognize the size and height of the man as belonging to Cotton, Barbosa's henchman.

Burt's decision to rush Cotton wielding the unloaded shotgun came too late.

Cotton raised his pistol and shot Burt Mc-Coy in the chest.

"No!" Sheriff Maxwell cried as he spun to see McCoy slide to the floor. Then a bullet split the wood over his head, and the sheriff had no choice but to continue shooting out of the window next to him to hold Barbosa's men back.

At the sound of the gunshot, Ethan had immediately begun to move. He raised his pistols and discharged them both. Cotton leapt back into the yard, but Ethan did not stop. He charged at the open door and threw himself against Cotton before he had a chance to see what was coming his way. The two men collided, grappling with each other in the yard.

Hope checked Burt for a pulse, first his neck and then his wrist, but couldn't detect the all-important thread of his heartbeat. The gunshot had killed him instantly. McCoy's eyes were shut, mouth clamped tight. His brow was furrowed, no doubt by the last thing he'd experienced — the pain of being shot, of not being able to get one last breath into the wreckage of his chest; the last seconds of his life probably too awful to imagine.

Maxwell let off two more shots and pulled the door closed. He watched from the window as the three gray dusters turned to look to their left at something. "Wait. . . ."

"What is it?" Hope asked, trying to see.

A lone figure stood in the middle of the street, snow falling gently around him. Squinting in the cold white sunlight. Dash Cassidy eyeballed the three men before him.

"Who the hell are you?" one of them demanded, spitting on the ground.

There was a long silence. Then Dash spoke, his voice edged with grit. "I'm the man."

"What the hell's that supposed to mean? What *man*?"

Dash's hand hovered over his sidearm. "The one who's gonna put you boys in the ground," he said, pulling his pistol free of its holster.

He shot at the man who'd addressed him, leaving smoking holes in the man's sternum and punching him back. The other two dusters cut away and fell back to the saloon.

Dash stood over the man he'd shot, who was writhing on the ground in agony. Dash aimed his gun at the man's head and unceremoniously pulled the trigger, ending his torment.

Barbosa appeared on the porch, eyeballing Dash Cassidy as his men retreated. "This ain't your fight, stranger!"

365

Dash glared at him. "I'll say it is."

"That's a good man you killed," Barbosa growled.

"Good men fight fair," Dash told him, stepping away from Barbosa's fallen minion.

Barbosa's hand flexed over his gun. "It's only you and me out here right now, ain't it?"

"Seems that way," Dash said, moving carefully to the right, not taking his eyes off Barbosa for a second, his own pistol already in his hand. "But I'd hit my mark quicker than you could pull that shooter, fat man. And you're not mine to kill. Besides, like I said, a good man fights fair and right now I have the clear advantage."

"How's about you holster that pistol and let's have us a duel on equal footing?"

"I done told you, you ain't mine to kill."

Hope took the shotgun from Burt and reloaded it with her trembling left hand. He'd bravely chosen to make a stand alongside them, to rid Fortune's Cross of Barbosa once and for all. She watched the standoff taking place between Barbosa and her uncle Dash, and knew she had to do something to break it. So she took aim at Barbosa and fired the shotgun.

The blast obliterated the window in front of her, showering the street in an explosion of glass and pellets. Dash used the distraction to find cover two stores up from the saloon. Barbosa cowered away, retreating inside the saloon with what was left of his men.

She looked for Dash. He gave her a thumbs-up from the other side of the street.

Hope heard scuffling going on outside in the yard and turned to see Ethan strike Cotton on the jaw with a right hook, throwing his entire body weight into the punch. If it had connected, Cotton would have been out cold on the floor, as he had been back at the café that night. But Cotton ducked away from it, and using Ethan's momentum against him, he pulled him to the side, sending the gunslinger sprawling into the fence surrounding rear yard. Ethan landed against the stiff posts with an "Oomph!" and then careened over onto his back in the dirt and snow. He groaned as he got slowly and painfully to his knees.

Hope hastily reloaded the shotgun. "Come on," she said, beckoning the sheriff out back.

Cotton loomed over Ethan and was about to take advantage of his opponent being on the ground.

Ethan looked up at him. "It's been a while since I fought someone your size," he said.

"You killed my friend Ed."

"It's not personal," Ethan said, trying to get to his feet. "You just picked the wrong employer, is all, and you're too dumb to realize it."

Cotton pounded his fist into the palm of his hand. "I will crush your skull with my bare hands!"

"No, you won't," Ethan said, and pointed to the back door of the store.

Cotton turned around.

Hope leveled the shotgun at him, the long barrel supported with her bandaged right hand. "He's right. It's not personal," she said, and fired.

Cotton took both barrels to the stomach. The force of the shotgun blast sent him flying backward, crashing into the other side of the same fence Ethan had struck moments before. This time, due to Cotton's sheer size, he went through the slats and landed in a heap the other side, his torso a mangled bloody mess.

He did not move again.

Sheriff Maxwell lent Ethan a hand to get back to his feet. "You held your own," he said.

"I tried to," Ethan said, rubbing at his jaw.

Hope reasoned Cotton had managed to land a few good hits against Ethan in the short time they'd been fighting.

"We lost Burt," Hope said.

"Really?"

"Afraid so."

Ethan looked to the roof. "The kid?"

"Up there still, I think," Hope said. "Haven't had a chance to check on him yet. My uncle is here. He took out one of Barbosa's men."

Maxwell cupped his hands around his mouth and shouted, "Jasper, you all right up there?"

They waited a second for a response, then Jasper called back, "Yes, sir."

"Your uncle okay?"

Hope nodded. "He's taken up position two stores down from the saloon. He got into a standoff with Barbosa a moment ago. I don't know why he didn't just take him out."

"Saving him for you," Ethan said.

Hope knew he was right.

"What now, eh?" Sheriff Maxwell asked Hope.

"There's two gray dusters left, by my count, and the big man himself."

"That's right. I watched 'em fall back," Maxwell said. "Either Cyrus made a huge error in judgment coming at us the way he did, or this is all part of a ruse to draw us over there."

"I noticed he didn't show his face in the fight. He stayed back there to see what happened," Ethan said.

"True," Maxwell agreed.

"Well, if it's a trap, I say we do him a favor and spring it. How's about we get over to that saloon and take the fight to them?" Hope said, pushing another load of fresh cartridges into the shotgun. She snapped it closed.

"Could be exactly what he's hopin' we'll do," Ethan said.

"Well, I say we hit him on all sides. I mean, the place has a front and a rear like any other building. What if one of us let's them have it from out front, and the other two get around back, try and surprise 'em? Not forgetting we have Dash with us now, too. We've got 'em pinned."

"Sounds like a good plan to me," Maxwell said. "Ethan?"

"I'm ready," he said, picking up his guns, which had scattered to the ground during the fight with Cotton.

"If only the people of this town had the guts to take a stand themselves," the sheriff said, his voice tinged with regret.

Ethan laid a hand on the older man's shoulder. "Sometimes deciding to take a stand is harder than actually following through with it. The people of this town did the right thing by getting out of here, out of harm's way. Now it's up to us to run Barbosa out of here . . . and ensure he never comes back."

Cyrus Barbosa ran a hand over his face. Of his six men, only two were left. Russell, and a relative newcomer to the unit called Peterson. He'd watched them get picked off, one by one.

Bad planning on my part, or a lack of gun-fighting experience on theirs? he wondered. The answer was most likely a little of both. And they'd paid the ultimate price.

"Cyrus?" Russell asked. "What's the next move?"

"They'll come for us," Barbosa said. "We sit tight."

Peterson stared at him with wild eyes. "We're gonna wait here for 'em to come on over, get us cornered?"

"That's right. You got any brighter ideas?"

Russell turned to Peterson. "Mister Barbosa calls the shots. We talked about this before."

"But the others —"

Barbosa leapt with a growl, grabbed the man by the front of his duster and shook him like a rag doll. "Just like he said, I call the damn shots around here!" he shouted, pushing Peterson back. "Now get behind the bar. I want you watching those swinging doors. The minute one of 'em comes through, send 'em straight to hell."

Peterson straightened himself out, then went to the bar.

"Do not fear death, Peterson. It is said: 'Cowards die many times before their deaths. The valiant never taste of death but once.' No truer words were ever said. Be valiant, man. Be fearless in the face of this threat! We will prevail, I swear. We will see this day to the end."

"I will stand my ground, Cyrus," Peterson said, swallowing hard.

Barbosa turned to Russell. "You and me are gonna be on the back door."

"The back?"

Barbosa nodded once, slowly. "If I were them, I'd cause a distraction out front, and sneak in at the back."

"What about Cotton? Reckon he made it?"

"Not likely. But hopefully he took one of 'em with him," Barbosa said. He walked to the back door, and as he caught sight of the barn, a fresh idea occurred to him. He smiled and said, "Slight change of plan."

Hope, Ethan and Sheriff Maxwell went back inside the feed store, walking respectfully around the body of Burt McCoy to the obliterated front door. The owners were still safely bound and gagged on the floor in the corner, looking petrified by what had happened around them.

"Either of you got a knife?" asked the sheriff.

Ethan pulled his free and set to work cutting the man and woman loose. "Now get outta here," he said, pointing them to the back door. "Get!"

The owners of the feed store needed no further encouragement to vacate the building as fast as their legs could carry them.

Ethan put his knife away. "Now that I think about it, it might've been the charitable thing to let them go earlier."

"Hindsight's easy," Hope said. "How're you two lookin' for ammo? Better reload now."

They made short work of restocking their weapons, Ethan snapping his glimmering pistols closed and twirling them around his fingers in a gunslinger's flourish.

The sheriff was far more sober, his face

set with determination. "I'll take the front. Give you two a chance at gettin' around to the back."

"Are you sure?" Hope asked.

"Never been more sure in my life," Maxwell said. He advanced on the open doorway, with Hope and Ethan close behind. "Let's get this done, once and for all."

They started across the street.

"Jasper, you up there still?" Hope called, peering up at the roof of the feed store.

Jasper's head appeared above the fascia. "Sure am."

"Lay down some cover fire on that saloon. Don't let 'em pick us off."

"On it," Jasper said, rising and aiming at the windows of the saloon.

Sheriff Maxwell led them across the street. Hope ran with her pistol in her left hand, cradling the shotgun against her right shoulder with her bandaged right hand. Hope and Ethan broke to the left, heading for the alleyway at the side of the saloon building. The same route she'd followed to scale the building up to her room the night of her altercation with Barbosa's men in the café.

"Jasper! Let 'em have it!" Maxwell yelled.

A fraction of a second later, Jasper shot at the saloon. Maxwell stopped short of the porch, using the raised platform for cover as he shot through one of the front windows, firing blind in the hope he might get a lucky hit. Return fire followed. The sheriff ducked down low as the bullets whizzed past and Jasper continued to shoot through the windows.

Barbosa stood to the right of the back door, using it both for cover and as a vantage point. He turned for a quick look at the bar, where Peterson was bobbing up and down to avoid the rifle fire coming from across the street.

"Peterson. Get upstairs. Take that kid out of action."

"On it," Peterson said, keeping a low profile as he ran from the bar to the stairs that led to the second floor.

As Barbosa looked on, he spotted the sheriff peering over the side of the porch platform. The old man was squinting through the smoke and dust to peer inside, no doubt wondering why the return fire had ceased.

Barbosa looked outside. He caught Russell's eye from his hiding spot in the barn.

He communicated with the same moves he'd used since the old days: he tipped his head to ask, *Anything?*

Nothing, Russell said by shaking his own head slowly, and clearly, from side to side.

No mistaking the question and no mistaking the answer, either. The rifle fire stopped as Sheriff Maxwell climbed the steps of the porch, holding his left fist up in the air to signal for the shooting to stop.

Barbosa clung to the wall as he moved up into the saloon, keeping to the shadows, gun drawn.

Upstairs, the floorboards creaked.

A gunshot reverberated throughout the saloon.

Outside, the sheriff sprang back, looked up at one of the front rooms, then turned on his heel to peer across the street at the roof of the feed store. Barbosa looked, too — in time to see Jasper clutch the side of his neck, stumble back onto the roof and slide off to the side. He thudded to the snow-covered street.

Maxwell cried out and ran toward him.

Barbosa saw his opportunity and took it. He burst from the saloon at a speed that belied his size. Brought his gun to bear on the sheriff's back.

Fired once, twice. Sheriff Maxwell was blown forward onto the snow. He lay still for a second, then tried to push himself up to his knees, but his arms trembled and he collapsed back down. He had to drag himself forward toward the kid.

It was almost sweet.

"Hey!"

Barbosa turned to his left in time to see Dash Cassidy step out from behind a set of snow-encrusted barrels, gun raised.

Barbosa brought his own weapon to bear.

The men fired at each other.

Dash's bullet whipped past Barbosa's ear with a *zip!* Barbosa's shot caught the other man's upper arm. Dash took cover again, grimacing and clamping his hand over his wound.

The sheriff continued to drag himself across the street, leaving a trail of red in the dirty snow. Barbosa checked that the coast was clear and advanced on the sheriff. He aimed his weapon at the back of Maxwell's head and pulled the trigger without a moment's hesitation. Any other man might have cast his eyes away from the shot, but Barbosa saw the bullet pass through Sheriff Maxwell's skull, exiting from his face in an explosion of flesh, bone and blood splatter. The old man lay in a heap, a pool of red widening out from beneath him.

Barbosa turned at the sound of a gunshot at the back of the saloon. He headed back, but not before spotting movement up the street. He turned his gun on the local doctor running toward him with her medical bag in one hand, the other hand waving for his attention.

"This ain't the place for a lady doctor such as yourself."

"Let me help the boy," Dr. Bell said, holding her hand to her mouth at the sight of Maxwell. She swallowed her revulsion down. "I implore you, Mister Barbosa. I can see him moving still. He might survive if I give him medical attention right away."

"He knew the risks when he joined their cause."

"Please," Dr. Bell said. "Be merciful."

A door opened. Barbosa's eyes flicked toward the tailor shop as Margaret Hatchett appeared in the doorway of her own store. Something about her presence gave him pause.

Miss Hatchett's eyes fell upon the body of the sheriff. "I never thought I'd live to see the day a lawman was gunned down in this town."

"He weren't no lawman. Maxwell didn't have no qualifications for the job."

"Well, he wore the star. That's qualification enough, I'd say."

"I don't have time for this." Barbosa said.

"The boy doesn't deserve to die," Hatchett said, stepping out into the cold, pulling her shawl about her. "Hasn't enough blood been spilled?"

Barbosa did not say anything in response, but his face said all that words could not. He looked at the kid. Another gunshot ricocheted off the buildings. Barbosa sighed in exasperation.

"Fine. Get him out of my sight. If he's still out here when I come back, I'll finish him just like I did the sheriff."

Dr. Bell pressed her hands together as if in prayer. "Thank you, thank you."

Miss Hatchett nodded in approval. "You're doing the right thing."

"Please, get back inside, Margaret. The street is far from safe."

"I can't. I have to help," Hatchett said, trudging through the mud and the snow to assist Dr. Bell in moving Jasper. "As you just said, the street isn't safe."

"It's your life," Barbosa snarled, pacing back toward the saloon.

He glared at the barrels where the newcomer had fallen after shooting him. He was about to go over there, with the intention of finishing the job, but the unmistakable sound of a shotgun being fired made him change his mind. He realized the implications and hurried up the porch steps.

A second later, Dash rose from where he'd taken cover. He could have easily taken Barbosa out, right there and then. But he knew it was something Hope was meant to do. He looked across the street to where the sheriff lay in a circle of red and sighed with regret. As much as he might have wished it otherwise, he'd never have been quick enough to stop the sheriff's murder.

He walked out into the street and signaled the two ladies attempting to move the kid between them. "Lemme help."

"You're shot!" the lady from the shop said.

Dash brushed her concern away. "Passed through. I've had worse. Let's get him in the warm where you can help him."

The doctor was more than willing to accept his assistance. "Thank you kindly. It's not far from here."

"I hope you can save him," Dash said.

"I'll certainly try."

While the sheriff and the shootists inside were trading bullets, Hope had started down the alley next to the saloon.

Ethan yanked her back by her arm.

"What?" Hope whispered.

"Look."

She followed Ethan's line of sight and, through the gaps in the timbers, saw the

380

man hiding in the barn. "Ah. I see him."

"It's a trap. He's reckoned on us following his lead. Got his man waiting for us to run straight around there and get the jump on us."

"What do we do?"

"I don't know," Ethan said.

As he pondered he looked across to the roof of the feed store as Jasper fired over the top of the fascia. It was then he caught a bullet from one of Barbosa's men, clearly positioned on an upper floor. Jasper clutched the side of his neck, stumbled back onto the roof, tried to maintain his footing, but slid off despite his best efforts. As Ethan and Hope looked on helplessly, Jasper plummeted to the ground.

Sheriff Maxwell cried out.

Ran toward him.

Barbosa emerged from within the saloon and shot the sheriff in the back.

"Come on," Ethan said, dragging Hope with him down the alley. He stopped at the corner — the same part of the building Hope had scaled to reach her room before.

"We have to help," Hope said urgently.

"The sheriff is already dead. Give me that shotgun."

As soon as he had it in his hands, Ethan ran forward to the spot where the man was hiding, and jammed the shotgun through a gap in the timbers. Ethan yanked hard on the trigger and the shotgun erupted, obliterating the man in one go.

He propped the empty shotgun against the side of the barn.

Hope cut around the corner of the saloon, heading for the rear entrance. She and Ethan took up positions on either side of the door. There was one shooter upstairs, and there was Barbosa. The playing field was finally level. Both sides had lost thus far — lost far more than could ever be replaced.

Ethan said, "Let's finish this."

"That's the plan," Hope replied.

CHAPTER TWENTY-THREE

They ventured inside. Ethan first, both pistols drawn, Hope close behind, gun in her left hand. Both walking through the dust-strewn wreckage that would have had McCoy weeping to see the state of his saloon.

Ethan took each step cautiously, as if the floor could have given way beneath his feet at any moment. Hope crept to the stairwell, preparing to check the upper floor, while Ethan sidled over to the bar and looked behind it, moving with the same studious attention Hope had observed in domesticated cats.

She ascended the first step carefully, trying to make no noise.

They did not need to speak. Hope was to find the shooter upstairs — the gun hand who'd shot Jasper in the neck and made him fall from the roof of the feed store. And Ethan was on the lookout for Barbosa, who had butchered the sheriff when he was distracted by Jasper's fall.

Hope reached the top of the stairs and paused there, listening. The only sounds were of the building itself, settling after getting shot up.

Then the floorboards in one of the front rooms creaked from the weight of someone walking on them. Hope looked down the flight of stairs at Ethan, whose eyes were turned up to the ceiling, watching as a handful of dust filtered down in a line from the spot where the shooter stood.

He pointed upward and to the left with one of his pistols.

Hope nodded. She took a silent step toward the door to her left, knowing she had one shot to catch the gun hand off guard.

Bang! The saloon doors swung inward and Barbosa barreled in with his gun outstretched, teeth bared like a wild animal.

Ethan turned to the side, ran and dove for cover.

Barbosa shot the empty air where Ethan had been standing a second before, the bullets hissing overhead as he crashed to the floor behind the bar. He smashed into the boards so hard that he felt several of his ribs snap like twigs from the force of it.

Hope jerked back, spun around, took aim at Barbosa from the landing. But he saw her and dashed beneath the cover of the stairwell.

Hope hesitated, unsure which killer to go after. Then the floorboards exploded upward around her as Barbosa shot at her from below.

At the same time, the door to the front room opened. A man in a gray duster stood there, pistol in hand. Hope raised her left hand and pulled the trigger. The bullet struck the man's head and he fell backward into the room.

Ethan managed to pull himself up using the bar as leverage and fired at Barbosa. Caught the big man in the side but knew it was a bum shot. The bullet punched all the way through but didn't hit anything vital. Snarling, Barbosa fired back as he retreated toward the back door.

Ethan could not duck behind the bar quickly enough. He was knocked back on his feet as the bullet caught him in the left shoulder, knowing it hadn't passed through but had buried itself in there. Ethan returned fire though he could barely hold out his arm, but Barbosa was a blur as he careened through the back door.

Hope clattered down the stairs and looked

around for Barbosa. Not seeing him, she made for Ethan.

"No!" he said, pushing her away with his good arm. "Don't let him get away."

"Will you be all right?"

"Yes. Just get out there."

Hope didn't need to hear any more. She ran across the saloon and out the back. She edged toward the corner of the building and peeked out to see Barbosa moving as fast as he was able up the street. He glanced back, spotted her and fired off a shot that went wide of the mark.

Hope raised her pistol to shoot back . . . and the gun clicked through the empty chambers.

Damn.

Dr. Bell was carrying Jasper up the street with the help of her uncle Dash and a woman she didn't know. The doctor looked up in shock as Hope dropped the gun on the porch and gave chase, even though without a gun she wouldn't stand much of a chance; all she had was her bullwhip. Her only thought was to put an end to the man who'd ordered her father's murder. Nothing else mattered.

"What in the world is she doing?" Dr. Bell wondered aloud.

"Finishing this," Dash said.

386

■ ■ ■ ■

Ethan exited the saloon on rubbery legs. He attempted to navigate the steps down from the porch and misjudged them, falling forward into the street.

"Can you hold on?" Dr. Bell called over as she and Dash carried Jasper's limp form toward her office.

Ethan rolled over onto his back. He looked up at the big white sky. Flat and featureless.

"I can wait."

"We'll be as quick as we can," Dr. Bell replied. "Just stay where you are."

"You got the kid the rest of the way? I'll go drag that one along," Dash said to Dr. Bell and the other woman.

"We've got him."

The two women carried Jasper into the doctor's building between them, the doctor kicking her own door open with one sharp blow of her boot.

Ethan felt the cold working its way into his extremities. For the first time in his life, he truly felt as though he was going to die.

Then he found himself looking up at Dash, upside down.

"You're not dying, friend. Not on my watch," Dash said. Then he reached down, took Ethan by the armpits and began to drag him up the street.

Barbosa limped into the church and closed the doors behind him. He ran a hand over his face.

His hand was not steady.

It trembled.

He stood in the aisle, wincing from the pain in his side. All his people had been killed. He himself had been shot. Everything had fallen around him — all the walls of his kingdom crumbling inward. " 'My hour is almost come, when I to sulfurous and tormenting flames must render up myself,' " he said aloud, wiping at his eyes. For every situation, for every great fortune or tragedy of his life, there was a line of Shakespeare. They always kept him grounded, allowed him to discern meaning where there was little to be seen.

Barbosa touched the wound in his side. His trembling hand turned crimson. " 'Bloody thou art,' " he said, swallowing the taste of fear on his tongue. " 'Bloody will be thy end.' "

He heard someone coming.

Barbosa moved up the aisle to distance himself from the entrance.

The church doors creaked open and Hope

stalked into the holy building, brandishing her bullwhip.

Barbosa aimed at her and pulled the trigger.

Click.

The weapon was empty.

Damn.

His greatest skill was in the taking of human lives. Snuffing them out like candle flames. Sometimes he felt like the man who goes along at the end of the night extinguishing every lamp to embrace the darkness. There was an office at the back of the church, and a private door the other side of the office that would afford him an opportunity to flee. He would not let an empty pistol be the cause of his downfall. Barbosa resolved to bludgeon Hope Cassidy to death with the weapon if need be — if she would not let him go on his way.

"It's over," Hope called to him.

His hand tightened on his gun. "Nothing is over until I say it is."

"You have no power anymore. It's over," she said again.

"No, it ain't." Barbosa turned to run for the office.

Hope threw her arm back, and then out. She flicked the whip at his ankles. and its tapered tongue snagged the left one. With one swift pull, Hope had Barbosa hitting the floor hard. He managed to pull the end of the whip free, crawled forward and reached up, gripping the pulpit with both hands.

With great effort, the former outlaw pulled himself up, grunting.

"Stay down," Hope said as she stalked up the aisle, readied the whip again, then flung it out with deadly precision. The tongue struck Barbosa's back, producing a crisp *whip-crack* sound — as loud as a gunshot. Then she struck again.

Barbosa's legs crumpled beneath him. He had to lean on the pulpit with all his weight just to remain upright.

"I said, stay down!" Hope yelled. She brought the bullwhip back again, then snapped it out, catching him right between the shoulder blades.

Barbosa cried out in agony. He clung to the pulpit for a moment, then collapsed to his knees on the dusty floorboards.

Hope continued to advance on him, the sound of her boots echoing throughout the church. "This is for my pop," she said, flinging the bullwhip out once more, catching Barbosa around his big, fat throat. She pulled tight and his head fell back so she could see his huge face turning from red to purple.

Staring up at the high ceiling of the church, Barbosa croaked, " 'I shall fall . . . like a bright . . . exhalation . . . in the evening. . . .' "

Hope yanked the whip again and he fell on his back. She stood over him with the bullwhip in her hand, watching him fight for oxygen with complete dispassion. "For all the people you killed, all the people you had killed by others. All the people who didn't deserve it, and all their loved ones."

Barbosa's massive face turned blue. In desperation he looked to her for something, *anything.* Some kind of mercy.

It was not forthcoming.

"Die," Hope said. It was all she could think to say to him in his last seconds.

Barbosa made a strangled noise that could have been a protest at the last word he'd ever hear. He convulsed, eyes rolling into the back of his head, legs jerking out against the floorboards as he fought death. Then his chest became still and he ceased to live.

Hope breathed a sigh of relief. The world no longer had to abide his cruelty and his malice, and neither did she.

Hope felt she had, at long last, honored her father. She heard movement behind her

391

and turned to find Dash in the doorway.

"Is it done?" he asked. He was covered in blood: his own running down his arm, and the blood of others.

Hope looked at Barbosa. She felt peace settle within her. "It's done."

"Good," Dash said.

"How is he?" Hope asked Dr. Bell.

Dr. Bell blew the hair out of her eyes. It was toasty warm in her office compared to the frigid air outside. The doctor's face even had a sheen of sweat.

"Jasper is stable. I think he will make a full recovery so long as infection doesn't set in."

"What happened?"

"Luckily for Jasper, he lost a lot of blood but the bullet did not sever an artery or major blood vessel. Half an inch one way or the other, and we'd be having a different conversation."

"I am so glad to hear he's going to be okay," Hope said.

"He's made of tough stuff, that kid."

"And . . . Ethan?" She was almost afraid to hear.

"Come with me," Dr. Bell said with a smile, showing Hope to a side room. She opened the door. Ethan sat on a bed, his bare chest and shoulders covered in bandages.

"You made it."

Ethan cocked an eyebrow. "You sound surprised. Surely you didn't think he'd gotten the better of me."

"Just for a second or two."

"Really?"

Hope ignored him. She turned to the doctor. "Did you get the bullet out?"

"With a lot of effort. It wasn't easy. And the recovery time is going to be long. I've told Ethan how it is, and I'll tell the same to you since you're here — that shoulder may never be right after this. It's just one of those things. I can only do so much."

"And I already told you, Doc, I get it," Ethan said. "I'm just lucky to be alive."

"There it is. Lucky to be alive," Dr. Bell said. "If only all my patients were so levelheaded. I'll leave you two alone for a moment."

Hope watched her go and close the door behind her.

She turned to Ethan. "So. We did it."

"We did it," Ethan replied. "We lost Burt and the sheriff, though. I regret that. They were good men."

"Believe me, I've seen my fair share of the bad sort."

"You and me both. It was your uncle pulled me up the street so the doc could fix me up."

"I know. He told me."

Ethan frowned. "Where is he, anyhow? I wanted to thank him."

"Left already. Dr. Bell patched him up and he went on his way. Guess he felt he'd done what he came here to do. He never sticks around in any one place for too long."

On the walk back from the church, Hope had presented her uncle with the worn silver marshal's star that had belonged to her father.

"What's this?" Dash asked, before reading the word *marshal* etched into the metal. "Was this —"

"Yes. It was Pop's. They took it off him when they killed him. And Barbosa tossed it at me last night. He'd had it all this time."

Dash went to pass the star back to her.

Hope shook her head. "No, I want you to have it."

"But it belongs with you, Hope. I can't accept this."

They stopped walking. "I know you had the chance to kill Barbosa yourself, but you left him for me. Because as much as you wanted to avenge your brother yourself, you knew it was important for me to do it. You gave me that. You made sure I had that."

Dash sighed. "I knew that you'd never leave the past behind without seeing things through to the end. It gave me just as much satisfaction knowing you did it as doing it myself. So I feel like we can both leave the past where it belongs now."

"Well, I want you to have that. It'll remind you of him when you're out on the road, going from one place to another," Hope said, reached over and closing her uncle's hand on the star.

"Thank you. But how will you remember him?"

"He'll never leave me," Hope said, tears spilling from her eyes.

Dash reached up, wiped them away. He smiled warmly at her as he held her face in his hands. "You did him proud."

They resumed walking and Hope watched as Dash tucked the marshal's badge in his pocket.

"What will you do now?"

"Get back to my camp. Pack that up. Head on my way," Dash said. "Make some progress before nightfall. You know the drill."

"Thank you for helping me."

He looked at her and winked. "Hey, us Cassidys gotta stick together, don't we?"

Her uncle climbed up into the saddle of his horse, turned the beast around, then rode out of town. Neither of them believed in goodbyes. To say goodbye was far too final. Why say goodbye when you'd see each other again?

"Some folk are like that," Ethan said when she finished telling him. "Hell, what am I saying? I've been like that my whole life." He shifted on the bed, wincing from the pain in his shoulder. "So what next?"

"Next?"

"I believe you mentioned a pub?"

"Yes," Hope said. "If you're still up for going into business with me. Being partners and all. I mean, we've only just met. Some might think it strange."

"Do you think I give a hoot?"

"Can't say I do."

"I know you well enough. You didn't shoot me out there in the street when you could have."

"Did you think I might?"

"No," Ethan said. "I didn't doubt you for a second."

"I'm glad we met. I never expected it. It was just . . . I don't know. Good fortune, I guess, that our paths crossed."

"I'm glad we met, too," Ethan said.

He held out his right hand, and despite

her reservations about letting her guard down in such a way, Hope rested her own hand in his. Ethan slowly closed his hand around hers and they stayed that way for a moment, getting used to the sensation of contact after being alone for so long, in the wildest corners of the land.

It felt new.

It felt good, to both of them.

It felt like home.

EPILOGUE

Many Years Later . . .

A new century, but the cemetery at the edge of New Devon looked no different, save for the additional headstones that had been erected since Hope and Ethan settled there.

She'd arrived a young woman. Now she was old. Hope did not feel the years in her spirit, in her will to do what she wanted to do, but she felt the burden of time in her physical self, in her muscles and in her bones.

I am old and I am slowing down, she thought as she left the cemetery surrounded by her children and grandchildren. *Even walking is becoming a strain at times.*

Ethan's headstone had remained nice and clean, despite a year of exposure to the elements, to the salt air rushing in off the sea and to all the wet weather New Devon seemed to attract.

At the time, she'd wondered if she could

go on without him. They'd been together so long, they were almost like two facets of the same person. To lose one half of yourself, it was a hard thing to get over.

But Hope was a survivor. She knew Ethan would expect her to go on without him. In fact, he'd want nothing less than for her to outlast him for a long while yet.

And in truth she was not ready to go.

One of her grandchildren had taken off from the cemetery ahead of them. Now she ran back, red in the face, barely able to get a word out.

Hope raised her hands. "Slow down, little one. Take a breath."

Her granddaughter sucked in the chill air. "There's a man waiting for you at the pub, Grandma."

"A man?"

"A black man. He says his name is Jasper and he's come a long way. He has a horse and carriage."

Hope felt light all of a sudden. "Jasper? I must hurry back so that I don't miss him."

"He said he'll wait."

Hope held her hand out for her granddaughter to take. "Here, help pull me along so I can get there quicker."

"You came," she said as she rushed into the

399

pub to find Jasper waiting there. "He would be sorry he missed you."

"Sorry it took so long," Jasper said. He looked out of the window at all her children and grandchildren approaching the pub, chatting and smiling and surrounded by numerous romping dogs. "You got busy."

Hope laughed. "We did."

"Can you still shoot?"

"I wouldn't know. I never had cause to fire a gun after Fortune's Cross. You?"

"Only to hunt."

Hope said, "You never did tell us how you knew to shoot like that. We always wondered."

"Maybe I'll tell you later on."

"I'd like to hear it," Hope said.

Jasper smiled. "Remember that whip you carried?"

"I still have it," she said, pointing to the bullwhip on the wall.

Jasper whistled through his teeth. "Well, I'll be. Can you use it?"

Hope stood. She crossed the room and reached up to retrieve the whip from the rusted nails on which it hung. Her fingers just skirted short of it. "Damn it."

"Allow me," Jasper said, coming to her aid. He reached the bullwhip with ease and handed it to her.

"I must have shrunk over the years," Hope chuckled.

"Haven't we all?"

Hope grinned. "Not you, Jasper. You're taller, I believe. Now then, set a glass on that table over there and be sure to stand back."

Jasper fetched a whiskey glass and placed it in the middle of the table. Then he stepped back, well beyond the reach of the whip.

Hope ran the whip through her hand, familiarizing herself with it after so long. "My father used to jokingly call it a cat-o'-nine-tails. He knew it irritated me. But now when I look back on it, I find it amusing. A lot of the past is like that. Do you find it so, Jasper?"

"Do I find the past humorous?"

"Yes."

Jasper mulled it over. "I guess some of it, I do. Now that I can look back on it with the hindsight of many years."

"Have you forgotten any of it?"

"Some, I've forgotten. Some I've chosen to wipe from my memory."

Hope looked at him. "There's much I've forgotten. Or I *think* I have. But then it comes back to me. Captain Quinn used to tell me that out on the sea, in a storm, the

401

water comes up green. That's how they know it's a bad one, because the sea is bringing up all the green water from the bottom. Bless him, the captain passed twenty years ago."

"I remember Quinn from when we got here. You know, after leaving Fortune's Cross."

"I always favored his company. The man could hold his rum, for sure."

"I know it," Jasper said with a chuckle.

"Sometimes I feel like the past is slipping through my fingers," Hope said thoughtfully. "Like the sand on that beach out there. Just slipping through and falling away. But every now and then, I find it again. I remember. Is anything I'm saying making a blind bit of sense, Jasper?"

The man's eyes glistened with tears. "Yes."

"Ethan died this time last year. I know you were going to ask. We had a good life here. He was good to me, and I was good to him."

"Did he pass *well*?"

"He died very well. He passed in his sleep and knew nothing about it, which is how I think we'd all like to go if we had the choice," Hope said, her voice soft, vulnerable. She looked down at her hands, unable to maintain eye contact with Jasper for the emotion flooding through her in that moment. Thinking of Ethan drawing his last breath felt too raw still. "D'you know, he had a terrible time as a boy. Much like yourself. He lost his family. But somehow, from that tragedy, he found the strength to live. It made him the man he became, the man I loved. And that's just what you did, isn't it, Jasper? Used that tragedy to build a life for yourself?"

"Yes, but I had a little help along the way. Burt at first. Then you and Ethan."

"*Burt . . .* Oh, dear Burt. I haven't thought about him in a long time. Him or the sheriff." Hope sighed. "There I go again. More sand slipping through my fingers."

"You didn't have it easy yourself, did you?" Jasper asked.

"I did not. But look at me. I'm still here." She smiled. Wriggled her shoulders. "Now, then, about this whip. Ready to see that glass over there shatter? Ready to believe I've still got what it takes?"

"*Shatter?*" Jasper asked, wiping at his eyes. "Hope, are you sure that's . . . safe?"

"Safe!" Hope cackled. "In case you forgot, I was never in the business of being safe! I didn't get shot, nearly drown and track down my father's killers to be safe."

With a sudden movement of her arm and

wrist, unexpectedly fluid for a woman of her advanced years, Hope struck the glass with a single lick of the whip. Jasper flinched as the glass exploded on impact, scattering fragments across the tabletop, where, seconds before, it had stood whole. All that was left were the broken pieces, caught in the dusty sunlight from the pub window.

Hope coiled the bullwhip back into a loop. "Not bad for an old woman, eh?"

Jasper took a folded piece of paper from his pocket to sweep the shards of glass off the edge of the table and into the palm of his hand. He looked down at the fragments twinkling against his palm as he turned it in the light. Sand was born from stone, and if glass was made from that same sand, Jasper wondered if he might be crazy for thinking he held time in his hand. Or a *memory* of time.

"What do you see?" Hope asked, drawing near.

"Years and years," Jasper said.

Hope stepped forward. Looked at the glass. The light was reflected in her eyes. "I see it, too," she said.

ACKNOWLEDGMENTS

Thanks as ever to Tracy Bernstein and the team at Berkley. This is our fourth Western together in the Ralph Compton series, and I couldn't ask for a better collaborator than Tracy.

Thanks, also, to my wonderful agent Sharon Pelletier — Team SP all the way.

Thanks to all the readers who have picked up my books so far. I hope you have been entertained, and that my efforts have resulted in something that is akin to eating a good meal: satisfied but wanting more. I always wanted to write a villain who is larger than life and has a penchant for Shakespeare, so I was glad I got to do that with Cyrus Barbosa. And it was nice being able to have Ethan Harper (from *The Devil's Snare*) help Hope Cassidy in her quest for vengeance. I hope the ending I gave them is to my readers' satisfaction.

It worked for me.

Until next time, take care of yourselves, whoever and wherever you are.

ABOUT THE AUTHORS

Ralph Compton stood six foot eight without his boots. He worked as a musician, a radio announcer, a songwriter, and a newspaper columnist. His first novel, *The Goodnight Trail,* was a finalist for the Western Writers of America Medicine Pipe Bearer Award for best debut novel. He was the *USA Today* bestselling author of the Trail of the Gunfighter series, the Border Empire series, the Sundown Rider series, and the Trail Drive series, among others.

Tony Healey is the author of the Harper and Lane mystery series, featuring Detective Jane Harper and Ida Lane, a survivor with a gift for reading the dead. The Harper and Lane series has been favorably reviewed by the authors Blake Crouch, Mark Edwards, and by *Publishers Weekly. Hope's Peak* and *Storm's Edge* are available from

Thomas & Mercer. Healey independently published the crime novel *Not For Us*, young-adult thriller *Past Dark*, science-fiction series Far From Home and is currently at work on a Western.

The employees of Thorndike Press hope you have enjoyed this Large Print book. All our Thorndike, Wheeler, and Kennebec Large Print titles are designed for easy reading, and all our books are made to last. Other Thorndike Press Large Print books are available at your library, through selected bookstores, or directly from us.

For information about titles, please call:
(800) 223-1244

or visit our website at:
gale.com/thorndike

To share your comments, please write:
Publisher
Thorndike Press
10 Water St., Suite 310
Waterville, ME 04901

For my niece, Eliza